DI

OF
THE
LAST
MAN

P.R. Brown was educated at University College, Swansea, and later at St. John's College, Cambridge, where he gained a PhD in Philosophy. He teaches English as a Foreign language in Cambridge and has published articles both in this field and in philosophy.

His books include the non-fiction trilogy *The Gods of Our Time*, *Dreams and Illusions Revisited*, and *The Mountain Dwellers*. His writing for DB Publishing includes *The Mirror Men*, *The Treadmillers* and *The Shadow People*.

DIARY OF THE LAST MAN

P.R. BROWN

DB
PUBLISHING

By the same author:

Non-fiction

The Gods of Our Time

Dreams and Illusions Revisited

The Mountain Dwellers

Fiction

The Mirror Men

The Treadmillers

The Shadow People

Circle Walker

First published 2022 by DB Publishing, an imprint of JMD Media Ltd,
Nottingham, United Kingdom.

ISBN 9781780916293

Printed in the UK

Contents

And we may think on this and perhaps profit from the debate, that the heights to which man may occasionally rise fall hopelessly short of the depths to which he sometimes sinks. On a vertical and volatile moral continuum, the descent of man is all too often infinitely and grotesquely faster than his ascent, which may well suggest a law of human nature the converse of which is yet to be satisfactorily proved.

Foreword

Given that it might be of some relevance to possible future research and of interest to historians of science, an assumption which is, under the prevailing circumstances, increasingly questionable, it has been decided by the Institute for Scientific and Pathological Research to publish in total the following so-called 'Diary', by one of its recent trial patients. The pages that follow constitute a record which, albeit fragmentary, contains certain insights into the gradual cerebral breakdown of the subject Ref.No.P101148 during the vaccine trials which have by now been regularly conducted in an effort to discover an adequate solution to the most virulent form of the Virus (COVID133X, otherwise known as the Omega Strain) that we have yet experienced, a complex mutant variant whose daily death toll now runs into the many hundreds of thousands in central Europe alone according to the last set of statistics available. The termination of effective national and international communication precludes certainty, but, since, as far as we know, no vaccine has been developed to counter the Omega Strain, it is likely that these statistics are now conservative.

Since the future of human life on this planet now depends on how successful we become in our efforts to discover an effective vaccine, the drastic step has been taken to conduct experiments on human subjects by conscription and not, as formerly, voluntarily. Unfortunately, many patients do not survive the ordeal of experimentation and are disposed of humanely having suffered cerebral and psychological damage to an extent that incapacitates them from rejoining normal, civilised society even were the Omega Strain no longer a threat. The important work of research must however continue at all costs in the interests of re-establishing at least a semblance of former civilised life. We have no qualms about this simple fact, that since the dead are beyond all help we should focus attention on those that still live and on those that follow them. This principle underlies all our work for as long as this work can be undertaken; and despite the obvious importance of this research there is, tragically, no guarantee of its continuance.

Even a cursory glance at the so-called 'Entries' that follow will demonstrate the slow and irreversible decline in the cerebral capacity and capability of P101148 after a trial lasting several months, during which time the patient in question was kept under close surveillance and increasingly sedated as the effects of the trials became more pronounced. Like every trial patient, P101148 was kept in an isolation cell throughout to prevent cross contamination. The patient began to experience hallucinations from the very outset, which became more pronounced at each stage of the trials. In the earlier part of his period of isolation, P101148 was permitted to take daily walks in the compound that skirts the walls of the Institute; however, external access was later denied due to his physical deterioration and as the hallucinatory effects of treatment became more pronounced, as is instanced in his repeated references to journeying north and in his narrative concerning people and animals encountered en route, all of which is, however graphic, entirely hallucinatory and in keeping with the deterioration of his state of mind, a cerebral decline which is in his case, as in that of so many of his predecessors, quite irreversible.

It is clear that both the substance and direction of his reflections have no basis whatsoever in fact, and there are indications throughout that the patient was himself critical of his own abilities to reason; hence his repeated references to a 'defective brain'. Indeed, it is not a little surprising that he seemed to retain the ability until the very end to form sentences of relatively sound syntax. His linguistic ability might be explained by sheer force of habit, which formed deep cerebral tracks in Broca's area, located in the left hemisphere of the brain, or possibly Wernicke's area in the posterior superior temporal lobe which connects to Broca's area via a neural pathway. The left hemisphere of the brain, the so-called 'dominant area', is generally responsible for language and speech, and it is here that we expect to find an explanation for the linguistic resistance to the more aggressive effects of the vaccine trials conducted on this patient even when the drug dosages administered were increased to very high levels. Confirmation of this theory awaits a satisfactory postmortem analysis, the results of which will hopefully be published by the Institute should time and circumstances allow.

A resistant linguistic capacity concerning the formation of linked words and sentences is not, however, evidence of their intellectual and logical validity. It is abundantly clear that patient P101148 has produced nothing whatsoever that can be attributed to correct observation and deduction from what he has observed. His references to and description of the Raiders is of course correct, since Raiders have been in existence for some considerable time before he was brought to the Institute for experimentation. However, his cerebral faculty for moral judgement is naturally adversely affected by the trials to which he was subjected.

His moral evaluations are therefore to be disregarded as having no basis either in science or in general fact. In general, his reflections are highly repetitive, often inconsistent, vague, fragmented and entirely irrational, which is precisely what is to be expected in consequence of the virulence of the drugs to which he has been daily and increasingly subjected in combination with the powerful sedation which has proved necessary to control his increasingly erratic behaviour. It will be clear therefore, even to the most generous of readers, that his reflections, should we dignify them with this title, are a confused web of irrational ideas, in short quite nonsensical. His reflections and his logic are unquestionably the products of an irreversibly diseased mind.

P101148 was allowed writing materials on request. After his final 'Entry' it was decided to be in the interests both of the patient and the Institute to terminate the trials humanely. Further trials on this patient were considered fruitless and were therefore not entertained. It was believed that his irreversible hallucinatory condition would constitute a threat to the physical and psychological wellbeing of both researchers and ancillary staff, which, especially now in view of their dwindling numbers, has become increasingly important to preserve and sustain.

The scientific fraternity at large, and we fervently hope that such a fraternity is still currently in existence, would be delighted to learn that the Institute continues its vital work in the most trying conditions and despite the inevitable and rapid decline in trial-patient conscription figures. There is still, unfortunately, no immediate end in sight to the daily ravages of the Virus. But given the quality of the research conducted there is always some lingering hope that an eventual end may one day be in sight. We few researchers, our own numbers having fallen rapidly, are yet firmly of the conviction that our researches are well worth pursuing; we are wedded as necessity dictates to the principle that the end justifies the means in all our endeavours. We have, we consider it fair to say, acquired and so far sustained the moral courage necessary to continue the sacrifice, if need be, of the few remaining trial patients in the attempt to ensure an inhabitable world post-COVID133X, an outcome which nothing but the discovery of an effective antidote can engender. Human life may exist without science; but science cannot exist without mankind, and *civilised* mankind cannot exist without the progress of science. Our efforts at the Institute have been dedicated to the future advancement of civilised man through the efforts of science. The progress of civilised mankind and the progress of science are therefore inextricably linked.

The Raiders are naturally a constant threat which must be taken seriously, but we feel relatively secure behind the walls of the Institute, albeit nothing can be guaranteed beyond the short term.

This document is necessarily stored in paper format, no other format having been available for at least the past two years by our calendar reckoning.

Institute for Scientific and Pathological Research
(Doc. P101148)

Addendum

Since the above was recorded and in the weeks following the demise of P101148, it has become increasingly clear that our work at the Institute cannot continue, partly due to the enormous difficulties involved in finding and conscripting additional trial patients, and partly because the encroachment of Raiders threatens the safety of the few remaining personnel. Despite their dwindling numbers in the indigenous population due to the ravages of the Virus, Raiders have nevertheless increased their ranks greatly due principally to the daily coastal influx from foreign shores, our own coastline having been inevitably unguarded and neglected. It has therefore been decided with the greatest reluctance to abandon the Institute and with it all attempts to discover an antidote to the Omega Strain. Each remaining member of staff will now abandon the growing insecurity of these walls separately and endeavour to make his way to a place of relative safety. It is not possible to write more.

Entry 1

Well, it was touch and go last night. Very much so. I must have dozed off upstairs and then, waking with a start, sleepily and stupidly lit a candle to light my way down to the basement, though, God knows, I should be able to feel my way down after all this time. Luckily, nothing happened. No raids. No Raiders. Raiders? They were human once; now they are wild animals, taking human form, with the power of speech, or what's left of it – they are the children of the Virus, and they spare no one but themselves, and sometimes not even one another. Had they seen the light … No, I must never do that again. It comes to something when I can't move about freely in my own house.

I say 'my' but really nobody possesses anything these days; you get attached to something, you begin to think of it as your own, and then it's taken away, stolen by the Raiders, old and new, but especially the new ones who come from further afield and forage around here and there picking up whatever they like and taking it away. They stop at nothing, so there's no stopping them. They hunt in packs, like the wolves of the ancient forests, and they'll tear anyone apart who stand in their way. They've lost it – everything, in particular their humanity, though they still look human enough. So, it's important not to be caught out, thinking that appearances must count. There are no friends these days, not even in the loosest of senses. Times are harder than granite. I vaguely remember reading a poem in which it was written that the skies rain the tears of a God of Love, a God who made us all and bitterly regretted the human template He had constructed – I suppose He was imagined to be crying for the pains suffered by His creations, very much including the pains they inflict upon one another. Well, there is as much to cry about now as ever there was.

The poets said that rain is the tears of a loving God. Tears for what? Well, it might be said, if you were in such a mood, that a man's life is a pitiful thing: that it should begin with helpless innocence, that it should proceed with expectation and promise, that it should continue with hard work and no small degree of disillusionment, and then decline with pain, and grief, either for the loss of your own life or for that of another, for well do we know that grief is the costly price of love – love for another, or simply love of life; so costly that some may even be tempted to ask whether love is vastly overrated. But into this sufficiently doleful mix we must add the observation that despite the ferocity with which one animal might pursue and devour another when following the simple and unreasoned instinct for survival, only man can commit genocide and kill en masse, only he can kill for an half-baked ideology or for riches and the baubles they buy, or for jealousy and revenge. Despite man's much vaunted and complacent superiority over them, the animals of the forest compare pretty well. Yes, I know. There have always been those in whom the flame of love thrives most naturally and cannot easily be extinguished, a fact for which the wise and the good should be eternally grateful. For all that, I often feel constrained to admit that the heights to which man may occasionally rise fall hopelessly short of the depths to which he habitually sinks.

Yes, but let us ask this: who would *want* to be an animal of the forest or to live like one? Such creatures may be bereft of human vices, but they lack the warmth of human virtues, too – despite those that we affectionately attribute to them. An animal cannot celebrate Christmas. And as for the downsides of life and living, the pains and stresses and the fact that it must have an end if it has a beginning, all we can say is that we must make the best of it and do the best we can.

Well, we have not made the best of it. I cannot help but think thoughts, but why I persist in writing them down I cannot say – except that they help to pass the time; but no, the very act of writing is like a temporary exorcism, one that must be repeated again and again. As for validity, veracity and truth – well, they are of little relevance now.

Courage. Stamina. Fortitude. Selflessness. Yes, I know. They are all well-documented human assets. And they were much in evidence during the first two years of the Virus. It would seem cowardly and immoral to deny it. And I do deny it. It would be disrespectful to all those then and before to underplay the acts of enormous self-sacrifice that were shown not simply in more recent times in the face of the Virus, but before that, in times of war or national and global catastrophe. Yet, there are limits beyond which such assets cannot be exercised – rather like birds who will lose their power of flight if they fly where the oxygen is too rare, or like fish if they are deprived of the element of which water enables them to breathe. Such was and is the tragic and grievous effect of the Virus – pushing the capabilities of man too far beyond their limits, beyond the limits of the saintly let alone those of lesser men, as though appeals to some loving God became quite hollow or as senseless as inarticulate sounds.

I scribble the word 'God', and my scribbling is as good as any on that subject. After all, what does belief in God, appeals to God, the whole language of God actually mean? Is the existence of God something provable either by science as we know it or by science as we might imagine it might become – as though the proof of the existence of God awaits an 'advanced' science, so advanced that it tests the limits of man's imagination and capabilities? No, no not at all. Which does not mean that God is something 'superior' or 'beyond the limits of man's understanding', however 'advanced' that understanding may become, or whatever that understanding or the methods of science might achieve. Which suggests that God is not a 'something' at all.

(Therefore … Yes, but I must be careful about my use of the word 'therefore'. Wisdom dictates that courage is required to use the word even when you are convinced that it is the right one, and even conviction is a shifting constant. When you use the word, it's like moving your front line forward when you are still unsure of the strength of opposing forces. Even when you are certain, uncertainty bites at your heels.)

Therefore, all religious conflict rests upon a monstrous piece of illogic. Appeals to God might resemble cries for help, appeals for comprehension, expressions of otherwise indescribable pain, or they may be joyful appreciations of things, people and events. Or they may be none of these at all – sometimes hitting a block of wood with a blunt axe is as much an appeal to God as High Mass. In any case, the significance of a heartfelt appeal to God can only be truly understood by an understanding of he who makes it and his relation to people and events. God does not enjoy the luxury of an independent existence – as star can be said to exist apart from those who observe it. He exists in language, but language is a human phenomenon and lives, moves, changes and fades with the commerce of human life on this planet. God is not a superhuman being of which a portrait can be made. All mental identikits of what God is are therefore absurd, illogical and irrelevant. All religious wars and exchanges are immaterial, primitive, barbaric.

Why I take the trouble to make these scribbles is hard to say. Should anyone ever read them, they will not understand them. And if they understand them, they will not need to be instructed by them. Who now amongst the remnants of mankind could possibly take an interest in the written or indeed the spoken word? Language itself is on the brink of extinction. No one, through fear and an irreparable sense of hopelessness, dares think of tomorrow; as for today, it might rightly be said that sufficient is the evil thereof.

As for hope, when the Virus became a threat to everyone and not just simply to someone in the next street, town, parish or distant isle, and when it came to threaten the very survival of mankind itself – yes, then hope was replaced by Faith, at first myopic and then increasingly blinder; so that many atheists, agnostics and cynics of every hue became fervent, not to say fevered, believers overnight, and at a rate beyond the wildest dreams of the Jesuit Fathers, while those who held strong religious beliefs long before the Virus became problematic considered their convictions amply validated. Amongst the latter were those of a more morally spurious orthodoxy, claiming that the Virus was none other than the iron fist of their God aimed at the ungodly, the ungodly consisting primarily of believers of alternative Faiths.

And for those of no religion and who could not bring themselves to change the habits of a lifetime, the only hope they entertained was that the sandman would allow them a pleasant dream or two so that they might wake on the morrow with at least a modicum of gratitude for having survived the night. They might also have wished that the experience of day and night could be reversed, so that the horrors of the day might become the nightmares from which they would escape in pleasant dreams at night, and then they might achieve a liveable life at night and discount the horrors of the day as simply so many insane but dismissible fancies. There was no end to such confused and confusing notions – all of them the products of fear and unsustainable despair.

I speak of my 'scribbles'. I must say, I ask myself *what* I should write. For it is a great responsibility to put pen to paper, even if, as is the case here, what you write will never be read. Putting pen to paper is an act of faith. Perhaps someone somewhere will find what you say in some way instructive, in some way illuminating, in some way readable. Or perhaps you write in the half belief that in the very process you may find the answer to those questions that trouble you, or as though the problems you thought troubled you will dissolve away in the very act of writing. Omar Khayyam spoke of the moving finger that writes and moves on. But such is the time in which we find ourselves, in which we can do no more than subsist temporarily, the moving finger must also stop and never move again. And so, what we write, if we write at all, becomes all important, and as final as the full stop that ends all full stops.

Anyhow, as I say, I reached the basement safely, without, as far as I can make out, being seen. Of course, from the small window at ground level I could hear the familiar shouts and screams, thankfully not too close – no doubt one pack of Raiders was battling it out with another, like dogs vying for bones. I saw the flicker of red flames in the distance, too, and I could smell the smoke from a fire or fires. It reminded me of much more civilised days when people would take an inordinate, and worrying, amount of pleasure from watching an effigy of Guy Fawkes engulfed in flames. But Raiders burn the real thing now, maybe a Raider from a rival pack, or even one of their own to whom they've taken a dislike, and they're always vying with one another for leadership. They've lost everything, in particular their humanity, and, having lost that, they are hardly distinguishable from the wolves of less familiar places. I can't be sure they burned anyone last night, but that ghastly smell of barbecued flesh was in the air – or so it seemed to me.

Anyway, I've decided to write things down – makes me feel better, I suppose. I don't know why I didn't think of it long ago. Technology, of course, has long disappeared. There is no electricity. There are no computers, laptops, tablets … no, not even manual typewriters. But I've kept a supply of paper, and I've some pencils, and that will do nicely for my diary. I'll call it a diary. I shan't call it a journal, because that sounds too pompous. But even calling it a diary is problematic if, like me, you still have some respect for language. I used to recite the days of the week and the months of the year, just to keep them in mind, like the names and addresses of old friends. I don't do that anymore. There's simply no point. Days and months have no names, I suppose because there's no way of telling one day from another, one month from another. All that can be distinguished is light from dark, with the most obvious gradations between. And that's why the word 'diary' is a bit of a misnomer – after all, a diary is meant to distinguish between days and months to note appointments, birthdays, important personal events, and so on. But so little is left now of what life used to be. So, my diary is not in the strictest sense a 'diary' with the names of days and months, because I don't know what day it is or which month – this would be pointless guesswork – and I shall simply number my entries; one entry will follow another, but not as one day follows another.

It's funny. I've just wasted paper explaining this. Of course no one will read my diary. No one needs to read it. And, no doubt, the time is fast approaching when people, those that are left, will have forgotten how to read and not even know what reading is. Well, that would be a logical development from what has happened, a very natural sequence of events. It's just as well. If Raiders found it and could read, I wouldn't rate my chances of survival. My chances would be slim anyway, but the diary would unambiguously seal my fate.

Fate! Not a word to be used lightly. What Fate decreed as I made my first entrance on the stage of being I now fully acknowledge. I now know unambiguously that I am a prisoner of Fate. For there are those who feel that from the moment they are pushed, pulled or cut from the womb their lives were never their own, that there is no escaping Fate. The walls of his dungeon are too thick; the windows are too high and too small; the door is sealed and bolted from the outside. I have bloodied my hands against the confines of this cell. I have forced circumstances, and now I know why it has all been entirely and necessarily in vain.

Amongst its edicts, Fate has ordered that I should live and die anonymously – this at least is one decree that I can most readily embrace. How sweet is complete anonymity! I have moved through life like a shadow, without substance, with nothing to say and nothing useful to do; never in the light; in perpetual shadow; I admit, I have preferred dark corners and shadowy places. I have always felt that I am not of this world, nor have I wanted to be part of it; in this, Fate and I are at one – perhaps this edict is a gesture of generosity. For one consequence is that I should not fear death. For why should one who has never truly lived fear the negation of life? Such comic irony to fear the loss of what one has never really possessed! Just a small corner of the tapestry that depicts the comic tragedy of our little lives; lives infinitesimally small, far too minute to be taken into account in the vast, unfathomable depths of the universe – specs of dust blown hither and thither by winds we can neither comprehend nor control. Is it good or bad that people don't generally take an interest in the skies above and beyond their heads? The silence of a starry night is capable of putting arrogance and complacency in their place; but when reflection upon it goes far enough, human worth may seem a hollow concept. Are we really no more than dust in the wind – minute particles that can't resist the urge to annihilate one another despite their eternal insignificance?

If such are we, then what are our words? If such is our being, then of what value is what we say and do? If we are nothing, then when we die we are less than nothing. What kind of mathematics can encompass that? And we know that nothing can come of nothing.

The time comes when rhetorical questions are the only kind of questions that can be asked. A time when what once made sense is now no more than inarticulate sound, and a time, like now, when vaunted civilised life is turned on its head. Yet there is a time for everything under the sun, so long as the sun shines.

No matter, my diary is for me alone. I can pour out my thoughts on to the clean pages, thoughts arising mainly from my walks. Well, I know it's risky, but I take a daily walk, quite brisk, round the park not far from the house – if we can still call that overgrown, unkempt mass of undergrowth and tall dark trees a 'park'. I complete one circuit just before daybreak. It helps to keep me fit and alert. Yes, risky! But the alternative would be to vegetate in the basement with the ever present risk of being discovered. But fit and alert for what? That's a question, like many other questions, I thought I'd never ask. I try not to ask it, but it haunts me every day.

Thoughts come to me as I take my daily walk. I suppose it's all part of trying to make sense of everything, of trying to get my head round everything that's happened and giving everything some kind of chronology, some kind of framework of cause and effect. It helps to keep me sane, if that's not too large a claim. Where and how did it all start? My circuit round the park, through the dark trees, made darker and foreboding in the half-light before daybreak, reminds me of circles. It occurred to me that civilisation might itself be a circle, starting from nothing, and then achieving everything that human nature, with its dire limitations, will allow it to achieve, only to turn back on itself again to some primitive state. So, am I now living at the beginning of the world? If so, I can find absolutely nothing to commend it, like a lawyer without a plausible, sustainable brief.

Did I say 'lawyer'? Now that's another anachronism. How can there be lawyers where there is not law? Perhaps my diary is a kind of personal reassurance that all is not lost, that the civilisation that once was can one day return – if only I can find adequate cause for what was happened, and some hope that these tides, though seemingly relentless, can be reversed.

Entry 2

I took the usual route this morning, down through that tangled mess, the remains of a garden that used to be her pride and joy when she … Well, then I made a dash into the park. But then I did two circuits instead of the customary one, darting quickly between the trees like a man on the run. Come to think of it, that's just what I am – a man on the run. Constantly on the run. Doing two circuits instead of one might seem like an act of bravado, of resistance, of protest. No, I was angry, ready to throw all caution aside – something had stuck in my craw, and I didn't seem to care whether I could make it back to the basement before daybreak. But there was no one there to see or be seen, as far as I know; and I did make it back before daybreak, just! Oh, I'm forgetting – yes, I did seem to see some movement through the trees, some shadowy thing, perhaps walking along what used to be a public path parallel to the trees and dense foliage. But I must've been mistaken. Nobody in their right mind would dream of walking exposed along that path at any time night or day – unless, of course, it was a Raider. If it was a Raider, I can only hope he didn't sense I was there or that he took me for another Raider.

In those early hours when everything is in shadows the trees look taller than ever they were, dark sentinels of the night, stronger, more resistant, more enduring than human life and civilisation. They seem to mock human weakness and stand tall in testimony of it. They are survivors. They have outlasted us. Ironic, when humans were so hell bent on cutting them down! Some there were who advocated a benevolent reciprocity between man and nature, a state of mutual respect, the idea that nature nourishes mankind and mankind in return serves it well. But such wisdom cannot find roots in the human jungles of the world, where self-interest holds sway like a god above all others, where human bestiality, so often masquerading as pragmatism or the requirements of necessity, demands centre stage. Such pious notions as benevolent reciprocity are now as irrelevant as they were hollow, as hollow as the burnt-out trees you sometimes find here and there, destroyed for fun by the Raiders – like the buffalo shot for sport from the windows of stationary trains, their carcasses left to rot on the plains of Montana.

But, yes, here in the park most trees have outlasted the disrespect shown them by more transient forms of life. And in the branches of survivors the crows congregate, like messengers perched for rest en route. This morning there were more birds than usual and they began their cawing just as the curtain of the night was lifting. Their conversations were deafening, the din intimidating, and I was incapable of clear thoughts. Perhaps they were warning me, reproaching me for my second circuit and urging me back to the basement. Or were they messengers of worse to come? No, how could things possibly get worse? I suppose we reach the limit when all beauty is extinguished or, if not extinguished, we become incapable of seeing it, of feeling it. The insanely hurried pace of life before the Virus struck inhibited the appreciation of beauty even amongst those capable of perceiving it.

Now there is no pace, hardly life itself, and only the lingering beauty of nature, to be barely perceived by those whose continued existence is in grave doubt from one moment to the next.

'The world will be saved by beauty' – a line from Dostoyevsky. But when our appreciation of beauty begins to fade, hope fades with it, and then Dostoyevsky's sentiment weakens, gradually, perhaps at first imperceptibly, but inexorably all the same. First, it is transformed into a conditional sentence, and one which becomes progressively tentative, gradually cautious and reserved, until we arrive at a grudging hypothesis:

If the world is saved, it will be saved by beauty.
If the world is ever to be saved, it will be saved by beauty.
If the world should ever be saved, it will be saved by beauty.
Should the world ever be saved, it will be saved by beauty.
If the world was ever saved, it would be saved by beauty.
If the world were to be saved, it would be saved by beauty.
Were the world to be saved, it would be saved by beauty.

And when, may the gods forbid it, all is utterly and irretrievably lost, the inevitable declaration would sting like a poisoned dart: *Had the world been saved, it would have been saved by beauty.*

I said 'beauty'. Now *that's* a word! Who, I hear you ask, is to say what beauty is or where beauty resides? Beauty is in the eye of the beholder, is it not? But do you trust the eye of the beholder? Does he trust it himself? In art I have seen beauty, though I know nothing of the theory of art and lack all artistic skill. In music I have heard beauty, though I know nothing of the theory of music. I have recognised the beauty of reasoning in teachers like Socrates, though he would find me a poor pupil. There is a clarity and a grandeur that is undeniable and irresistible in a work of beauty, be that work simple or complex; yet why is it that time after time I have met people who simply shrug their shoulders and walk on, oblivious to everything but the mediocre and the praises showered upon it?

Perhaps it is possible to *feel* beauty, to *sense* it and to *love* it, which is why a simple man might be moved by it even more than an artist, a musician or a logician, and why an artist, a musician and a logician may be oblivious to the beauty in their own productions. Rightly or wrongly, it's as though we wanted to say, 'It is given to some men to know beauty, but not to all.' Pablo Casals, who knew the beauty of Bach and Dvorak and was above all men capable of reproducing it, called himself a simple man who preferred simplicity in all things. In a letter to Coleridge, Charles Lamb rebuked his friend with the prescription, 'Cultivate simplicity Coleridge. There are not hotbeds in the gardens of Parnassus.' But in a world in which people seem ever more impressed by the complex, simplicity it seems is not so simple either to understand or to achieve (but, I must confess, I have exchanged the world of youth for that of old men; I now live in the world of old men in which the tastes, smells and sensations of sight, hearing and touch are not what they used to be; at least in this way, the so-called generation gap is inevitable and unbridgeable).

According to Plato in the *Republic*, the purpose of education is to teach us to love beauty. Might it not be objected that I've taken this statement out of context? Yes, I have, and on purpose, because I should like to think that what we call education is designed to teach us to love beauty. To philosophers and others of an inquiring disposition the idea begs questions about what beauty is and what education is – questions that are so seldom asked, either because there are so few capable of asking them, or because the answers would seem far too obvious. Cutting through this Gordian knot, I might assert that education teaches us to love beauty; but then it needs to be explained why so many who have successfully made their way through the artificially illuminated forests of academia, where paper qualifications hang from the branches of synthetic trees, fail to love it; they fail to love it because they fail to see it; and they fail to see it because it is so rarely in evidence.

But, whatever it means, the beauty of nature remains unquestioned, even when shrouded in the half-light of my morning walks – in the majesty of those tall, dark sentinels and the conversations of the black-winged messengers who sleep amongst their branches; is there not a beauty in the persistence of nature, in the continuity of the theatre of nature? On the battlefields of Ypres and the Somme, lives were lost forever, but nature recovered and flora flourished as never before. Yet, beauty is a house of many mansions and the perception of the beauty of nature is only a by-product of a much larger imagination. Wasn't it an old Roman proverb that true progress amongst mankind can only be achieved when one can imagine the pain of another? But a sense of hopelessness belongs to those who have seen too much of the worst in man and too little of the good, while blind optimism is for those who have been lucky enough to see the good in man and too little of the worst.

But what kind of progress can make man 'better' than he is, since we must rule out of court the progress of technology? Progress may be a house of many mansions, but we look in the wrong place if we turn to scientific man, for science cannot bring about a moral improvement in his constitution any more than a law, rule or sanction can, any more than a new suit of clothes can turn a monster into a saint.

If viruses are defeated, or at least subjugated, and if man does not bring about his own demise through war or relentless environmental abuse, what then? Is it at all possible that nations will achieve maturity of soul, some more some less, some sooner, some later, an achievement of moral intellect that will look upon war and violent divisions as items fit only for the infancy of primitive man and as morally objectionable as a Chamber of Horrors.

Ah, too many 'ifs', too many 'buts'. Such speculation is an idle pursuit when what must be assumed is such a profound transformation of human nature that would render it quite unrecognisable and alien. It is rather like attempting to improve a chair by turning it into a table: we have now a table, but what we wanted all along was a much improved chair! And so, we find ourselves attempting to envisage an improved human nature by imagining something quite different. Therefore, this kind of speculation is not simply idle but utterly misconceived.

Enough of these idle ramblings.

I still have some batteries left. When I got back to the basement this morning I played an old cassette – some pieces by Handel. I played it low and quiet. Maybe one day I'll have the courage to turn up the volume. This morning it was barely audible and its beauty was as loud as thunder.

Stupidly, I ask myself why, if things are so bad here, I haven't yet left? Of course the answer is too obvious for words. For everywhere is just the same, one place is as bad as another; besides, travelling is dangerous, especially when done on foot; the longer you travel the higher the risk. Buses, trains, planes are all things of the past – the

Virus and the Raiders have seen to that! Oh, there were various names for it bandied about by scientists and the medical fraternity – but the phrase which gained popular currency was 'The Virus' – and I suppose we might almost say that what became known as 'The Raiders' was an offspring of the Virus which caused humans to lose their humanity.

But the real reason I can't leave is … No, I couldn't bear to part from her – deep in our garden where I put her. For as long as she's here, I shall stay. Rousseau said that slaves in their bondage lose everything, even the desire to be free. But it is not only slaves who lose the desire to be free; those who love also lose the desire to be free, if only because 'freedom from what you love' makes no sense to them.

Even so, more than once I packed a small bag, ready for a road I was reluctant to take – until I was pulled up by the thought that the garden I was to leave was hallowed ground, that leaving for that reason alone was out of the question, and that a man in his sixties would do better to stay put, having seen long ago the best his life could offer. When you no longer have a hand to play, you stop dreaming of what luck might bring your way.

Entry 3

Got back to basement without incident again this morning. Did only one circuit – better to play it safe.

The irony struck me as particularly poignant as I walked through the morning haze, namely that people were so wound up about saving the planet from a largely man-made environmental disaster here on Earth, little thinking that the human race would itself be wiped out by the Virus which many now think to have had its origins in space, and that the end should come long before the global environment has become uninhabitable. Well, that's how it is: you focus on the front door, and your enemy enters through a back window. The irony is worth underscoring: the predicted destruction of the ozone layer has been beaten to the post by a viral Armageddon, one which threatens to wipe out humankind as effectively as the oversized meteor is said to have destroyed the dinosaurs. Trees, shrubs, vegetation – everything now is thriving in a world which is finally bereft of human pollution, while human life is in irrevocable decline. Humans had to give up the ghost so that the environment could recuperate and outlive them. What a trade-off! Jesus Christ had to die so that he could make a mark worth leaving. Socrates had to submit to his accusers so that he could be remembered. The mind boggles. Fred Hoyle's *The Intelligent Universe* received a boost in popularity when the idea got round that if human life on this planet began with microbes from space, it may very well end in the same way. Hoyle's estate must have enjoyed a noticeable increase in royalties. Not of course that his or any other estate matters now.

True, there was for a time a period of moral respite. In the early days after the Virus first struck people became more selfless, adopting what they referred to as 'a wartime spirit' or the 'spirit of the Blitz'; but when the Virus took more lives and promised to stay around far longer than the Blitz of 1940, nerves began to fray and the thin veneer of 'other-mindedness' began to develop first hairline cracks, and then fissures which would only add to the confusion and lack of social cohesion, elements that were vital to keep a sense of proportion and goodwill.

The so-called IR factor declined and quickly became irrelevant: 'I' stood for Initiate and 'R' for Response: you say hello to someone and thereby initiate an appropriate response; or in a meeting, you make a suggestion and the act of doing so generates a response. Well, anyway, this IR factor was just a fancy way of talking about the importance of civilised communication. But civilised communication declined to well below zero, which is just about where it is now – which is what might have been expected with any marked decline in civilisation: language and behaviour are the first to suffer, and then so does everything else, when despair replaces hope and finally overrides humanity. In the early days of lockdowns, national, regional, total or partial, people were told to suppress the instinct for social interaction, an injunction which most followed with difficulty and many under protest; but when hope turned to despair, suppression became second nature and social avoidance assumed the status of an instinct which was followed with the utmost vigour.

Despair grows like a cancerous vortex, like a maelstrom dragging and drawing down even the strongest who attempt to resist it, down into the deepest, darkest depths of the ocean. If you see it early enough, you just might, with a few strong breaststrokes, reach the calmer waters at the whirlpool's edge. But great strength, courage and temperance of mind are required, a trio that is in short supply at the very best of times, but in times of fear and panic is virtually non-existent if only because the third element is almost invariably absent. They said at first that we were all in the same boat, but they forget to distinguish between the upper and lower berths, for the poor of the so-called Third World, who constituted the masses, were left out of account altogether – a tragic error of omission, pragmatically as well as morally, since the virus could never be effectively opposed unless a policy of 'All for one, one for all' were adopted. And, since there was no end to the virus, despair ran rampant and sucked everyone into its vortex.

Despair was rampant and ran deep, but in the early days there were those who, like myself, did our best to nourish the thought that despite all appearances things might change for the better. After all, is it not true that sometimes we are obliged to turn a corner and, having done so with the greatest reluctance, find before us an unexpected avenue of hope, a ray of light where hitherto only darkness reigned, a fresh prospect which, though perhaps in the event fleeting, fills us with a new and brighter resolve?

But despair continued to reign supreme.

The poor are always neglected, as though subject to an unwritten law. Good writers have always known it and struggled to point it out, as though the mere pointing might end it. Meanwhile, the law prevails as Primo Levy described it, '*Nella storia e nella vita pare talvolta di discernere una feroce legge, che suona: a chi ha, saro` dato, a chi non ha, a quello sara` tolto.*' It seems a law of universal injustice that to those who have their share more will be given, while from those who have little will be taken the little they have. But when good writers wrote they did so for themselves or for the converted; larger readerships preferred the suspense novel or entertainment for entertainment's sake. Now, no one writes at all. Even in more civilised times, people like Levy were largely unread, and consequently the law to which he referred slept like a sleeping giant. Now, reading is a half-remembered irrelevance – a vastly insufficient balm for the loneliness and isolation that the Virus has engendered and quite incapable of nullifying the universal sense of despair and dejection.

Yes, there is such a thing as 'human spirit', courage and selflessness beyond measure. But people need people. Isolation and loneliness were the handmaidens of despair. A garden may boast the most beautiful of blooms, but gardens must be cultivated lest the most beautiful of blooms fade, wither and die – and once dead they will not return. Human virtues are also blooms in need of cultivation. Isolation cuts off the heads of flowers and leaves a sea of stalks. It was written that no man is an island unto himself. No man can possibly be an island and at the same time exemplify those virtues that depend for their being and their sense on the existence of his fellows. Isolation compounded despair, which grew at an exponential rate.

Let me state it simply: People Need People!!! These three words pack a greater punch than any axiom of geometry. Yet, they are so frequently forgotten and almost always undervalued – like something you don't throw away but hide in the bottom drawer or shove in the attic. *People Need People*. Perhaps these words should be written on our foreheads so that we can be constantly reminded when we look at each other or in the mirror, as circumcision is supposed to remind the mutilated of God in moments of their ungodliness, moments that are anything but few and far between.

Here, outside gangland, where interaction is below zero, those of us who are left avoid each other like the plague, if the pun can be forgiven. People have become synonymous with 'carriers' and with the Virus they are believed to carry. The Roman dictum 'Divide and Rule' could never have been so effective or so cruelly applied. The advice of governments and health authorities, at first fairly faithfully followed, became ineffective. Nobody listened. Nobody wanted to listen. The whole thing had gone on for too long. The patience of the best of us had been tried, and was found wanting, especially when despair at finding a solution was compounded by the deaths of loved ones and the consequent destruction of families. Things started to unravel – as they would have done in 1940 had the Nazi pounding of London continued much longer, or, even late in the war, had Hitler's much vaunted 'secret weapons', the V1 and V2, been unassailably long-term.

And so it is that Nature survives and Man does not.

Entry 4

The crows were silent this morning. I spotted one in silhouette sitting stock still on one of the lower branches, and not even my hasty movements below, brushing against bush and branch as I passed, caused it to ruffle a feather. I later realised it must have been asleep. I was amused by the thought that those noisy fellows must also sleep; perhaps they were all there, up in the highest branches, asleep in unison. I wondered whether they dream, and, if so, of what? I dream nightly – confused patchworks of scenes and events none of which make sense, causing me to wake fearful and morbidly alert.

When it all started and lockdowns were imposed, cars in the early morning were few and far between. One or two would gingerly pass me on the road that skirts the park, the road I need to cross to enter it. Now cars are equally scarce, but unsurprisingly they aren't driven with care; Raiders have taken most of them, just as they've taken over petrol stations, and they drive them with the aggression that comes with a loss of humanity. Nobody drives anymore, unless they're a trusted member of a gang. Cars are to be avoided as are the Raiders who mishandle them. I once saw a bus driven at speed and crazily entertained the thought that it was a benevolent thing – a semblance of normality, perhaps, and therefore a piece of welcome nostalgia. But the speed gave the lie to such a thought, and I knew it must be Raiders. Roads are best avoided. I cross in semi-darkness from the road to the park as quickly and as deftly as I can. Because I am a man on the run!

But in the early days it was different. Then I took my morning walks outside the park. The park was in darkness at 5am; the entrance was pitch black, no doubt a foreboding aspect to which the dense tall and leafy trees contributed much. I chose instead to walk the roads that skirted the park; in those days the roads were still lit at intervals and the houses were still inhabited and untouched by Raiders. Residents were nervous and apprehensive about the events that were unfolding and tried their best to follow the official guidelines that were designed to protect them from the Virus; though nervous and uncertain about the future, they were still human and mindful of the sacrifices they were asked to make in terms of what was innocently called 'social distancing'.

The road I walk was bounded on one side by these houses, and, on the other, by the dark, deep, dense blackness of the park. People were fast asleep in their houses, not one light could be seen in any of the windows. But even the houses themselves seemed in repose. I remembered Wordsworth's lines, written on London Bridge, and agreed that 'the very houses seemed asleep'. But those were the good days, days of hope, however fragile. Now the houses are empty, their occupants dead and gone – or at least dead. I once picked up the courage to enter one of these houses after knocking first respectfully then frantically on the door, which of course was locked. Fortunately, I should say unfortunately, a door to the rear was open, and I entered. The place smelled of death and decay as I entered the living room – no,

I had seen enough and will not open the wounds of my memory here. I quickly decided that the park would be a better option for my morning walks, be it ever so dark and foreboding – better the trees in deep shadow and the crows in their black mantles than the sight of corpses in varying stages of decay. The only house I enter now is my own, and then only because it has a basement.

Suffice to say here that in the days when hope turned to utter despair, the hospitals were overflowing with the dead and the dying, which included the medics themselves, losing their lives not only to the Virus itself but to those equally deadly conditions that had perforce to take a back seat or be neglected entirely in favour of Virus patients. With the first partial and then total breakdown of the health services people stayed at home and died there. The exponential transmission of the Virus was inevitable. The deadly outcome, at first confined to the elderly and those with serious existing medical conditions, then spread to younger and stronger generations who had thought themselves immune to fatality. Even those who had suffered the Virus and recovered were subjected to it again, this time fatally, probably because the Virus had mutated into a stronger strain, one that was determined to have its way. Faced with transmission and mutation with overwhelming force, few were likely to survive.

I try not to think of the houses I have to pass en route to the park. Bereft of all life, they are not merely asleep; they are deceased; they have become mausoleums. I have no curiosity. My steps quicken as I approach them. Despite the darkness in which they are enveloped, the trees and their inhabitants seem almost amiable beings.

Once inside the park, and to my right and not far from the entrance, there is a particularly dark cluster of bushes and trees, black as pitch inside. It strikes you as a pitch-black patch in the lesser darkness of its surroundings. I can recall times when the sight of such a place would have filled me with horror and foreboding; a somewhat diseased mind might have imagined it as a place of foul deeds – the sight of some horrible doings, or of a witches' coven or a heinous crime, some unspeakable crime. I would have recoiled at such thoughts and walked passed it with quickening pace, or found an alternative route. But now this black dingle is a safe haven, standing in contrast to those sepulchres of red brick, those tiled boxes of death and abandonment that line my route to the park's entrance and which I must inevitably pass – daily reminders of how far man has fallen, from his high estate and vaunted superiority over nature to a state of helpless servitude to his baser instincts, while trees from their commanding heights yet stand tall and pitying.

How far we have fallen since the early days, weeks and months! But even the best of us are crushed by events. Repeated reassurances from even the most respected of authorities are subject to the law of diminishing marginal utility and begin to fall on deaf ears when events continue to take turns for the worst. The Virus tore families apart: mothers from children, husbands from wives, friends from friends, followed by the pains and anguish of total isolation, contributing to widespread mental deterioration, forcing thoughts into minds that had had no place in them, corrupting the spirit, perverting logic and distorting the capacity to think – and therefore to feel. People said forced goodbyes to loved ones as they were hurried away first to hospitals, and then, when hospitals failed to cope, to the so-called 'isolation units', never to be seen again.

In the early days some of those who had been whisked away returned, having 'survived' the Virus, but survival was temporary, therefore illusory, and this time they were left to die at home, infecting those loved ones who had been so overjoyed to welcome them back into the fold. In this way, whole families were first dissected and then terminated, reminiscent of events at such places as Auschwitz, Sobibor and Treblinka where the unspeakable evil of separation and extermination was practised as though it were a straightforward question of expediency – though, since Holocaust survivors and those who had lived through the 'blitzkrieg' were now extinct and since schools had closed their doors, there were very few who were minded of Man's unspeakable track record when separation and disintegration again became a question of expediency. This time the evil might of course be blamed on an impersonal Virus, at least at first, but the swift, detached efficiency with which the process was soon to be conducted inevitably fuelled comparisons with the human inhumanities of the preceding century.

Since the word 'God' is never far from the lips of believers and nonbelievers alike in times of either abundant joy or insufferable pain, there were those who appealed to Him for succour; and also those who denounced Him and his appellants, for no God worth his status, certainly no *loving* God could possibly allow the Virus, or indeed anything else, to wipe out his beloved creations. Oh, dear, the same old disputes, as ludicrous as that between the Lilliputians as to which end to break an egg. If only they could have resolved the dispute by stepping outside it and removing its legs right from under it. If only they had decided that God is neither a something nor a someone, but an idea, and that the best idea is the idea of love! Then God as an object of blame would be absurd, what some philosophers might have called a 'category mistake', and then all religious differences would have melted away in volleys of good-natured laughter and a flurry of warm embraces. Centuries of conflict and bitter resentment would at last have been seen to be entirely, not to say wickedly, groundless.

Instead, competing religions sharpened their responses. The Christian Church appealed to believers to cling to their faith in a benevolent and loving God, while Imams argued that their God was out to seek revenge on infidels while, since believers of all faiths were subject to fatal viral outcomes, securing a place in Heaven for all Muslims who succumbed to the Virus. Others who were sickened by such nonsense simply hoped for the best in an increasingly hopeless scenario. As mental health continued to decline and social isolation and lockdown cut off any and every recourse in the shape of holidays, pubs and other recreational facilities, racial tensions, until then kept largely in check, began to increase and were further exacerbated by religious zealots on all sides. Fear and a lack of confidence are the food of fanaticism, which now grew apace and threatened ever-widening social and communal divisions especially in the industrial and manufacturing heartlands. An at first weakened and eventually non-existent police force was replaced by a cobbled-together militia, a rag-tag substitute for a domestic army already impoverished by former economic exigencies and, now, irreparably weakened by viral upsurges in all ranks. Riots were at first put down by force; then they were tolerated; then they ran their course.

Then came the Raiders.

Entry 5

I didn't venture out this morning. There was too much external noise last night, and I thought I heard something upstairs this morning, some kind of moving about, which woke me up and went on for a bit. Thankfully no one discovered and tested the basement door. I've disguised it as a set of makeshift bookshelves; I've stacked the books on it flat so that they don't fall off every time I open and close it, which I must do gingerly. It's worked so far – God help me when it doesn't! If they discovered the basement and me in it, they'd be more likely to burn me out.

The only reason I need to venture upstairs is to replenish my water, which I keep in plastic bottles. But I've got a good supply down here. And plenty of canned food, which we started to accumulate bit by bit as soon as the outlook began to look bleak. In those days, shops were still open and supplied most of what people needed, but when things got rough and no antidote to the Virus was in sight, people lost hope and conspiracy theories of all kinds, largely promulgated on social media, started to take hold. I remember laughing at the suggestion that beings from another planet were planning an invasion and that the Virus was the equivalent of Hitler's blitzkrieg and was designed to eliminate all organised opposition. I laugh at it still, though less convincingly. Nobody knows anything, but one conspiracy has become as plausible as any other, and now people are ready to believe anything, however incredible and implausible it may once have seemed.

It's all about panic and despair. Crime was bound to increase far beyond the capabilities of the police and the army. At first, most people toed the line, but the prospect of inevitable death outweighed any penalty that could be devised for looting, and, of course, no one listened to the Church with its pious pronouncements against selfishness and greed. The police and the army progressively lost their voices until, at last, they broke ranks with public order and formed the very gangs they were designed to protect everyone against. It's as though a beast were released from its cage and couldn't be recapture. The old weapons against hopelessness, fear and despair have lost their edge.

Bunyan's *Pilgrim's Progress* is the only book left from my father's small library; I have it here with me in the basement. I still repeat to myself my favourite line, 'Be ye watchful, and cast away fear; be sober, and hope to the end.' But the Virus carries with it an end which is infinitely more certain than the hope which is here prescribed – unless of course you believe in Heaven and are sufficiently complacent to believe you are assured of a place in it.

Seems quiet outside and upstairs now. Tomorrow is another day. As for today, doubtless sufficient is the evil thereof.

Entry 6

There were the remains of a large fire in the park, and bits of other stuff which I couldn't clearly make out, and a great many beer cans littered about. I dared not stare in passing – but left it all in my peripheral vision. I walked quickly and made for the dense foliage which skirts the central square of grass completing my circuit as much under cover as possible. Sounds carry from the park, especially the inhuman ruckus made by Raiders; I heard late last night and tried to block it out with earphones plugged into my DVD player – with Handel's *Messiah* at full blast. Bonfires and large crowds have always sent shivers down my spine, with thoughts of mad rampages and inarticulate protests. The roars of spectators have about them the echoes of a distant past and the gladiatorial ring. No doubt they had a good time last night, especially if others had to suffer for it. On my return I filled some extra bottles upstairs and was more than commonly careful when opening the door to the basement and closing it behind me.

When people were people and were still capable of thought, albeit unclear and twisted thought, conspiracy theories were rife. There was talk about biological weapons and experiments. But the underlying issue was that of survival and most people agreed that speculation, theories and investigations would have to wait under the Virus was well under control and an effective vaccine had been developed – until it was all over and done with. The problem was that it was never over and done with. It was however agreed that no one country could have engineered the pandemic on purpose, for all countries were affected and what country in its right mind would annihilate itself? Of course, something might have gone dreadfully wrong with a biological experiment which ended up as a global catastrophe. But in the absence of proof positive human beings are quick to draw cast iron conclusions from mere speculation. The stage was set for blame, and tension was in some cases created between a desire for positive and constructive cooperation in a global crisis and, on the other hand, the breaking of international ties following a spate of relentless reproach for the failings, real or imagined, of other countries to do or say the right thing. The Virus was therefore bitterly divisive, and states which had historical reasons to treat one another with more than a modicum of circumspection were now more resentful of each other than ever before.

Opinions within countries were also divided and, like a house divided within itself, each country was bound to suffer vacillation and decline. The Far Right and the Far Left were set on a collision course that would rock the foundations of the society which had until now managed to contain them. Even families were divided, so often irreconcilably.

One such problem arose when a test was devised to demonstrate immunity to the Virus. Those whose immunity was proven to the satisfaction of the medical fraternity were given identity cards; cards which became greatly coveted due to the favours immunity conferred upon the chosen few – those few chosen by Fate to be spared a most painful and undignified end.

Immunity cards became golden tickets to freedom of movement between the blocks or regions into which the country was now divided and heavily policed, and even to positions of authority and power. A new militia composed of the so-called Immunes began to replace the police and the army. Inevitably, they began to abuse the powers conferred upon them and became at first the butt of jokes and soon the objects of fear and loathing amongst the Vulnerables. This biochemical lottery replaced the powers traditionally conferred by birth or acquired wealth.

Even before immunity testing became mandatory for all, it was avoided by those who feared the implications of the outcome, for they dreaded the prospect of separation from loved ones. Those who tested immune were no longer permitted to cohabit with their loved ones unless these latter tested likewise. A new and dreadful class system began to raise its ugly head.

But it was shortlived. For the much desired immunity was anything but permanent, and sometimes non-existent despite testing negative. The Virus was indeed a resourceful enemy, adapting itself through mutation to strike the Immunes down or disguising itself as benign, as resourceful as a sniper in camouflage. The theory was that the Virus was simply lying dormant and undetected due to temporary mutation. At first, those who tested 'negative' were happy to receive their immunity cards, which ambiguously read 'Virus undetected'; the phrase unfortunately tended to suggest either that the Virus was absent or that it might indeed be present but was unseen; since there is a world of difference between 'absent' and 'undetected' card-holders felt uncertain about the reassurances the card was meant to provide.

The ambiguity was sooner for some, later for others, resolved with crystal clarity. When ready, the Virus struck the Immunes with a vengeance with its customary disregard for gender, age or status. Next to death itself it soon proved to be the greatest leveller known to man. Little wonder the Virus was then credited with a super intelligence of which only super beings could be credited. The little green 'men' who had inhabited a moon made of cheese, and the more complex but equally fantastic variations in *Star Trek* and *Doctor Who*, all amusingly familiar in the imaginations of a human and therefore inferior species of being brought up on a diet of complete but harmless fantasy, were now replaced by an infinitely more complex creature, invisible to the human eye, intelligent beyond human comprehension and, worst of all, very real. But from this confusing and mind-blowing picture of an adversary which could only be seen under a microscope, a 'corollary' was entertained to the effect that the Virus was merely the tool, the weapon, of creatures from another galaxy – and (who knows?) these creatures might after all be little green men!

The truth, of course, was that no one knew anything, and are none the wiser now.

Entry 7

I've made no notes for two days – no three; two or three, I'm not sure. Yesterday, I heard footsteps following behind me on the path which leads out of the park. Well, I'm not certain of that. I *thought* they were footsteps – at least, they stopped when I did and then seemed to start again when I moved on. Whenever I turned round, I could see nothing – hardly surprising in the half-light of the morning. Whoever it was might have sidestepped into the bushes where it's even darker. I could have called out – but no, I wouldn't do that; I don't want to invite any kind of intercourse at all; I just don't want to know. In any case, I might have been completely mistaken, and then calling out might have attracted some kind of unwanted attention; it would have been a signal that I was there – I don't want that; it's safer to be absolutely incognito. There are no friends these days. You just can't make a friend in the jungle that this whole place, this whole country, this whole world has become.

Well, my worry was that someone might follow me home and to the basement – I'd be a target, and then it's all up. So I made a detour, through the overgrown hedges and gardens slowly, looking and listening all the way – and ripping my jacket and scratching my face and hands in the process. I made it, I think safely, to the shed at the bottom of the garden. I waited inside, until I remembered that I didn't want to move in daylight from there to the house. I crept out of the shed just before the light was fully up and made a dash for the house and then to the basement. Come to think of it, it might've been better to make the return journey in the usual way – the detour might itself have attracted attention. It's hard to think straight when you feel up against it and for so long. If they find out the house is still inhabited … But anyway, all's well that ends well.

I'm definitely not what I was. My nerves are shattered. How many are left like me – hiding away and afraid to move, afraid to be seen? I don't know. I can't afford to know. So this is what the Virus has done – it really is a house divided against itself. It has separated people so well … better than an isolation block in a security prison could do. At least in prison you could do with friends and you might try to make them – you might knock on your wall, and then someone might knock back; you wouldn't be averse to some kind of communication, however basic it might be. But in this hell hole, you daren't make a sound that could be heard by anyone else. After all, you wouldn't want to be heard by the Raiders. It's lucky I've managed to escape attention so far – just as well the house is tucked away at the end of a long cul-de-sac, almost out of sight. Even so, luck is in the habit of changing.

We had a car, once. Stolen, of course, and no prizes for guessing who stole it. But, as I keep saying, no one really owns anything anymore.

Entry 8

I spotted the shadowy figure of a muntjac deer darting across the parkland, followed by the dark shape of a fox, its brush trailing behind it like a rudder. Animals are always on the run, as are humans now, and as am I. They were hell-bent on running, one to escape, the other to kill. If they noticed me amongst the shadows of bush and tree, they obviously couldn't have cared a fig. Animals and humans seem to have equal claims to the land now and are all equally at home whether in overgrown parklands or rundown suburbia. All those well-kept gardens are now unkempt bush and thicket and home to every species of wildlife; dogs and cats have lost whatever domesticity they had, becoming beast-like and hostile; so much so you could be forgiven for thinking they've contracted the Virus, too, which may, if not killed them at least changed their natures; who'd have thought that poodles and pussy cats could ever become ravenous little beasts; their growls and screams can be heard throughout the night, mingling with the shouts and obscenities of the Raiders when their blood is up. Not a pretty account of what was once called a green and pleasant land. Domestic animals, which were once affectionately considered the companions of man, have become his adversaries and his equals in the struggle for survival.

Living in isolation from one another was and is the worst thing. It begged questions about the whole point of existence when all human contact had no place in the equation. It was like a huge tapestry which had at one time been taken for granted and seemed to make sense but which was now tattered and torn with bits falling off. What, for example, was the point of education when you felt that all was absolutely lost? In the early days, students were in colleges and universities in a state of lockdown, separated not only from their families but from their teachers and one another. What was the point of that? Then, further down the line, when hopes of finding a conquering vaccine were beginning at last to fade, all students who had not themselves succumbed to the Virus returned to their families, or what was left of their families, whether family members were infected or not – just like people bunching together when all is lost and the end is inevitable; the kindest thing, the obvious thing, was to end your days with loved ones who were ending theirs.

Human contact, preferably benign contact, is essential. For that reason alone retirement should be abolished. People able and willing to work should continue until they decide otherwise; age, other things being equal, should be no barrier to either work or education. But the Virus puts an end to all options.

It's strange to think that there were schools, colleges and universities, with students and teachers and books and all the paraphernalia of learning. When you're facing certain death and the extinction of human life, education of whatever description really has very little to offer.

It used to be hoped by some that the pandemic would result in a morally improved world, a kinder, more compassionate form of civilisation, one that would bring people closer together and give a lasting boost towards a global utopia. Much the same, of course, had, by been said time and time again about political revolutions, despite the rare voice of wisdom which described such dramatic events as no more than one man holding a gun to the head of another, or, just as graphically, as the substitution of one rider for another on the same horse. Anyway, such hopes have not been realised; *hope* requires material to work with, and *faith* requires something to believe in; the pandemic has left scope for neither. Humanity has behaved rather badly in their absence, supplanting them with the primeval urge for survival, however temporary that survival may be.

When organised religions which promised an eternity in paradise for those who behaved well declined and tended to be treated as relegations to the nursery of mankind, the baby was thrown out with the bathwater; for most people virtue is by no means its own reward; vice so often *is*. When the incentive to do good is removed, well, why bother? Even before the Virus reduced people to quivering wrecks the chances of the majority recognising beauty where beauty truly resides were pathetically slim, thanks to the unprecedented rise of technology in the form of personal computers, laptops, smart phones and the fanatical obsession with the so-called 'social media' that inevitably accompanied their widespread use. Mediocrity on such a scale replaced the worship of a loving God and made it harder to distinguish between wheat and chaff. Talk of 'true beauty' had almost invariably seemed a lost cause when confronted by a rapidly burgeoning dependence on the tools and gadgets of mediocrity. But when the Virus began to dissect and devour us, no one knew what the word 'beauty' could possibly mean talk of the beauty of nature and, more particularly, of the human soul, seems perversely hollow now and just so much cant. Is there anyone left capable of distinguishing between the compositions of Bach and the beating of a drum?

The truth about mankind, its limitations and its propensity to make the worst out of a bad job, its fickle, unreliable nature, is heavy; strong, broad shoulders are needed to carry it, and courage, too, when hope is so scant and so fragile. As Augustine well knew, 'There may be some light in men, but let them walk fast, walk fast! lest the shadows come'; and again, 'He who is wise knows pain, and a heart that understands acts like rust in the bones.' If the wise must shoulder such pain, would it not be better to live in ignorance, like an animal which has no knowledge of the slaughterhouse that awaits it and is incapable of being comforted by the promise of an afterlife? J.S. Mill thought otherwise, 'It is better to be a Socrates dissatisfied than a pig satisfied.'

But the thoughts of the wise, like those of the unwise, have no place here now. Such a waste of human life is war and man's unspeakable inhumanity to man; but the waste laid by the Virus to which all without exception, good, bad, vile or saintly and all the rest of us in between, are subject was unasked for and undeserved. But what do we know? No one knows anything.

It was never the so-called successes but the so-called failures that merited my attention – I mean, the stories of all those good people who had worked hard and honestly and yet ended their wretched lives with nothing to show for all their sacrifices except a name on a piece of stone that no one reads. Why, even a snail leave behind it a signature of its existence. Instead, that wretched god Mediocrity saw to it that those who refused to bow at its altar would live in oblivion, while those with nothing to say and little of value to do were the subjects of high acclaim, cradling in them a false belief in their own worth – like those who subsist on junk food thinking it to be high cuisine or at least a simple but reliable source of nourishment.

I remember being told, 'You can always stoop and pick up nothing.' And 'nothing' is also the fruit of Mediocrity and those who vaunt the hollow achievements of mankind without counting the cost for others or for the future of the human civilisation or that of the planet on which they strut. Perhaps the Virus has thrived on our own misdemeanours, our encroachment on animal life and our consequent adoption of their own diseases. How far we are ourselves responsible for our plight is still unknown and, now, will never be. All we reap is the whirlwind.

Bertrand Russell waged a war against nuclear weapons and their proliferation, believing them to be a wicked; he would have said the same about chemical warfare; and about war of any description. Why? Because he thought the planet and its human civilisation was worth preserving; not of course on account of its evils but because of the beauty that man is, after all, capable of achieving, in thought and in deed.

But our decline has come so far that Russell's position would now stand on hollow legs.

Our education, good or bad, wise or unwise, could not have prepared us for the world as it is now. 'Education is a preparation for life' was the old cliché, though I always thought that 'Education is a preparation for a *better* life' would have been a vast improvement. Either way, education has become an irrelevance. I've almost begun to envy the muntjac and the fox, risking Mill's judgement about Socrates and a pig – but the muntjac and the fox can't speak and are therefore immune to the reproach that they don't.

Communication in any meaningful sense has ceased to exist now – although one might well ask to what extent meaningful, let alone profound, communication was ever achievable between members of the species *homo sapiens*. Still, there was a time, long before the Virus was dreamed of, when men doffed their caps or inclined their heads as they passed one another in respectful recognition of one another's existence, and this might have passed for communication of a kind and was very welcome as such. When the Virus tightened its grip, such forms of acknowledgement were even more sought after; but then, when hope was gone, even this rudimentary form of respect went with it, for people became excessively inward and lived with extreme caution, on a knife's edge of nerves, as a man might walk half expecting the ground to open up at his very next step and swallow him whole into a pitch-black and bottomless pit, never more to see the light of day and the smiling faces of those he leaves behind.

What passes for communication amongst the Raiders may well decline further into the grunts, squeals and shrieks familiar in the animal kingdom; be that as it may, they are at least subsisting in groups or packs which may loosely be described as 'social'; all those who are not with them subsist in bubbles of isolation, most dreading death, many considering it a form of blessed release, though not wishing it to come without an uncomfortable degree of ambivalence; 'tired of living and afraid of dying' must have become a common refrain – but I'm in no position to do other than guess, projecting my own emotions on those I cannot see and have no wish to see.

With a sense of hopelessness came a loss of humour; even trench humour had a short life and disappeared when total isolation and unmitigated fear was in the ascendant; after all, trench humour must be shared, and therefore becomes pointless when individuals are in total isolation from one another. I myself had a sense of humour; in fact, I believe it was an enviable sense of humour, one which won me friends, true friends, not mere associates. But I've forgotten how to laugh, and even smiles are hard to form. I remember, from long, long ago, an uncle of mine who, reproached for being consistently solemn, would remark, 'Well, I smile when there is something to smile about, and laugh when there is something to laugh about.' I thought very little of that at the time, yet now I respect him enormously – that was a man with uncommon intelligence, and I reproach myself for not understanding him better.

'A good philosophy book might consist entirely of jokes,' said a prominent philosopher. No one is joking now. Philosophy, art, history, yes and even much-vaunted science, is at an end. No one is laughing. No one knows how to laugh. Eyes are as blank as the eyes of the dead. And no doubt you know, the eyes of the dead are blank indeed.

And did I not say, the eyes of my mother were as blank as a starless night?

She died many years ago, long, long ago, long before this pandemic, and her eyes, her sharp and beautiful eyes, closed upon an ordinary morning in April, a morning which was anything but normal because of her passing. I am glad she didn't live to see all this. Her poor, sensitive soul could never have endured this – this isolation, this road to nowhere, this total abnegation of all that is loving and compassionate. I looked upon her lifeless eyes, and, ever since, I wish I had never done so. A spell was cast which, it seems, can never be undone. I guess she would have said, 'May God save us all' – though her faith in God had all her life through been only half formed and half entertained, like someone who bets on a horse without studying 'form' – who bets on hearsay and simply hopes for the best.

Entry 9

Last night I believe I dreamed of hope – if it is possible to dream of such a thing, to dream such a dream. I dreamed I walked to the top of White Tower Hill and in the full light of a summer's morning, something I have not be able to do since I can't remember when. I took a good look round from the top. Everything was refreshingly clear, and the air was pure nectar. Yet there was no wind and nothing moved, no movement below, either, on that winding road below. No movement, and no noise; not a sound, none of the customary skylarks; but none of the angry barking of dogs, either, that roam in packs as though in emulation of the Raiders. Everywhere was a still and vivid canvas, lifeless but for the vistas of grass and bush and the cluster of small trees at the summit. It felt like a new start, as though a nightmare had ended. Perhaps I had a feeling, vague as feelings are when recounted from dreams, that the sky, the grass, the whole hill, was the same as that seen and walked by former generations, that it was somehow better and purer than what we see around us now, as though what man has called progress is in fact a retrogression of at least a thousand years. But, well, dreams are like memories – they both cheat us in the telling.

At least it was a brighter dream and a complete change from the dreams I now so often suffer: nightmarish, confused and confusing excursions which cause me to wake in states of fear and anxiety – as those the fears and anxieties of my waking hours aren't enough! It seems as though our brain cells store and then in sleep release, like barbed arrows, the disturbing sights and unhinging feelings of the day, to give us a double dose of painful visions. Our reflections are hardly ever salutary, simply because there has been so little to be hopeful about. Whenever hope is kindled, something happens to extinguish the flame. There was the call, for example, for Community Groups to help the elderly and the infirm who, confined to their houses, were obliged to depend on others for food deliveries, medical supplies and some temporary relief from the monotony and evil of loneliness. It worked for a while, until hope was knocked on the head by a growing and irreversible sense of despair and fear, and some CGs responded by looting the homes of the helpless, no doubt thinking it to be a far better proposition. The CGs were formally disbanded, but the looting and the systematic abuse of the helpless continued to run unabated. Even when voices could still be raised against the bestial nature of such unspeakable developments, there was no authority to back them up; law when it cannot be enforced is no more useful than a wallpaper pattern.

When hospitals were unable to function (due primarily to the unstoppable ravages of the Virus which began to kill off the medics faster than their patients, and then the absence of electrical power when the generators failed, and also the total lack of clean water) and were consequently abandoned, the thread by which social care hung was finally and irrevocably cut. They became places the least safe to work in, unsafe to stay; those inmates who could leave, did so; those who could not remained where they were and, presumably, died where they lay. Large hospitals became labyrinths of utter misery and desolation. They became the castles of the Middle Ages which, it was said, could be smelled from miles distant. What human remains may be found in them now I shudder to think – visions of skeletal remains are like unwelcome guests in my imagination, since I never dared venture inside these huge brick mausoleums, even when it was still possible to venture out into the light of day. People gave them a wide berth – so that far from being safe havens of treatment and cure for the sick, they became infinitely worse than the slums and ghettoes of the Middle Ages.

There was, presumably still is, a winding and leafy road which, if pursued far enough, begins to run alongside a large hospital visible to the right and well above it. There were times when I walked that road, taking in the fresh spring air in the early mornings, happy to breathe deeply the mixture of aromas that nature freely provided. It was as if that enticing road led to a better world, a Land of Oz, where everything might be put right – perhaps there on the horizon where the hospital stands. I dare not walk that road now, not in the light of day, and to do so at night would be pointless, even if safe, which I doubt. Should a stranger even find himself upon it, he would do well to walk in the opposite direction or get off it altogether. The beauty of that road seemed to make a promise which it cannot now keep.

Its beauty partly consisted in its power to evoke memories of better times and places, of names and faces long gone. What an album of ghostly things memory is! It's pictures and the ways they are arranged can hardly be trusted – all twisted into shapes invariably better than those they were born with. You hardly know whether the things and people pictured there are representations of what they once were or are merely products of your wishful and so often pained imagination – figments over which you have very little control, as much products of feelings as of substance; and feelings shift and change, their shapes like demons from an ancient mythology. Are we masters of our fate? We are not masters of our memories; they hold sway over us; we are their slaves, and at their beck and call.

The world is full of haunted men; for memories, twisted, embellished, perverted though they may be, may have about them the curse of witchcraft; the source of fears incalculable or of siren calls from a paradise forever lost, they will not loosen their grip. We pine for what once was, and, as we age, our memories, entirely reliable or not, become sharper, even in a reality half-imagined, as long-term memory outperforms our ability to recall what was said or done some moments past. Objects and things remembered, though of little consequence in themselves, seem invested with the feelings left far behind and now irrecoverable: comfort, security, peace, familiarity, tranquillity and a settled peace of mind; such feelings make for bittersweet recollections and may be as much to be feared as recollections of doom and disaster, of great loss and unspeakable inhumanity. And so it is that the longer a man's years, the less he lives. His memories ensure that he will shake and shiver with fears beyond his control and far beyond his comprehension. Is he not to be pitied? Or is he simply a lost child of his own dying egoism? Such is the world of old men, full of lost souls yearning for the simple sensations of youth.

My cerebral self hardly lets me rest. The brain in the machine presents me with objects from long, long ago, emotions duly attached:

chair, table, corner, lamp, book, pipe, wine, Dorcas and the modest tin of tobacco she brings, like a kind woman bearing a small gift to one who is unable to treat himself. Simple objects. A simple memory – but why, then, does it burn, sting and rend the flesh like a barbed arrow? Any answer I give would be no more reliable than the memory it seeks to explain. And that is because both the answer and the memory come from the same source – me!

Dreams, like memories, may be twisted further in the telling, but I'm happy to have had that glimpse of the world from the top of White Tower Hill. How it acquired that name I can't say. Perhaps a tower had stood atop it. Or perhaps a white tower could have been seen from it. I saw no tower, white or otherwise, nor the remains of one. If a dream is a foretaste of the future, might a white tower yet be built there? Tonight I can expect something less uplifting.

Entry 10

Mornings are decidedly colder, and the trees have begun to shed their leaves. Our lives follow the broad pattern of the seasons: we have our beginnings like the first shoots of spring, then we bloom, if at all, in our summers, and then like leaves, my mother used to say, we fall, our exits and our entrances on nature's stage – not a hopeful reflection, just a fact, and not a pleasant one. Our ends seem hardly a fitting conclusion to the gruelling journey we have made since the cradle. Aram Arax, an Armenian poet of note, once asked what he gave his mother for all her self-sacrifices, for all her acts of self-denial, for all her labours and trials, for all those things she'd said and done to comfort and encourage him, for all those selfless efforts she had made to care for him and keep him safe, for all her quiet sufferings and unspoken indulgences on his behalf, for all the love she'd shown him.

He says she was given 'a splendid funeral, with many floral sprays and bouquets', and asks, 'What if those flowers could speak?'

A mother, good or bad, is an individual made significant by her individuality. If all we give to the best of mothers is a floral tribute, what do we give to everyone else?

This morning I felt once again that I was being followed, but the wind repeatedly rose and fell, and the leaves rustled in the half-light, so that it's hard now to tell fact from fiction. I sensed that I was not alone – that's all I can say. It's been too long; nerves are frayed and judgement is unreliable. Grief and loneliness made thin, ethereal, hollow creatures of all of us who survived the first wave of the Virus. The survivors, many falsely believing themselves to be endowed with more than a modicum of luck and unaccountably immune to the Virus, some others believing themselves protected by the imagined efficacy of prayer and religious devotion, became the victims of a second wave. The fact that the Virus attacked in waves was reminiscent of the bombing strategy adopted by the Luftwaffe over London and other major cities: in the first wave came the incendiaries, forcing inhabitants to vacate burning buildings for the safety of the streets; then came the second wave, with high explosives, to decimate those who had congregated in the imagined safety of the streets and open spaces. The Virus was being used to similar effect.

Little wonder that in the imaginations of many they were being attacked by a biological weapon wielded by an enemy, terrestrial or otherwise, hell-bent on wiping out the human race – or at least large sections of it; added to which was the brilliant stroke afforded by a weapon which was transmitted amongst humans, one to another, at potentially exponential rates, so that humans were actually doing the work of their enemies for them by wiping out each other with a weapon that was *invisible*. A masterstroke if ever there was one! Evidence indeed of a higher intelligence! And the more you thought of it, the more masterful and unstoppable it became, so that a rapid decline in morale could be added to the armoury of the invaders. Here was an enemy with no chinks in its armour ranged against the defenceless and helpless. This was no contest.

Other, even more deadly, waves were to follow. But it was during this second wave that she … No, I can't! I can't even bring myself to write of it, not even one word. The thought of it is. But I shall never leave her. That's one promise I've made that I'll never break. Never! But things are hard here, in the silence. Man wasn't made to live alone – here in this silence and this darkness. Which reminds me – I must go easy on the candles. Go easy. Maybe if I write during daylight hours – but even then I need more light, here in the basement. I must learn to write in the shadows. Very appropriate.

There is something else I hardly dare write about. I think … I think my brain is giving up. Those dreams – I've already mentioned them – well, they seem to be getting more frequent – taking me to places I don't want to go – strange, twisted places. Sometimes the most painful are those that take me back to places and faces long ago – yes, these are the worst; places and faces that mean me no harm; on the contrary, they were the places and faces much better times, times of hope and pleasant expectations, of kindness and humanity. But to dream of them now is to suffer the pain of contrast. Those places and faces have gone, never to return. Instead we have the last waves of the Virus – which means the last of everything. Then there are the dreams without faces; only places I can only half recognise, winding roads and paths, all full of trickery, leading nowhere except to solid walls of grey concrete or to cliff edges where there is no return but only falls into the blackest of depths.

If I were a drinker, I'd have kept that box of whiskey instead of throwing it away. But that was down to her … and, yes, I'm glad of it. Drinking that stuff now would only fog things up even more than they are already. I remember reading that thing about Sam Johnson. He was near his end but declined to take a drink though he'd been a keen tippler all his life; he said something about wanting a clear head – something like that; well, I think I understand him well enough.

Entry 11

The walk this morning felt particularly oppressive, I guess because of the silence, made more intense by the frosty air and the crunch of icy leaves underfoot. No birds sang, and the crows were nowhere to be seen. It's as though everything had been sucked into a black hole, leaving behind a blank, soundless canvas. Will the world ever be repopulated?

During the first wave of the Virus, amongst the weird, half-humorous remarks made was that the additional time spent in isolation at home would occasion a greater propensity to copulate, and that this would serve to repopulate the planet should the Virus decimate human life – though no one at that time believed it possible that the Virus could possibly wreak that amount of havoc, confident that science would produce an antidote well beforehand. But when it finally dawned on everyone that we were in for the long haul, with no guarantee of deliverance, and, even further down the line, when the death toll topped millions, those who had contemplated families began to question whether it was right to bring children uninvited into a world which offered little or no hope of salvation from the Virus – more than this, into a world whose population was panicking and growing ever more hostile. Sex for the sake of sex had become not merely defensible as an antidote to boredom but a morally laudable alternative to that which sought to create life.

Morally speaking, bringing a child into the world had always been somewhat risky. A child might turn out to be very bad, thus increasing the world's already burdensome stock of undesirables, or else very good, in which case it would suffer at the hands of the very bad; most likely, the child would, like most of us, be neither very good nor very bad: neither saints nor bastards, they would simply live like the faceless masses and live out their lives like predesigned automata – eating, drinking, copulating, working, sleeping, and worrying about their ability to do any of these things, finally ending their depressing existence without reward or recognition, while those who lorded it over them are feted, remembered, or at least die with smiles on their faces.

Anyway, those humorous commentators gave up their talk about how lockdowns might replenish the stock of human lives lost – at just about the time when humour itself, in all its forms, was seriously in decline, a process which was aided and abetted when language itself was delivered a series of death blows.

However, the whole subject did raise questions about why men and women would ever want to have children. Was it to preserve themselves vicariously in the faces of their offspring – as it were, to go on living without actually living, a step towards immortality without actually being immortality? Surely not because of some moral or intellectual conviction that human life is worth preserving! – such a form of reasoning would belong to the very few, those capable of a sophisticated appreciation of man's intellectual accomplishments in science, philosophy, literature and the creative arts; no, not something that is expected to appeal to the majority of mankind, let alone to those, and their number is legion, whose mission in life is to rip off as many people as possible and live off the spoils of ill-gotten gains. If all human life went the way of the dinosaurs, what would be so extraordinary about that? Wars, not an act of nature but of *human* nature, certainly tend towards extinction. Perhaps human stupidity is the mechanism of human built-in obsolescence. Would the loss of human life be a loss to the universe or to the myriad galaxies that surround it, if 'surround' is the right word? Some questions are worth asking even when they are unanswerable, even when they are not *questions*.

Human beings certainly appear to be designed in ways that ensure their downfall, despite everything that might be said about the instinct for survival. That instinct might be a far surer thing for the animal kingdom than it is for humans, for the ways in which it is customarily played out in human life tends against it! Cordial feelings, even those of brotherly love, were in the ascendant in the earlier days of the Virus; they grew weaker as the Virus progressed, and finally became non-existent. Limits of endurance were reached and breached. Anyone who came to the attention of the authorities for even minor infractions of lockdown rules was treated with toxic abuse through social media, with much greater scorn and reproach than that formerly meted out to proven and suspected paedophiles, even to the extent that they merited police protection – until, that is, the police became the very last refuge for those seeking a helping hand.

The invectives published through social media were egged on and in many cases occasioned by the press when so-called journalists seemed to be more interested in whipping up hysteria than in the objective reportage of fact – always a rather lame concept, 'objectivity' fell off the shelf and shattered into a thousand pieces. Minor transgressions of the rules were elevated to the status of unforgivable forms of subversion against persons and state, punishable in the early days by ostracism and, later, by lynching in parks, town centres and other open spaces – people paid for spaces above shops or in offices so that they could get a good view of the grim proceedings, roaring their approval when bodies fell and writhed and necks snapped, all horribly reminiscent of the callous satisfaction of the masses who had come to watch Madam Guillotine more than three centuries before and relished the inhumanity she remorselessly doled out on a daily basis. There are times when history seems to have reformed itself beyond recognition but in fact is waiting in the sidelines to repeat itself all over again – as when children were encouraged to report their parents for breaches of lockdown rules, just as the Nazis encouraged children, in obedience to a wicked doctrine, to report their parents to the Gestapo. The repetition of history is the greatest indictment imaginable of our much vaunted human kind.

Yes, when the police and the approved militias were thinned out and eventually disbanded, the inhuman treatment of proved or imagined 'lawbreakers' was entirely bereft of recourse or correction. The callous blandishments in the press and on social media stopped only when these laudable organs of communication themselves ceased to be, thanks again to the Virus.

All is silent now. All the talk has stopped, all the debate, all the wrangling, all the accusations and criticisms to and fro. Everything came to an end when language itself ceased to be either relevant or useful beyond the most primitive and inarticulate of sounds. And language died with communication, like a couple in love who decide to end it all together.

This basement is a small square room in which I am quite alone. But I can imagine it bigger, much bigger, and in each corner I imagine a small group of people sitting round a table. In one corner they are discussing some aspects of the human condition; they are animated but everything is in good order. In another, they are quietly playing cards, with a little good-humoured banter, for the game is not in the least serious and they do not play for money. In another, there's a couple exchanging 'sweet nothings'. And in the last corner they are listening to music from a battered radio; the music is not loud; two of them decide to get up and dance a little – unintrusively. Yes, this large room might be part of a recreational centre, a good place for quiet social exchange.

Yet, it is all too easy to imagine how volatile the situation is – how quickly things might turn from cordial social exchange to bitter and unrelenting conflict. The discussion of the human condition becomes a rabid political debate and voices are raised; the game of cards abruptly comes to an end when one of the players is accused of cheating; it wasn't a serious game – but then, it's the 'principle of the thing', and this phrase is bandied about like a demonic slogan, a pretext for division and war; the sincerity of the 'sweet nothings' are questioned because perhaps they are considered insufficiently sweet, or perhaps they are thought to catch someone out in a lie – maybe he called her Susan instead of Julie; and maybe the couple who decided to get up and dance are disrespectfully dancing to the wrong kind of music, maybe the partnership was a misjudgement, or maybe those sitting it out have strong and opposing feelings about what counts as good and bad music.

Yes, all too easy for a picnic to become a war zone. All it needed was a virus. And not all viruses are biochemical. That room – the one I imagined – is it not a microcosm of the world? A simplistic microcosm, I confess. In the room I imagine there are far too few corners.

Entry 12

It occurred to me this morning that rats appear to be rather less in evidence these days – perhaps because there's much less to feed on now, at least in this vicinity. At first they'd scuttle off when you approached; and then they didn't, becoming increasingly brazen, no doubt considering passersby meals in waiting – and they wouldn't have been far wrong. There were plenty of corpses to gorge themselves on – in homes and hospitals. They'd received invitations to dine earlier, when refuse collections ceased, together with the cessation of all other services designed to maintain infrastructure local and national infrastructure. The streets were crammed with over-spilling trash receptacles, and the rats had field days. Formerly considered a serious health hazard, the creatures began to be ignored as though they were just another feature of a declining social environment and certainly not the worst of our worries. But the fact that they were bigger than ever was noticed.

Theories about how the Virus responded to seasonal changes were vague and naive. The general idea was that the Virus would fare less in the summer than in the winter. But the winter exacerbated common seasonal ailments to the extent that they became life-threatening, especially in the absence of proper and sufficient medical attention. All eyes were focused on the front-door Virus while back-door varieties added to the death toll without opposition; and people who were already subject to long-term chronic illnesses, especially respiratory, were left to their own devices. The hot summer months were no respite, especially given the incidence of bacterial infections to which the breakdown of refuse collections substantially contributed. Diphtheria, dysentery and tuberculosis became competitors in the race to cause as much mayhem, fear and despair as the human spirit could stomach; what dark ends they failed to accomplish, the Virus would most assuredly bring about.

In the early days the elderly were more susceptible to the Virus, youth more resilient. But it was hard to imagine a better future in the faces of the young, who assumed a robotically resistant character, refusing to respond to any advice which emanated from authority and failing to treat with respect anyone outside the gangs they eventually formed. I've not forgotten the days, now long gone, when two strangers passing one another in the street would nod their heads or doff their hats in casual but respectful reciprocity. This was hardly ever the practice amongst the younger generations, and the Virus ensured that it would never become so. The young were not forever immune to the Virus, which soon enough began to decimate their ranks and erode gang membership. Those that survived the gangs presumably joined the Raiders.

Such reflections about the errors of youth are useless now, as are the words of the wise that ring down the centuries. What have we learned? It's not so much that man's stock of wisdom has been forgotten – rather, it has, for the bulk of mankind, been entirely unknown and therefore not a subject of rational and profound deliberation. Such stuff has always been confined to small academic or pious coteries. Or else, ironically, wisdom, simply expressed, has been rejected as a primitive novelty. Very little practical acknowledgment has been made of Native American Wisdom with its repeated emphasis on the preservation of the natural environment and its insistence that the earth must be held in trust for future generations and not abused as though it were a transitory plaything. Such forms of wisdom have obviously not caught on. Instead, what has impressed mankind most is technology with all its gimmickry. No one seeks to use the wisdom of wise men as templates for emulation and application in the devising and execution of policy.

But how pointless now is all this talk about opportunities missed. Wise men who burned the midnight oil writing sentences pregnant with ideas for the salvation and improvement of the human condition might have been better off using the oil to turn a profit in the market place. Socrates should have grovelled before his judges and Jesus Christ should have recanted before those who so bitterly opposed him. Keats's 'hungry generation' has not been hungry for wisdom. True, human life on this planet is in its geological infancy, but much should have been learned in the school of recorded history, from which few, if any, have even managed to graduate, let alone *summa cum laude.* Has history taught men to despise one another for their weaknesses? If some deity wanted to create a being likely to draw the wrong conclusions from the correct premises, or the correct conclusions from the wrong premises, it could not do better than devise homo sapiens.

Repeatedly the saddest tales are told of those who begin with demonstrably unassailable sentiments and principles but become in their turn every bit the tyrants they sought to displace, committing injustice in the name of Virtue, or, infinitely worse, of God. And so, every crowd which assembles to demonstrate for right contains within it the seeds of its own condemnation. Do nothing, and evil flourishes; but do something, and it flourishes under another name. Paradise on Earth has always been a contradiction in terms, which is what I guess is meant by some who say that their God left the world to Satan and free will to mankind. And so, those who profess universal equality act as though their own superiority ought not to be overlooked, and those who denounce negative discrimination are all too ready to discriminate against others.

Sporting groups and their spectators have long ceased. Football is a thing of the past. But even when they existed I could never have attended football matches; crowds were in my mind too reminiscent of mobs and riots, and, even when watched at a distance, the roars of the masses were to my ears the roars of the gladiatorial ring. Football is *play*! Yes, but even a mere game can bring out the worst in those that watch and participate. And it seems that no game is a *mere* game when it attracts multitudes, for a multitude is the most dangerous beast on the planet, with a potential as destructive as an atomic weapon, for it is after all an *atomic* phenomenon. Sir Thomas Browne referred to the multitude as 'that great enemy of reason, virtue and religion' and 'that numerous piece of monstrosity'. Others of greater, equal and lesser reputation have made similar observations, acknowledging that a multitude in its separate parts may be as reasonable and as virtuous as can ever be expected of human beings, but as a conglomerate can shake beyond repair the very foundations of reason and goodness. Now, who was it who said that his compatriots were tolerable in the particular but repugnant in the generality? No matter, for the immorality of a multitude is defined not by national boundaries but by the irremovable and ineluctable failings of humanity.

Things are as they are. Expectations can play the devil with us; they can bring us down when they are too high and raise us up when they are too low. And love? Well, love is rare, no less so even in marriage let alone outside it. So what can we expect of love in the world at large and outside the compass of those who are incapable even of professing it falsely let alone truly? But expectations can be damned by their own weight. Excessive expectations are a mortgage I have never been able even to start paying off. My idiocy overwhelms me. I seem incapable of forgetting that I am an alien from some planet way outside any known galaxy; which is why what I would regard as true friendship is and must be chimerical, because I expect of it an uncompromising commitment quite beyond the reach of homo sapiens. How presumptuous can you get? But is friendship what I think it is? Do I really have an idea of it worthy of the name? My thinking is defective; the cogs in the cerebral machine are moving but make no contact; perhaps there is merely an illusion of movement. Or am I in good company with my expectations, so that I have every right to feel that they must be disappointed?

The old Buddhist sentiment entreats us to 'fare lonely as rhinoceros' since friends are few and far between. Is this an indictment of homo sapiens? Or is the entreaty underpinned by sheer illusion and defective thinking? Our biggest illusions are survival tools; we know that we die alone, but we are stubbornly reluctant to admit that we live alone also; true the world is full of good mothers, but no less is true of the beasts of the forest; mothers and wives, fathers and husbands, however close you feel they are, cannot live for you, and many have no desire to do so; worse, there are many amongst them who would be constrained to lift a finger to help children and partners in need. Yet our expectations of others seem to know no bounds. Expectations are the devil, and they play with us and trick us, trading upon our loneliness and our inflated egos. What Shakespeare says of the gods we may say of our expectations – as flies to wanton boys are we to the gods, they kill us for their sport. But now the rise and prevalence of Raiders have mightily dulled our expectations and brought them down from their dizzy heights.

(Expectation and perfection are fond bedfellows. If you believe perfection doesn't exist, you will expect less and your expectations can be properly chastised. But things can be perfect in their imperfection, and this muddies the waters. Are things perfect when we can't find anything worth complaining about?)

Are we really to conclude that the world is indeed a cold place despite the heats of summer and the passions of poets? Well, life is hard even when there are blessings to count. Our joy at the arrival of a new-born babe is matched by our grief at the loss of the elderly; the trade-off is hard to bear, and of course impossible to justify. And as for grief for the loss of those we love, surely few things cost more than love. Love we must; love we should. But we love at our peril, and the more we love the higher the price that must be paid should we outlive those loved. True love demands a kind of courage unexampled elsewhere. We love. God help us.

We must never in any case become blind to the best in people, and we must never become incapable of loving them for it, lest civilised man becomes totally and irrevocably lost. Is this a platitude? If so, it is not one platitude amongst others. It is capable of saving the world.

Entry 13

I thought again this morning about taking a knife with me on my walks, for self-defence should the occasion arise. But again I changed my mind – a weapon can be taken from you and used against you, which is likely in my case. The safety a weapon gives you is illusory. Illusions are thought to be dangerous; the very word 'illusion' carries with it a negative or critical connotation – 'I have no illusions about …', 'He entertained the illusion that …', we say. But illusions can also be beneficial. In fact, I'm inclined to think a life devoid of all illusions is a cruel thing, leaving us cold and comfortless.

The old world has passed away. But remnants remain, like the trees, and these feed the illusion that everything will return and be just as it was. Trees? Yes, it's ironic that they should outlast mankind which ignored them, took them for granted, abused them, or destroyed them for *Lebensraum*. It was left to the wise to respect them, even to personify them; but the wise were in too short supply. People were treated in the same way: ignored, taken for granted, abused or destroyed for *Lebensraum*.

The Virus saw to it that in the end the worst in human nature stood victorious over the best; and so much so that those in whom goodness still managed to prevail began to detest even the human form, despise it and fear it, as so many learned to despise and to fear the form that was clothed in the uniforms of the *Schutzstaffel* (S.S.). But even the good are susceptible to a mob mentality. The Virus bred a nihilism, a moral anarchy, a rejection of the foundation stones of anything and everything that might be described as 'civilised', including the tools of science, reasoned, analytical thinking, the more sophisticated elements of rationality and standards of quality in the creative arts. Everything was abandoned in a sea of discontent and frustration which took as their watchwords such shapeless notions as 'racism', 'white supremacy', 'male supremacy' and 'cultural bias', to such an extent that what truth might have justified discontentment and frustration was rendered confused and meaningless in its very pursuit and expression. The foundations of anything that might rightly be called 'civilisation', in any acceptably normative sense of the word, were swept away in successive waves of hatred and contempt. Augustine's words had as much application as ever, 'There may be some light in men, but let them walk fast, walk fast! lest the shadows come.'

At last the darkness descended.

For all those who have prided themselves on their ability to see beauty and goodness where beauty and goodness lies, how doleful such a spirit becomes when it can no longer perceives these things upon which hope can feed and thrive. For such people it is either the end, or the primeval beginning, of the world for which they had harboured some hope.

Does that explain the tortured nature of my dreams – things mixed up in crazy patterns, with snatches of the past, nothing concluded, nothing complete, a distorted patchwork of mazes and labyrinths with no exits? If we are satisfied that there are no exits, it is pointless to try and find them. All speculation about meaning and sense has about it the aura of absurd comedy. We accumulate what wealth we can though we can't take it with us; we don't ask to be born and we have no wish to die. We just *are*, until we are *not*.

I must control my thoughts. I must think positively. This *isolation*! Perhaps it plays tricks, making a very bad situation seem entirely hopeless when it is not. But who now can tell me how distorted my own thoughts are; who is there to guide, to correct, to question, to admonish, to criticise, above all to comfort? We are poor measures of ourselves when the only measure we have is our own. It's getting harder to hang on to my brains.

Entry 14

Couldn't sleep last night – plagued with presentiments of danger and doom, and no better this morning. So much so I almost decided not to go out at all. But I managed to overcome it – walking the circle of shadows again, you tread on a twig and it sounds like a gunshot, a bird gets up in a flurry from the bushes beside you and you think you've been found out – but I made it back to the basement, in a hurry! Goodness knows how things will feel in the darkness tonight if my nerves don't settle.

It's funny. For years I'd lived like on who wants to attach to those who reject attachment, like one who seeks but is himself unsought, one whose love, or at least interest, is unrequited. But now I feel much sought out, and very much for the wrong reasons. I should be used to them by now, these feelings of vulnerability and unwelcome exposure – like a piece of fresh meat on a rock.

The Virus came, and when the wrong people had a little time to think about it, they put two and two together and made something that wasn't even a number. Religion, of course, had to have its say. The Islamists, and fanatics from a variety of sects, some calling themselves Christian, argued that the Virus was no more than divine punishment meted out to unbelievers and infidels; in vain was it pointed out that the Virus failed to distinguish between believers and unbelievers; the retort was that those believers who succumbed to the Virus were martyrs who went straight to Heaven to enjoy an eternal paradise, while unbelievers were thrown into the eternal fires of Hell; no one paid attention to an incisive sarcasm: Hell and Heaven are one and the same, for an eternity in either is equally unwelcome, the torture of the flames suffered in one, the horror of unceasing pleasure in the other. Heaven and Hell have forever been the final recourse in the confused attempt to justify good conduct to those lost souls to whom an external justification is required, with no advance being made from the Elysium and the Tartarus of the ancient Greeks; with the corollary that human nature has forever taken one step forward and one step back.

The nonsense of divine judgement missed the fact that a punitive God is quite unnecessary in a world in which men punish themselves and one another more than adequately; and it was missed because the monstrous notion of a punishing God rejected demonstrably and unambiguously the concept of a loving God, let alone the conceptual simplicity that God and Love are one and the same. It really does look as though Man has created God is his own image and that his template does not project the best in him but the very worst. The legacies of the wise are twisted and perverted in the hands of men. It is as though a child is given something priceless; but because it doesn't sparkle or shake, rattle and roll, he throws it aside as though it were a piece of junk, like a non-comprehending savage. Such are the children of men. And such are those who are bored with Bach and Shakespeare, find the study of history dry and irrelevant and believe a photograph an improvement on the Mona Lisa. I remember again the story of the old man who, they said, had lost his mind, and was placed in a care home because of it; whenever anyone said anything to him he had only one reply; even if you just asked him whether he was comfortable or wanted a cup of tea, 'I don't *like* human beings. I'm glad I'm not one of them!' Such a reply, at first amusing, and then incomprehensible, was considered proof positive that he was out of his mind, and, after a while, no one took any notice of it at all – rather like what happens when someone says, 'You know' at the end of every statement, or when someone writes an exclamation mark after every sentence.

The old man's brief against human beings was not entirely indefensible. The fact that people are capable of hurting, maiming and murdering one another either with malice or in the august name of justice demonstrates a serious defect of design in the species known as homo sapiens, a fault that neither time nor the teaching of the good and the wise has been able to correct. Of course the fault is improperly described as a 'design defect'. It is simply the ways things are, and the way things are is notoriously difficult to change for the better. The fault in the fabric is hard to improve, let alone eradicate.

The diseased idea of Divine Retribution set the stage for further acts of terrorism from the Islamist camp; it provided a licence, a free for all, which the police and military units were deployed to put down – until the Virus began to take such a toll that the efforts of the martyrs were hardly necessary, both believers and non believers falling like nine-pins; even the ranks of the clergy were decimated, a fact which people in general failed to notice.

Religious differences became irrelevant in the destruction the Virus left and is still leaving in its wake, as indeed they truly were before the Virus was even dreamed of.

Writing things which no one will ever be able to read does help. But whenever I stop I feel these presentiments of impending danger. Nothing has changed in the basement. My routine is the same as it was when the Virus was first admitted to be invincible. Perhaps I should change it – but I'm not sure how. I have noticed how painful my hands are when I touch them – I have developed hypersensitive skin. I suppose it's the effect of this continued isolation and consequent weakness. When, over time or through weakness, our defences are down, our natural imperfections creep out of their hiding places to taunt us and wear us down further. Courage is what is called for. After all, without courage nothing else can work however much you talk about things or want them to happen. Courage!

Your life can seem like a story you've written and are displeased with; but one you can't rewrite. You have only one story, and you find you're stuck with it, and the characters in your story are fixed and immovable, and they haunt you with their fixedness and immovability. What does this really mean?

Why do I still go on? But it's all part of the long goodbye. I didn't mind losing everything. But I can't abide losing everyone. And when that happened, it had to be the start of the long goodbye – saying goodbye to my own life, almost as though I was dead already but not quite. Long goodbyes are usually painfully drawn out, are they not? But it seems to me that in my own life the shortest goodbyes have been the worst – the ones I've regretted most, and the ones I can do nothing about.

Entry 15

This morning I walked in circles once again around the park: down the leafy path, past the pool, then through the huddled trees, over a slight incline, through the trees and down the path on the other side of the circle, pausing to take stock and ensure I was alone, and then round again. Two circles and home to the basement. Just like life now and before the Virus; round and round, appearing at a stretch to move forward, but walking in an arc nonetheless. However long the circumference, however wide the radius, we move as though in obedience to the seasons: spring, summer, autumn, winter. Even our memory moves in circles; with age out long-term memory, a bittersweet thing, improves and images of faces, places and events sharpen, even of things we had long forgotten, while we are unsure of what we did or said or saw a short time past; and so it's as though we are being pulled back to where we started, for the most part helplessly. It's as though we are completing a circle begun long ago.

In the early days and before I decided to walk before dawn, I would see another walker, or a jogger, even a cyclist; and that odd couple, a man and a woman, quite elderly, walking together arm in arm. Everyone looked ahead, except the odd couple, who looked down; no one spoke – no salutations, no greetings. Everyone kept their distance, as though afraid of catching the Virus at one hundred paces! Well, no one knew then that it could be caught in the air, without close contact transmission between humans. Very little was known. We know even less now. Insightful assertions were made at regular intervals which all too often proved contradictory; before long no one trusted the scientists, who seemed to disagree amongst themselves, and with the loss of trust in its exponents, science itself lost all credibility; it was as though people expected no less than absolute certainty, as though science was a form of mathematics; people mistrusted statements of the form, 'It is to be hoped that …' or 'It may be that …' or 'With luck …' , because they did not imagine these to be consistent with the certainty they expected from mathematics. Mathematics could leave no room for doubt, and if, in the popular imagination, science should equate with mathematics, then a science which offered less than certainty and could do no better than come up with tentative predictions was useless and above all bogus. And if you can't trust science then what can you trust?!

The scene was set for an anarchy of misinformation and illogic.

Entry 16

My dream last night was a most welcome rarity. I gave her a long and warm embrace which seemed to last the whole dream through. The only way I can meet her now is in my dreams; she's found again; she lives again. Shakespeare's couplet is bittersweet:

'Thus have I had thee as a dream doth flatter;
In sleep a king; but waking, no such matter.'

What must I do to dream like that again? No doubt the price will be paid over the next few nights. But such dreams remind us of what our priorities should be – or of what they once were. It's so important to get our priorities right – before we become incapable of preserving them, before we lose what we most treasure, because a regret that cannot be righted is a high road to Hell.

But it was a good dream. I have dreamed of her before, but usually I can't touch her, or I just glimpse her as she fades away, or melts into grey-stone, labyrinthine buildings, or runs down dark stairways, or through heavy wooden doors, bolted with iron, which slam shut, leaving me empty, hollow and weakened by an overwhelming sense of loss, or I am like a small child in a vast shopping complex, suddenly bereft of the loving hand he had just held, now alone and bewildered by the vast complexity of things and longing to be found by the one who loves him more than life itself. Oh, may I be saved from dreams such as these!

How I've managed to elude the Watchers, those who watch and wait for cruel gain, and the Raiders for so long, Heaven knows. Sometimes I wish I had been caught – then it would all be over, all this senseless striving for survival would end.

The thought struck me, not for the first time, that it is entirely irresponsible to bring children into this world; not because they are unloved by their parents, though many are, but because they are not loved by the world they have inherited through no fault of their own. If strangers loved the children of others, it would be a better world, and living and dying would be more tolerable. But death is something I have never been able to understand on anything other than a clinical level. How can human beings, beings who are so full of hopes and dreams, how can they be living today and dead tomorrow – dead, as though they had never existed at all? That they can be turned to dust, or rotting and insensible carcasses is quite beyond my comprehension.

To say that a god has created beings subject to such an end is to imagine a creator supremely wicked – and to think that so many human beings actually worship such a god! The promise of an eternal paradise in recompense for a Hobbesian life so 'nasty, brutish and short' and pregnant with the immeasurable grief of loss, is not at all good enough – it just won't do at all! If life is a gift, it is wrong to take it away. But there are some who say that your life is not a gift for you but for others, because you are given an opportunity to serve others, to do good to others. But whether we understand your life to be a gift for you or a gift for others, it is wrong to take that life away – especially if we are so loathe to lose it. That a god can suffer his creations to live and die in misery is incomprehensible – unless of course that god is made in the image of man, because for man all things are possible short of perfection. All such talk may be stuff and nonsense – if so, it is the stuff and nonsense that emanates from a distorted view of how we should live our lives; the fact is, most religions, from the smallest sects to the largest and unfortunately most immoveable institutions, give religion a bad name.

Entry 17

O, unfortunate coincidence! I must have had a presentiment of disaster. In the last entry, made the day before yesterday I think, I wondered how it was I had eluded the Watchers and the Raiders for so long. I've been lucky, very lucky, and luckier than most – many have been dealt a bad hand, and many more have not even been given a place at the gaming table.

Despite my caution I've obviously been watched and followed. While I cowered down in the basement, thankfully unheard, they rifled the whole house, ransacked what was left of the furniture – all in a vain effort to find anything really useful, and nothing edible. The noise was unsettling. 'Unsettling'? – hardly the right word! I heard doors slammed shut with a vengeance, and when I was satisfied that it was sufficiently safe, which took several hours, I emerged from the basement, but just long enough to assure myself that the house was empty again. Then I came back to the basement and I've been here ever since. Maybe I'll get back to my routine tomorrow – or, better, the day after.

I don't know whether I'm on their radar or whether the raid was just a one-off. If they'd discovered the basement they'd have taken the canned food and, well, I hate to think … Well, if it was just a one-off, they may never come back. But if I'm on their radar … That would explain the feelings I've been having that I've been followed. I've just got to work out my strategy – change my routine; just in case. I need time to work things out. Time to think things through. Maybe I should move out altogether. But I can't! I can't leave her all alone in that cold place. I promised I wouldn't. I've never been good at breaking promises, and this is one I just can't even dream of breaking. There have been times – times when I've packed a haversack, painstakingly putting things out that needed to be taken, carefully deciding against this or that – sorting out my priorities. Then, after what seems an age, when the haversack is fully and properly packed, I've taken everything out again and just as painstakingly returned each item to its proper place. Every now and again I feel I need to repeat this ridiculous ritual – perhaps it helps to keep me sane. But, no, I can't possibly leave! I just can't. It's absolutely out of the question.

Yes, what I need now is time. Time to work things out. Time to reckon how things stand. Time to work out how to go on from here. Time! We say that time passes, but we seldom stop to give this fact the weight it deserves. Yes, time passes, and as it passes much is gained and much is lost. You discover rusted tools – hammers, saws and the like, and you know they were once used and prized by someone, God knows who, someone who passed on long ago, and when they passed on there was no one to prize his tools, and so they were neglected and began to rust. The tools may be interesting, but surely infinitely less than the person who used and prized them! It's miraculous that people come and go, come into being, and then fall like leaves in autumn. Surely a most monstrous miracle! And before the Grim Reaper cuts us down, Time has its wicked way. I have looked upon the face of a pretty young girl and a handsome young man, and in the same instant I imagine them as they might look in their 80s – and the only feeling I can recall is pity.

Time passes, and I need it to stop – to stop long enough for me to think things out, to decide what happens next. For it stops for no man – a commonplace that is taken too much for granted.

What is time? Is it not a measure of movement? Can there be time without motion, without events? Yet events do not move through time in the same way that I move through the basement. Time is not a vehicle for events. But can time make sense in the absence of that which it measures? The clock ticks, the hands move. Time passes. Time is a tyrant and does what it pleases, impervious to out pathetic rebukes, deaf to our pleading to go faster or slower or stop altogether, indifferent to the degeneration of mind and body it engenders. It breaks down whole civilisations, breaks up loving ties, annihilates whole families and makes of a home an empty, cold, heartless, hollowed out wreck of stone. It never mends, despite the aphorism that states the contrary, for broken hearts once broken can never be repaired; time addles the brain before destroying it and then is praised by many as a 'blessing'. There is so little to be said for time that were it on trial for its life no reputable Counsel for the Defence would dare take up the brief for fear of losing both case and reputation.

Whether time passes or everything passes through time, everything changes. Blessings that were once counted cease to be so. Remembering is a mixed blessing, bittersweet. Yes, there was a time when blessings were counted, great and small: a warm bed in a comfortable house, favourite meals, favourite books, hearty meals and, above everything, someone to love and to be loved by, children perhaps, good health and a world of nature to wonder at and enjoy … But now there is nothing left that can possibly be counted a blessing; the bare fact of survival doesn't count, for you become like an automaton, or like an animal avoiding hurt – as when a sense of humour, that last bastion of defence, has finally petered out. All is solitude and survival for the mere sake of survival. Bertrand Russell's plea that human civilisation is worth preserving must fall on deaf ears when there is nothing left that he himself would describe as 'civilisation'. What, you are bound to ask, is worth preserving in the total absence of civilisation? Art, science, literature and a society in which you are free to ask and to question, to debate, to choose, to follow your harmless designs ... Yes, but when this clichéd definition is even less than a mere memory, what then?

Mankind is capable of losing so much. Once lost, those few who remain and can still remember, however vaguely, may feel like doing what a philosopher once said he wanted to do – they might want to utter an inarticulate sound, as an expression of utter despair and incredulity. The unbearable truth is, man's track record is not simply morally insupportable but quite beyond the imagination of the kind of god that is believed by so many to have created him. How could a god of love envisage the bestiality of his own creation? The beasts he has created cannot exist in a vacuum but depend for their existence, their sustenance and the thorough execution of their designs on the compliance of the ignorant and the simple, yes, and even on the assistance of those who believe themselves beyond reproach and anything but simple, anything but ignorant. Faced with the complexity and enormity of human wickedness, it is little wonder that the philosopher finds himself incapable of uttering anything but an inarticulate sound. Like pealing away the layers of an onion, he finds himself bereft of every emotion, and is left with nothing.

How did it all come to this? But when once the beast is uncaged the sequence of events is all too predictable. Outside those bars it finds food enough to sustain it and aid its monstrous growth. All it needed was to set itself a course and appeal to the worst in that delightful phenomenon 'human nature' and the rest was a fait accompli. Such a small step from the roars of the football stadium to the mass following of maniacs who, from some fearful trick of the human mechanism, now fail to tell the difference between a Jesus Christ and a fanatical demagogue.

Such are the Raiders and those who follow them, like twisted Pied Pipers and their blind entourage. Enough!

The candle flickers. Sleep … perchance a dreamless one!

Entry 18

The pungent aroma of burning fills the air this morning. The red glow of burning houses could be seen on the skyline last night. It's getting bitterly cold, and no doubt the Raiders are making bonfires of the houses that were once homes. If this practice continues, I'll need to be more vigilant than ever to avoid being burned alive. It would be an unenviable irony to be entombed in the basement while *she* is entombed in the garden.

I looked at her photograph again last night. I discovered that if I stared at it long enough I could fancy that her face moved or that her eyes did, as though she were alive and well but trapped inside the frame. I took some comfort from that. What an unwholesome thing a photograph can be – revealing a painful past that we have been struggling to forget, or a past infinitely better than our present, that we have been naively attempting to relive.

This morning I noted again that black hole of a nature reserve; I walked quickly as I passed it on the other side of the road, quickening my pace until it was far behind me. Why the place should haunt me, I don't know – raking together fears from unfathomed depths, like dead leaves from unseen places. Why?

It's bitterly cold today. I have blankets and there's still oil enough for the stove. Another winter. Should survive it, maybe. But it really is cold. I've always hated extremes of heat and cold – like my politics, if I have politics. I don't know. I think I have no political affiliations whatsoever. When I listened to politicians on their rostrums, I always felt they were less than they pretended to be; even those with the best of hearts and intentions got things wrong – a surplus of passion, maybe. I was always middle-of-the-road; but then. I wasn't sure what road I was on. Friends said, 'You can't sit on the fence.' But I thought that was the best place to be, not just for myself but for everyone else. Now there's no place in politics, because there's no politics but the politics of survival, and that has become a very personal, individual kind of thing.

It's too cold to write more. I have blankets; and oil enough for the stove, if I'm careful, very careful. Damned cold!

Entry 19

It must be a week ago, maybe more, maybe less, when I made my last entry, and a great deal has happened since then. It shows how just one person can make a world of difference – though whether that difference is entirely welcome remains to be seen. But the irony of it all is overwhelming.

I found it on the return from my morning walk – a bundle of rags; which turned out to be a small, hooded figure, squatting in the corner of the sitting room above the basement. At first I thought the game was finally up, that the Raiders had sent one of their scouts to reconnoitre. But the bundle didn't move or speak – just sat there on its haunches shivering with the cold. I gingerly approached and pulled back the hood. If it was a Raider scout it was the least likely looking member of that clan that you could possibly imagine. The muddied but sweet face of a girl in her late teens looked up appealingly into mine; her fair, tousled hair and light green eyes seemed out of place with the rags she wore. A striking face, a face bursting with innocence – and with fear.

I should think not many years have passed since she was bright and hopeful, before time and circumstance have made of her a shivering wreck. She has seen the gaunt faces of death and is now one of them.

No one, no child in particular, should have to see them and become one of them. I once heard someone say that the Creator – for he believed there had been one – made men mortal so that they would love one another more and not take one another's lives so much for granted, for they would know that the lives of their loved ones and friends must come to an end.

If this were true, we might ask how successful the invention of death has been. On intra-personal levels, it might well be said to have achieved some partial and grudging success. But on impersonal levels, the very fact of repeated and repeatable war and of man's repeated and repeatable inhumanity to man are the strongest arguments in favour of failure that I can adduce. As Plato so succinctly put it: Only the dead have seen the end of war. What's more, it's to be seriously doubted whether, on intra-personal levels, the success of endowing men with built-in obsolescence has been at all worth all the pain, all the grief, that the loss of a friend engenders! No, the jury is out. And he who endowed his imagined Creator with such a spirit of benevolence needs to think again.

Meanwhile, this poor girl sits in the corner and refuses to speak; and it's wasn't at all obvious that she could hear – until something, a it must have been a bird, hit the window and she looked up, eyes wide open. So, the bundle can see and she can hear. But as yet she hasn't uttered a word – not responded to obvious questions.

We couldn't stay up there. I had to get back to the basement, and I had to make her come with me. I opened the door and, to my surprise, she got up and shuffled right past me through the door and down to the basement. I thought it would be a struggle. My only explanation for the trust she's shown in me is that I must have been under her surveillance for some time – perhaps those times when I thought I was being watched or followed. Somehow she must have reached the conclusion, more hope than deduction, that I could be trusted – that I wasn't one of *them*.

Now there are two mouths to feed – more pressure on supplies, but it can't be helped. She gulped down her first meal – all out of tins, of course. But she seems to have settled down now and eats moderately – as we must both do. The Virus has caused a diseased form of isolation, but the girl's isolation is at least twofold, as though she's been living within herself for a long time even before the Virus, is stuck with it, and now refuses, or maybe doesn't know how, to come out – a creature imprisoned by its own shell.

It's ironic that I've longed for someone to speak to, longed to hear another voice. Now I have and do not have a companion. It reminds me of that boy who, in the naivety of his youth, would dream of sharing his life with a kindred spirit, reading poetry together by the fireside, and, in his diseased state of mind, he would foolishly picture a marriage bed as far less a site of passion or of mere sleep than a venue for the sharing of literary ideas. Oh, poor boy! No one told him his dreams were no more than puffs of smoke round a camp fire. He was destined to find out for himself. Yet all his life through he maintained a fondness for his youthful misconceptions, while Fate laughed at his naivety.

(Dreams may be wonderful things and powerful motivators; but the dreams of youth are also dangerous and a recipe for the deepest despair when unfulfilled and unfulfillable. A dream is as a fire is said to be, our dearest friend, our bitterest enemy. And it so often happens that the dreams entertained by one are the nightmares of others. Ultimately, age defeats us all. I guess there comes a time when, our fondest dreams unrealised, we need the courage to abandon them and instead do the best we can to facilitate the legitimate dreams of others, especially those of our loved ones.)

The girl needs to be looked after and fed. Is that all? Maybe she finds it impossible to speak words of beauty. But can she still hear them? Shall I feed her poetry and philosophy? Or, am I like the boy – grown up but still a slave to my naivety?

Yes, it's ironic that I should have acquired a companion who is little more than a bundle of rags. But life is full of irony; it seems to stick burr-like to human life. *Si vis pacem para bellum*, said Vegetius, advising that those who desire peace should prepare for war, and war has itself been considered a high road to peace; love, too, or what is often called by that name, can kill, while a surfeit of hate is believed to be akin to love, the line dividing them apparently too fine to be detected. All very confusing – but, infinitely worse than that, also very true! And the trick is how to live with the multiple layers of irony with which life presents us. Perhaps to be blind to them all would be a kind of Elysium; the only justification for blindness that might hold water; but no one wishes to be blind; there is enough blindness already. Blindness would be a kind of ignorance. And, despite everything, I still agree with Mill that it is better to be a Socrates dissatisfied than a pig satisfied.

Irony! It forms part of the tragic comedy of our lives. Its bite is deep, its sting is lethal, emerging from its murky depths when we stop doing what we should not be doing; as when a roofer who has been effortlessly climbing ladders all his life for only a pittance, develops rheumatism and arthritis soon after he retires; as when a heavy smoker gives up his addiction, only to fall under a bus; as when an alcoholic finally abstains, only to become a compulsive gambler.

'Save us from irony' is a belated and unanswerable prayer.

Entry 20

I went out for my walk this morning, leaving her (what can I call her?) alone in the basement, huddled as usual in a corner. Once again I tripped along in a circle, round and round and through the dark shadowed trees, with here and there a crow call, one crow to another, as if to herald the morning on this planet now apparently devoid of human intervention. All the while, I was thinking of her, there huddled in the basement; and the thought occurred to me that it was like it used to be, long before the Virus, when, returning home, I would think of her who was waiting for me and who now lies cold in what has become the hallowed ground that I cannot leave. But it was a cold, dark, foggy – like a scene in an old horror movie – in fact, that sums up our situation quite well, for the Virus has created such a scene for real. People used to say that it was natural to be afraid of the dark; now the light of day is equally horrific, equally objectionable yet unavoidable.

The thought occurred to me that I might save her, the nameless girl huddled in a corner of the basement. Yes, and I thought that by saving her I might also save myself. If I can teach her beauty, then maybe I can learn of it myself, be reminded of it, for beauty is also easy to forget. Was it Dostoyevsky who constructed that sentence, that the world will be saved by beauty? Well, maybe not the world, but perhaps a single soul – and that would be worth something, wouldn't it? Teachers teach. But how many of their pupils learn? Should only one learn, and learn the finest thing, that would justify the whole system of education. I think, dare I say it, that I have lost sight of beauty – hopefully only momentarily. I want to bring it back, by creating, not destroying; by creating a sense of beauty in that lost girl. It is my mission.

I dread to think what happened to her. Perhaps one day she'll be able to tell me. She looks so forlorn and helpless and impermeable. But it has to be said that for some people happiness is just another's dream; that for some happiness is as elusive as that pot of gold at the end of the rainbow. But they can't themselves articulate this to anyone else. It is something that must be said *of* them and not *by* them. If it is said by them, they risk being judged arrogant, overbearing, full of their own importance, non-entities in party dress. No, if it is said at all, it must be said *of* them. But whether it is said by them or of them, the truth still stands, namely that some people have been born with such a degree of sensitivity, or have acquired it by some divine force unbeknown by man, that happiness has been rendered impossible or possible only by the qualification of a thousand cuts. Some reassurance may of course be provided by a religion; but while it may be presumed that those who adhere to a religion, like Islam or the more fanatical versions of so-called Christianity, will derive some degree of comfort from their beliefs according to the degree of fanaticism by which their beliefs are held, it is quite beyond mere presumption that the vast majority of so-called 'infidels' or 'non-believers' do not; that is to say, the vast majority of human souls must pay the price for the comfort derived by the minority – which is hardly fair when the infidels and non-believers are the subjects of physical abuse and attack.

Ah! the follies of mankind! All is irrelevant now as the planet reaches its zenith. Literary critics may discuss and debate as much as they like, but when the play is over and the theatre is closed never to reopen, there doesn't seem much point in further debate. In fact, debate seems not only irrelevant but almost irreverent – as though there is something above it that needs to be addressed. Yet, there is nothing at all above it. Just ending; just nothingness.

Can I help her? Can she help me? Or am I beyond all help? Is *she*?

Entry 21

The acrid odour of burning was more intense this morning, reminiscent of the mornings after bonfire nights celebrating the saving of Parliament and the execution of Guy Fawkes. I'm sure she senses the danger approaching like a dark enveloping blanket. I'm still loathe to move. I have my promise to keep. Yet, some promises are meant to be broken, because they never should have been made in the first place.

What is the most important thing – I mean, when it all comes down to it? I once heard it said that the most important thing was to love and be loved. But loved by whom? By the unlovable? By whom, then? And who should I love? Should I love the Raiders – those who torment others for greed, for pleasure, for the greed of pleasure? Should one love the Beast? Should one love the downtrodden simply because they are downtrodden? Reservations and qualifications, it seems, are very much in order. Was it not Plato who said that we should pray to have the right desires before we pray that our desires be satisfied? But should we not also be taught who or what to love before we allow ourselves the pleasure and the pain of loving them? If the question is nonsense, then so too is the whole debate.

To love and be loved – is this the most important thing? Is this what it all comes down to? Is this simplicity? – simplicity being that which the wise have advised us to pursue? And yet, this isn't simple enough. There are those who have said it is enough simply to love – to love without expectation and therefore without demands. All we need to know is what and how to love. But that is not so simple. I must confess, I do not know what the most important thing is. Except that it is not *fame*, for fame only elevates you to drop you from a height; the higher you get, the harder you fall. Besides, people are unreliable judges and tend to be economical with their praises on matters that far transcend the mediocre. President Ulysses Grant saved the Union, yet he is only remembered for being a drunkard, while Einstein was treated like a spent firework by those who owed him their hegemony – and Christ they crucified, Socrates they poisoned; not much chance for the rest of us, then! Beauty, like fame, also elevates, at least in the realms of mediocrity; but it fades, and so often causes more anguish and division than it deserves.

But there is another kind of beauty that elevates and cannot fade – it can only be hidden, and never seeks sanctuary or acceptance in the cold embrace of mediocrity.

The promise I made was made out of love. Would not love also relinquish me from it? Forgiving myself for breaking it would also be an act of love. Or, is this nonsense, too?

Must not a man be forgiven for withdrawing his hand from the searing heat of the fire? And it isn't simply my own hand that I must look to. This poor girl must be protected. I must help her to live for as long as Fate permits. And I'm sure that she, she who is buried out there, would approve and release me from my oath.

So perhaps the time has come. When I pack my backpack again it might be for the last time; it might be for real. The girl will come with me, I'm sure of it. She's seems to cling to me; after all, she found me out, and she hasn't sneaked off. Those eyes and the fear that sits deep in them tells me we should move out – though move out exactly where, I don't yet know. The bitter cold makes such decisions more difficult. We are between the anvil and the hammer. Stay and be burned out and worse by the Raiders; or go and face the worst of the winter God knows where – O, did I say God?! Well, I don't think God has much of a hand in any of this. We are left to our own devices and must face the consequences of the decisions we struggle so painfully to make.

There are two women in my life, one buried, the other still alive but largely unresponsive. One that has passed, one that still lives, but lives inside herself. I shall explain everything to both. And then, it's the open road – or rather, the half-hidden byways by night and sleep and sustenance by day. The thing to be decided is which point of the compass to follow. North? South? East? West? Which way? Hard to decide with any confidence (no wonder the *moral* compass is a much neglected piece of equipment!). Well, south is warmer, but on that account alone is likely to attract the attention of the Raiders who may be likened to lions, which expect to find their prey at water holes. East and west lead more directly to the coast, the most obvious places for all those wishing to escape this island, and therefore an even stronger magnet for the Raiders. Besides, one place is much like another, which, to their cost, may be demonstrated to those few who manage to leave this once green and pleasant land. Despite the cold, north seems the best option. I have thought of delaying our departure until the thaw, but the risk of discovery seems too great. The Raiders are closing in. I feel it. We must move.

Entry 22

I have abandoned my twilight walks in the twilight of this world. I have prepared the stuff we should take north – not much in the way of clothes; we must wear as much as we can against the cold and hope that that's enough; a compass, which I'm using for the very first time; and I've emptied some tins, which are too heavy to carry, into small plastic boxes – this won't go very far, but it'll have to do, and then we must forage what we can; water is heavy, we'll need to ration carefully the little we can carry. I've even packed a pipe and some tobacco, as I always used to; I don't expect to smoke it, but it makes me feel better to have it with me; come to think of it, it's been quite some time since I've been relaxed enough to smoke a pipe – even here in the basement the aroma might have attracted unwelcome attention from someone, or something, passing by above; silly, really; but I've never been able to rid myself of the merest possibility of detection; interesting that acknowledgement of your fears is not at all the same as their abandonment.

We shall leave for the north at dusk tonight. I've done my best to explain to Bundle, which is what I call her. Her responses are minimal, but I've come to expect little else. And I went down to the bottom of the garden where my treasure is buried; I did my best; I explained why I must move on; I reassured her that she would stay safe where she was, and I made a promise (yes, another promise!) that someday I would return. I think she'd understand; yes, I'm quite sure of that. She wouldn't want me or young Bundle to fall into the hands of the Raiders. As for Bundle, I prefer to take silence as acquiescence. I will not force her to come with me – how could I? But I think she trusts me enough and is much more aware of the situation than her huddled, stiff and mute state would seem to suggest. What's going on in that head of hers? I started reading to her but ended up reading to myself. One thing is certain; if she stays behind, she'll be ravaged and thrown to the dogs or burned on a pyre for the sheer entertainment of her persecutors.

So, everything is ready, or as ready as it can possibly be. What we shall find, I don't know, or whether we shall get far. But I'm taking my diary. I'll try to take account of our journey. It's funny. First, I discarded the diary; and then I took it up again and stuffed it into my backpack. Why do I want to record what happens to me, to us? – when nothing, nothing at all, is of any consequence? Could it possibly be vanity? That would be disappointing. But it may be true. I should prefer it to be an expression of regard for posterity. But what form posterity will take, or whether there will be any posterity at all worthy of the name, is very much a moot point. If the Raiders refuse to do the decent thing and die off, they will represent a decline from which there can be no comeback.

Entry 23

We're on the road at last, travelling gingerly at night and resting during the day in whatever cover we can find. Yes, Bundle came with me, all right; she knew what was happening and followed me meekly like a stray dog. I write a few lines in my diary when we stop after a night's walk – we avoid houses, especially those with lights in the windows. Sad how things have turned right round – after all, a light in a window was once long ago a sign of warmth, of hope, of humanity. But now only the Raiders, notably their hierarchy, have the nerve to make their whereabouts known in the darkness. The advantage for us is that at least we have some idea of where they are, or where they tend to congregate, like packs of wolves – brazen and ravenous.

Likewise, we avoid fires – not now protection from the cold and an invitation to eat and drink, but scenes of lustful destruction, like the burning of witches in a past that can boast a marked improvement upon the present. Bundle sleeps soundly enough though struggles, as I do, with the biting cold. We must hurry north and to the thick woodlands there, as far as possible from houses and bonfires. A cave would be a luxury. But there are no caves hereabouts. We must hurry on each time darkness falls. We must find safe places to build a small fire.

At last we found a place to build a fire – we must risk the smoke; we had no choice if we aren't to freeze to death en route.

But I could have sworn Bundle smiled as she closed her eyes, huddled up as close as she could get to the small fire which crackled with twigs and the debris of the forest floor. She smiled, I felt sure she did. Some kind of madness came over me. I remembered the lines I learned as a schoolboy long ago:

> *Let me not to the marriage of true minds admit impediments.*
> *Love is not love which alters when it alteration finds,*
> *Or bends with the remover to remove.*
> *…*
> *If this be error and upon me proved,*
> *I never writ nor no man ever loved.*

I couldn't remember the middle part. Never could; and I well remembered being punished for it. Why I came out with these lines now and in these absurd circumstances, I can't tell. But I could swear I saw her smile. I wish I could have remembered all of it. Everything is fragmented now – especially the very best of things. But fragments are better than nothing.

Long before the Virus ventured upon its deadly course it was remarked by an uncommonly kindly soul that the world is a cold place. 'I'll tell you,' he said. 'If you ever find yourself in the wilderness, your cries of anguish would meet with deaf ears, save those of your God – *your* God, mark you, and no one else's! The warmth you seek is within your own breast.' I've been trying to figure out what he meant ever since.

I believe myself to be on the edge of madness. Only Bundle is my safe haven. It may be colder in the hearts of men now than in the cores of glaciers. But Bundle is my hope – that poor, emaciated, mute thing. Were we right to leave the basement? Already I begin to question the wisdom of that decision. Only from the foot of a mountain can you truly take in its height. Perhaps we are at the foot of a mountain and the lines I remembered were the measure of its height. Even if only one man can produce sentiments like that, there must be some good in everything that has passed and perhaps some good in what is to come – as a spark is to a fire. What though the world is lost to the Raiders; perhaps there is another, a world within a world, one to which the Raiders are, and must always be, quite oblivious; a world infinitely preferable to that inhabited by the glutinous hordes of soulless creatures who, even before the Virus, were only half-born into the light, their better halves still reluctant to join them.

Yes, I feel sure she smiled at those lines, as she huddled next to the meagre warmth of that small fire, as the sun began to rise.

Entry 24

A few more miles last night, I think – in the vague direction of north; that's fine, as long as we don't move in circles. It's cold, stressful, exhausting progress. Strength and courage is what we need; strength and courage, both together; the one is useless without the other.

We move through clusters of trees with naked, frozen branches like arms outstretched in postures of appeal or resignation. Interesting how the advent of the Virus seemed to bring with it a renewed emphasis on the importance of preserving the natural environment, of protecting it from the abuses of civilisation – I guess because the Virus showed us how fickle and uncertain things are, how weak we are when something comes along which we can't control or control only partially. But that renewed interest in the future of the planet never came close to those who had had an abundance of sense and sensitivity sufficient to say and to mean that there is no poem as lovely as a tree, or those, rarer still, who understood or at least wanted very much to understand, the sentiments of a man like Pablo Casals, who declared that he spent hours looking at a tree or was moved to tears at the beauty of a flower; if this was insanity, it was a vast improvement on the sanity of the vast majority of human kind. It was the kind of insanity needed to bring about a significant change in attitudes, a change sufficient to alter human behaviour to save the planet or at least significantly mitigate the effects of global warming. But of course not enough people felt moved to write songs about trees; Handel's aria, 'Ombra mai fu', was a rare human aberration. Anyway, all this is purely academic now, all this talk about how we all lived and how we all should have lived, what we did or didn't do. Soon there won't be enough of us left to make a difference to anything – no doubt the trees will be glad to see us all gone.

Entry 25

We're holed up in what must be a farmhouse. We came across it in the middle of the night. It took us a while to make sure it's uninhabited. But it seems safe enough. Some canned food was left in a cupboard – more than welcome since our supplies are running low. We risked lighting a fire in the grate using some sticks of broken furniture we found lying around – the wood is dry and makes less smoke. What a gift! Made me think of Christmases past – those times of sparkle and jingle and jangle, when people went crazy at the last minute buying baubles and things of no consequence, and justified every excess in the space of a week or two. Goodwill became prominent in that short space of time, which was at least better than at no time at all. In the first year of the Virus, Christmas was cancelled, and those who put a brave face on things preferred to say it was postponed. But it never came round again – forever lost, like humour, good nature and hope.

We can't stay too long here. We'll take what food we can and march on tomorrow night. It's risky staying inside the farmhouse during the day – but it's better than freezing outside. Yes, we must move on. On from what was once a family home, and if the pictures in some of the broken frames are to be trusted, it must've been a good family, content and hardworking. We have trespassed upon it; but there's no one left to object. These rooms which were once well kept are dusty now, all torn and crumbling with neglect – but no sign at all of corpses, just total abandonment. We must move on.

Entry 26

We've stayed in the farmhouse for two days, storms too severe and lasting throughout the night. We should reverse the plan, anyway – travel by day and hole up at night; this way we can see where we're going, and the risk of coming across unwelcome gangs in plain sight is less since we are in more open country now and further and further away from anything that can be called a residential area. Night or day, Bundle shivers herself to sleep – I've given her the last blanket from our pack, but it doesn't seem to help much. Last time I dreamed, I dreamed of Christmas, and I actually felt the warmth of a log fire somewhere deep down, and heard the laughter, and saw the smiles of friendly faces – I can't believe, *won't* believe, we've said goodbye to all that. There are some things that have no right to disappear forever, leaving nothing comparable in their place. Loved ones have no right to die.

We'll move by day – in the morning, still heading as north as far as we can tell.

Entry 27

The incident at the bridge held us up a bit. Intent on a northerly direction, it seemed a good idea to cross the river. Bundle went first, and then stood stock still, staring at something in the river below which turned out to be a floating corpse head down in the water. She just stood there shivering, transfixed; it took a while to get her moving again. I thought I saw another corpse, but I said nothing. Corpses in varying degrees of decomposition are common enough in the inner cities, progressively less so in the urban and peripheral areas, and thankfully rarer as you move into the rural regions which used to be farmland; the bare hills and crags of the north have become welcome sights for their relative dearth of human decay. Not like the days before the Virus was dreamed of, when people thought it 'cool' and life-enhancing, if not necessary, to head for the big cities to work and settle; the days when the metropolis was everything – until the big cities became the worst breeding places for the Virus and the homes of viral transmission.

We moved on, but she was obviously badly affected – the sight might have jogged her memory of something closer to home; but she continues to be mute, and anything I say, any explanation I give myself, must remain pure conjecture. We walked on, with me hoping to find some kind of shelter for the night; the skies were dark and ominous; but the hope is always that we'll find some kind of building, without the threat of human life. Walking through this once harmless land is like chopping your way through what a dark jungle was once imagined to be, with every step uncertain and accompanied by a feeling of uncertainty and apprehension. Once upon a time it would have been madness to question your every step or to treat every unfamiliar byway with suspicion and dread – but now it makes perfect sense, too much sense to take in.

(And is it not also strange that the unfamiliar might spark in us an *unaccountable* dread? In better days I might take a train journey, and simple passing scenes – a field, a rickety wooden shed, a row of houses, a broken cart in the corner of a farmyard, a small grove of trees on a hill, a crumbling building on the skyline, a railway platform or outbuilding – which in themselves were completely devoid of anything monstrous, being plain and simple and no part of any horror story known to me, would nevertheless fill me with an inexplicable terror and a strange feeling of foreboding. It was as though the unfamiliar was sufficient in itself to awaken the darkest of moods, which would dissipate only when the familiar was once again clearly in view. But perhaps this experience was an early symptom of cerebral breakdown, an early indication of a defective brain, and therefore not something that is widely shared.)

Entry 28

We found no shelter last night save a wall, which at least gave some kind of protection from a bitter easterly wind – but, as if to refuse us all respite, it became westerly sometime in the middle of the night, and we were just too cold to get up and move round to the other side. We went to sleep huddled close together. Yes, that memory is very clear. Yes, we were together, wrapped in each other's clothes; cold but together. Yes, there's no doubt at all about that. We were together – cold but safe. Yet, when I opened my eyes, the wind had taken her. God! The wind had taken her! I looked, I called, I called and I looked. Everywhere! It was madness, but I even backtracked, walked southerly for a good hour or so. Then I stopped, taking up the northerly route again, and I walked at a great pace, hoping and praying to catch up. But then it dawned on me that she might have gone east or west. People just don't disappear in storms in the middle of the night, with nothing or no one to guide them. It just doesn't happen. And she was so frail, so vulnerable – and it was just this, her frailty, that brought her to me in the first place and which kept her with me – her frailty, and her fear, and her vulnerability. So, where on God's earth is she, and where in the name of God did she go? Ah! I've caught myself out. Did I say *God's* earth?! And did I say in the name of *God*?! I'd forgotten that it isn't God's earth at all, and never, ever was! So anything said in the name of God is neither here nor there! Bundle! Where are you?

What can I do? What can be done? Is there any more I can do? Bundle has gone. She doesn't want to be found. I did my best to protect her, to save her from harm, to sustain her in this worst of all possible worlds. Perhaps I bored her, or the journey did. I can never know, for she never spoke, and left me in doubt whether she ever understood a word I'd said.

Well, it was not meant to be. She was not the best of companions – incapable of giving warmth, perhaps even incapable of receiving any. Should I lament? Should I grieve? For what? For *her*? For *me*? She's gone and that's that. I was meant to be a loner. It was written in the cold stars. And what's written there can never be altered. God knows I've *tried*. There goes that God word again. It's hard to give up old habits.

I shall keep moving north – alone again.

Entry 29

I move on – plod is a better word. I miss Bundle and look for her still, half expecting to find her huddled up and lifeless under a bush or the bole of a tree – the very idea is anathema, and the reality would stop me in my tracks, bringing me to an abrupt stop despite the fact that she was latecomer to my solitary world in the basement. She came to me without my bidding. But did she leave me or did I leave her? Who can ever answer such a question, if it is a question at all? If it's a question it's not about who was first to leave by the door – no, it's not a question about movement through space and time, but of change of spirit or of soul. Funny how you become so attached to people you never knew and never got to know.

So I plod on northward. What can anyone do other than this in this mere bubble of a thing called life? Well, I guess it's like the journey of life itself – you follow a point on your compass and then hope for the best. What a journey the journey of life is – full of twists and turns, more curves and bends than straight lines, full of false leads and dead ends, and many ways to stumble and fall; roadside cafes are few and far between, and no refreshment will be offered without a valid currency in exchange. But I plod on northward, despite all this, and despite the absence of fellowship or any expectation of respite in this green-brown-grey and unkempt desert.

It's all open country now, with a smattering of bushes and miniature forests scattered here and there on the hills – all growth, all life is frostbitten and ill-clad, like starving, tortured creatures whose blood's turned to ice. I must eat sparingly. My backpack was heavy when at first I set out, and I complained about that; now it is much lighter, and I worry about that. The lighter it gets, the more urgent it becomes to find supplies to fill it. I am not a hunter and in any case have no weapons. I saw three hills in the distance, one hill dwarfing the others with what looks like some sort of ruin on top. I'll make for them and should get there this time tomorrow with one slow, plodding march. Strange place to find a ruin! Maybe some kind of ancient outpost. Maybe some clues tomorrow.

Entry 30

Reached the hills after a day's slow plodding on a breakfast of stale bread and a cup of water. Must eat better tonight and go to sleep on a fuller stomach, otherwise tomorrow's march may not amount to anything at all. Must eat a full can of stewed meat and warm it up – the ruin will defuse the smoke to some extent. Yes, the ruin. Can't make it out. The remaining arches give it a gothic and religious aspect, but I have no idea what it's true function was. It's remaining walls provide a better shelter against the wind than I've had for some time. Who would have thought that a few cold, grey and roofless stone walls would be a welcome and comforting venue for a night's sleep. In the morning I'll take a good look round from my hilltop retreat before plodding on.

Entry 31

After a night far less restful than I had expected, crazy dreams returned, and I tossed and turned in a storm of half-baked ideas or visions, which explains my reaction when I opened my eyes in the grey light on a morning calm and unearthly quiet. Thinking it to be a lingering vision of the night, I simply blinked a few times and rubbed my eyes. But, no, there it was, a creature more wolf than dog sat on its hind legs staring at me as if waiting for my next move, which was, naturally, a start. I jumped up and made to shoo it away as I looked about me for some kind of weapon, a stone perhaps or a piece of branch.

Wolf or dog, I believed my visitor to have evil intentions, if the intentions of a mere animal can be properly described as either good or evil. A cool head would have discounted the idea of a wolf, for the country had not known them for at least 300 years. A dog, then. But rather larger, I thought, than a German Shepherd. Before I had time to think, the creature ran off, leaving me wondering how it had got there and whether there were more of them around. One dog like that might present a problem, but a whole pack could spell disaster. Then again, a dog might have a master, and that immediately brought to mind the Raiders. Were there Raiders here about? A frightening prospect, and hardly an improvement upon a pack of ravaging dogs! It was a relief that the dog had gone, but the prospect of his returning with either a pack of his fellows or a bunch of Raiders was persistently worrying.

I was determined to leave the ruin as quickly as possible, and without breakfast. Time spent building a small fire and filling my stomach would be much better spent getting away from the place without delay. Food had to wait, and lighting a fire would be asking for trouble.

But while I was fumbling with a poor blanket and stuffing it back into my backpack, the dog returned with something in its mouth. That 'something' turned out to be a rabbit, which he dropped at my feet. I looked round carefully, to make sure that he had come alone. There was neither dog nor man in sight. I made a decision which on reflection might have been very rash. I decided to stay put, build a fire and share it with the dog. Crazy, incredible, but that's exactly what happened. I gave the dog the bones and some of the flesh, which perhaps he construed as an expression of gratitude. And so we just sat there, round that small fire, waiting for the rabbit to cook, and as though we'd been together all along.

After the meal, I shouldered my backpack and made down the hill from the ruin to the open country below, the dog following behind. I stopped, turned and looked at him. I was not inclined to shoo him away. He wanted to be a companion. Who was I to refuse? That meal, poor as it was, was a feast under the circumstances, and it was all down to him. No, if he wanted to tag along, he was more than welcome.

And so, we both moved down the hill. I had found another companion – albeit another *mute* companion. I called him Dog, and he seemed happy with that. Before leaving the hill, I could see smoke way down south – lots of smoke, as though whole villages, maybe even towns, were ablaze.

Dog and I moved northward.

Entry 32

As we move north, the geese move south. Flying high in perfect formation, changing their pilot, as is their custom, to relieve him of the pressure of flight. Flying south, as if to defy the chaos there below, or as if to mock the mess of remaining human life. Why did humans fail to achieve the same perfection of response? Partly because the Virus mutated so many times that human science was incapable of catching up, one vaccine after another failing to deal with the mutations that followed at the rate of knots, multiplying, it seemed, at an ever increasing rate. Partly because human benevolence had reached its sad limits. Panic, disobedience and riot were then thrown into the mix.

Dog and I continue on our way; he supplies the food, and I cook it while he devours what I cannot digest. This doesn't happen every day; on days when it doesn't we must make do with the scraps I have left in my backpack, and we sleep as much as we can. On bitterly cold nights, he lies besides me, closer and closer still as the temperature falls, and I feel the warmth of his body.

On seeing the geese, I was reminded of New Year – it must be about that kind of time now. New Year celebrations were the most important item in the year for many people, dwarfing Christmas itself.

I remember the fireworks and the cheering, and the bonhomie which barely managed to outlive the first 24 hours. How ironic the euphoria which heralded the first waves of the Virus! Needless to say, such celebrations became just a memory, increasingly distant, increasingly vague, increasingly irrelevant, and permanently non-existent. Even so, long before the Virus, there were those, though no doubt in the minority, who were always gripped by a different reality, a reality that consisted in the silence of places devoid of human crowds – the strange silence that reigned outside bars and dance halls, the cold silence of nature, that kind of silence that seems to invest the icy fields in the darkness of winter evenings, the stillness that clings to the frozen branches of leafless trees and in the very sky at night; those scenes that exist outside the madding crowds and despite all attempts to blot them out with the noise and clamour of revelry.

The silence of nature in winter, all the more marked when the music has to stop – that silence that seems to mark the insignificance of man and all his puny attempts at self assertion. Yes, there were those who were gripped by such silences amid the revelries of New Year and who therefore could not truly partake in the excitement that was driven by the end of one year and the beginning of another. Such ends and beginnings are the invention of man and, without him, have no significance. The cold silences of nature were and are a reminder of man's place in the larger continuity of rock and earth, and even rock and earth will pass away in a future that no man will ever know. No wonder that those with sufficient sensitivity to such things might have stood spellbound outside the dancehall while those jigged and jogged within to the artificial rhythms of man – spellbound, but not quite understanding why, transfixed by something neither they nor of course those within could grasp and therefore even begin to articulate; transfixed, like a rabbit in a headlight; haunted by something uncomprehended and barely comprehensible. And those that are haunted by the silences of nature are also among those who gaze skyward in wonder at the immensity of space and the mystery of the universe, and it has been said that such wonder is the beginning of philosophy, or of philosophy worthy of the name. They gaze skyward, as distinct from the majority of mankind who look upward only to confirm the prospect of rain.

Dog, I have noticed, rarely looks skyward, but sniffs the ground to forage, only occasionally bothering to look round when he senses danger.

I ramble again. But the light of the fire is poor and the embers are dying. So I write quickly before the light goes. I find scribbling a kind of civilising thing, a reminder, perhaps, that Dog and I don't really belong to the same species of being. It's a discipline that Dog isn't capable of understanding. Writing has rules; knowing some of them, like the use of the simple comma, is a reminder of my humanity, which, I struggle to hope, is not altogether lost or defeated; and to think that Orwell said the semi-colon should be scrapped! Sacrilege! Was that tongue in cheek? With the decline of civilisation comes the decline of language, or is it the other way round? Even so, it's just as well I write in short bursts; our daily plod takes it all out of me, and progress is slower now; the less we eat, the harder our line of march. Incidentally, I notice that my handwriting is smaller now that it used to be. Does that mean something? Trying to get it all down before … Before what?

Anyway, Dog has already succumbed to sleep. So shall I. Surely, tomorrow he'll find something to eat other than the scraps from my backpack. Hope, or something akin to it, dies slow. Empty stomachs, like empty vessels, speak loudest.

Entry 33

Seems a long time since I made the last entry, but it can't be more than a couple of days. Dog comes and goes as he pleases, and pleases me best when he returns with something in his mouth. He surprised me yesterday evening, returning with a bunch of feathers which turned out to be a chicken – dead, thankfully. I did what I could with it; it was better than nothing, even when half-cooked. Dog ate the remains with greater relish. My last half loaf of bread is green with mould, and I spend most of my mealtime picking at it.

Dog's chicken suggests that there is, or was, a farm hereabouts, or maybe a small holding. I can't ask him because Dog can't say. But a speechless companion is better than no companion at all. I can't claim to exist in total isolation – not the kind of isolation that brought so many to an early end. That last call from Jon ended in a laugh that was totally unconvincing; laughter isn't necessarily expressive of joy or merriment; sometimes it's a signal that the end has come. I never heard from him after that. In the early days of the Virus his depression was thought to be treatable, with a visit from a psychiatrist, who prescribed an anti-depressant, and subsequent once-a-week phone calls from a social worker to check on his progress. He lived alone and in social isolation, so he welcomed any attention he could get in the circumstances. But pretty soon all such monitoring disappeared with the rest of social services. Jon never answered my calls, and then all electronic communication was cut. I can only guess what happened to him. He had found some solace in his work as a bio-medic, but the Virus proved too great a challenge, and he gave up hope, just like all the rest. Even before the Virus he'd had a tendency towards depression. The Virus completed the job.

I talk to Dog all day when he's around, and even when he's not around. If only he could shock me with a verbal response! I talk to him and ask his advice, and I even imagine him giving me some.

Entry 34

My crazy dreams have returned with a vengeance. I dreamed a Priest appeared and tried to take Dog away, claiming he was his. He stood there dressed in black with a white collar that seemed to be luminous in the dark, glowing like a white-hot coal. The priest seemed to make off with Dog having forced him to wear a collar and lead; off they went into the shadows with Dog glancing behind as if to ask whether it was right, whether I really wanted him to go. I was relieved to wake and find Dog at my feet.

I'm also plagued during the day by vague visions of things, especially animals or animal forms, which seem to flash past me now and then. They make me turn sharply, wanting to follow them in case they offer some chance of food for me and Dog. Reality seems to be merging or alternating with unreality. 'Go on, Dog! After it!' I once shouted. Dog barked and stood stock still looking at me as though … well, I suppose as though I'd lost it – which, in a sense, I had.

But that Priest! – perhaps the devil clothed as a cleric, I don't know. That's how it is with dreams – I can't remember his face, just his clothes and the shadows he cast. When the Virus proved undefeatable, priests were everywhere, online, offline, in the streets, on radio, television, all telling people that things would be all right in the end because the Virus wasn't part of God's plan. There was one prayer that was said everyday, and then several times a day, and it became a mantra, until it was repeated so often that people, even those who sets their hearts of it, came to forget that it was a prayer at all, but it was learned despite the efforts of the least religious to block it out. I remember it came after the Lord's Prayer:

'Holy Father, gentle lord Jesus, help and protect us all this day from the evil Virus and all its variants. Give us all strength and courage, yes, courage and strength. Protect us all from evil and wickedness whatever their form and whatever their source; and protect us from those who appear to be human but who rend the flesh and spill the blood of the innocent and the good. Give us all this day intelligence and wisdom, and compassion for all those less fortunate, and let us reserve a little compassion for ourselves also, since we are punished enough already and should not punish ourselves further. Protect us all from misadventure and misjudgement, from the misjudgements of others as well as our own. Give us all confidence and hope for the future. Resolve all our physical, mental, emotional, material difficulties so that we may live long and strong to protect our loved ones and complete our tasks before the end.'

That's the gist of it. The dirge was repeated every day, even after every news bulletin – and every news bulletin contained nothing but the progress of the Virus and hollow expressions of hope. The line about those 'who appear to be human but who rend the flesh and spill the blood of the innocent and the good' was a reference to the burgeoning number of Raiders who had begun looting and raping and were committing these crimes at a rate and with such aggression and such impunity that it would soon prove beyond the competence of the seriously dwindling numbers of police and military to offer effective resistance or deterrence; the situation was deteriorating so badly that your next cautious visit to the supermarket might well be your last; leaving your house not only exposed you to the Virus itself but to those 'who appear to be human', and how many people, not just the elderly, who succumbed to malnutrition and the weakening of natural immunity, can never be calculated.

The Virus had quickly found an ally amongst the rapidly fading ranks of humanity. Amongst the early Raiders were those who had argued all along that the Virus was a hoax, though with what rationale no one ever managed to explain satisfactorily; they stated, amongst other things, that the hospitals, far from being overwhelmed with people suffering and dying from the Virus, were either empty or subject to under-capacity; others said the Virus was simply nature's way of controlling the human population and that the process should simply be allowed to run its course without opposition, while the rest of humanity blamed the sceptics and the so-called 'Naturists' for aiding and abetting viral transmission, comparing them to those who had either doubted or condoned the Jewish Holocaust and the Armenian genocide that had preceded it as a template for Nazi strategies of annihilation. The virus was in one way or another tragically divisive at a time when unity was of the essence. But divisions festered, losing all shape and reason, and reached their zenith when, ultimately, people blamed one another for the very vice that each of them possessed in abundance, namely a savage, wild and unmannered craving for self-preservation – it was as though each looked into a mirror for the first time in a long time and was revolted by the reflection that met their gaze, believing it to be that of someone else whom they longed to despise.

Anyway, the prayer stopped with the implicit consensus that it consisted of sounds that seemed to fade into an ether of nothingness when uttered, and no one seemed the worse for it, for the situation was beyond the help of prayers; and in no time at all, those of us left forgot how to pray and even what to pray for. Plato said somewhere that we should pray to have the right desires before we pray to have those desires fulfilled; but desire eventually gave way to the instinct of brute survival – the only desire recognisable, and even God shook his head in disbelief to see what had become of his protégés in the sad ruins of what had once been the Garden of Eden. And so, the online priests fell silent, for the situation was more than enough to test the faith of saints – and no priest was a saint.

Entry 35

Haven't scribbled for days. Dog barked this morning and woke me up, pulling my arm this way and that and wouldn't stop 'til I followed him out of the thicket where we'd bivouacked for the night. He stared into the distance, clearly wanting me to do likewise. It's a house, a whitewashed house, standing alone – as conspicuous as a landmark, maybe three, four hundred yards away on low-lying hills. We stared at it for ages. Stupid, really – as though I would be able to make out any signs of life at that distance and without binoculars! But it's the first remotely looking civilised thing we've seen for days. But is it occupied – and, if so, by whom or by what? It would be a luxury to shelter there – maybe treat it as a launching pad for something else, like a change of direction. Not to mention food – could there be food there?

We'll make for it – cautiously, step by step. We've come so far – this could be our salvation, or our undoing. I've told Dog not to bark, and I hope he gets it – if he betrays our presence prematurely, it could be a bad thing, a *very* bad thing. It's funny, though. A whitewashed house standing there all alone in the middle of nowhere. Reminds me of my boyhood days and my ramblings on low hills just like these, and of a house that was whitewashed and inhabited by two brothers who were seldom seen down in the village and were therefore the butt of jokes and the objects of common suspicion; naughty children were sometimes reprimanded by the prospect of being sent to 'the brothers', though I'm absolutely sure there was nothing at all untoward about them – but it was an oddity, just like this oddity now, a whitewashed house in the middle of nowhere. Anyhow, we must plod on, trying not to be seen or heard, and hoping there's no one there at all – but is this a real hope? It would be quite something to meet someone else as distinct from a Raider as it's possible to be.

Entry 36

My hand trembles. There's so much to say. I mean, about the house.

As we approached we came across hazel trees in the garden – is it a garden? No matter. Is the hazel as magical as some of our more imaginative ancestors believed? I remembered reading something about hazel trees, about hazel nuts being givers of inspiration and wisdom – and about hazel trees standing between the magical border between one world and another. In extremity we may begin to believe anything that strikes our fancy. I say no matter. I took them as a good omen, even before we found the house to be empty and more than I had hoped for. I suppose because I remember that time, as a small boy, when my father cycled, with me perched uncomfortably on the crossbar, to a kind of garden or open space full of hazel trees, and we each picked a handful of nuts, as like as not too unripe for the picking. It's one of the very few enduring memories of my father I have, of what we did together – and I guess I remember it because it was one of the very few things we ever did together. He died young – his reward for having survived Dunkirk with only a minor bullet wound (if ever such a thing can be called minor) and for presumably having pleased the gods.

But the house itself! Abandoned (apparently – it's safer to keep an open mind!) But no human corpses and no sign of struggle – thank goodness. No electricity, of course – the fridge is empty; everywhere covered with dust – another good sign! There are tins of stuff in a larder, and this should keep us going for a while. Even books in a bookcase, each one raising clouds of dust when touched. Haven't bothered to read the titles. Upstairs there's a bed, though curiously little sign of dust in the bedroom, and it seems like a godsend to my aching bones – Dog too has taken to it and lay on top of it with me as I stared at the ceiling wondering what to make of it all and thanking the stars for our luck. We need to look around more. The dust covered laptop downstairs is of course quite useless, as is the old radio in the corner of the living room. But we have adequate shelter, a bed and the prospect of what we can at last call a meal. Above all, the chance to rest and maybe take stock as to our next move. All too good to be true – maybe.

Entry 37

Spent an unexpectedly restless night despite being indoors and in a bed for the first time since I left the basement. Taking stock of the situation is wishful thinking – I don't really know how to go about it. It's dangerous to stay in one place too long – that I suppose must be true. But where to go is not at all clear. North, still? Not south. East? West? I feel like a piece on a chessboard with limited options or no options at all – or it feels as though the options are illusory. It's like a man in pain in a hospital bed, thinking that if only he could move on to the other side the pain would go away.

No, there are some things you're stuck with. That's the hell of it. That together with the fact that the Virus has generated the nightmare illusion that time doesn't exist – one day is indistinguishable from another, one week from another; days pass like seconds; days and weeks and months have been cloned, preceding and following one another with no discernible distinguishing marks. I once entertained the idea that the more conscious you are of how quickly time passes the slower it would pass, as though being conscious of it would somehow slow it down. Crazy idea! The opposite seems to be true – the more conscious you are of the speed at which time passes, the quicker it goes. That seems crazy too. But there's no yardstick anymore – neither for the passage of time nor for your state of mind, nothing to tell you how crazy you are or might become; anything seems possible, and this is not as liberating as it might sound; no, it's a nightmare. It's like waking up on a conveyor belt that keeps forever going round and round in the same place – and you can't get off!

Well, we'll stay here for a while, as long as it seems safe. But when uncertainty begins to bite, we'll move out with a toss of the coin as to which direction, excluding south. Whether it's a good omen or a bad, I found a 12 gauge shotgun propped up behind some old clothes in a cupboard and a box of cartridges on the top shelf. A gun like this is what you might expect to find on a farm of some kind. But it's amazing how many guns like this came out of cupboards in urban areas, especially after rats became an issue when refuse collection ceased to exist. Confusion and stark despair gave on to frayed tempers, and guns were just as easily turned on neighbours as they were on vermin – and those with guns became the first and most effective Raiders. The problem was not confined to the USA, a country constitutionally and traditionally more warmly attached to guns than any other. You might have expected the UK to be the least likely venue for such a rampant display of violence – but the issue was universal, no country was untouched, and the UK was no exception. There were even parliamentary calls for the temporary return of capital punishment; such calls were resisted mainly from the Left. But before there could be any reasoned debate on such a drastic issue, parliament itself had folded, debate and legislation becoming things of the past.

Looking out from the windows of this whitewashed haven on to the rolling fields and with the songs of skylarks gently piercing the morning air, it's painful to recall the devastation of civilisation we've left behind, Dog and I. I say we've left it behind, but I feel it all around. Neither house nor nature can erase the sensation of it; this house can't protect us for long, I feel it in my bones. But where should we go? What a question? If only Dog could say something. How long will the tinned provisions last? Maybe a week. Maybe more if we stretch them out, and then we must move out. The gun gives me some measure of security, though whether I could actually kill a person with it is doubtful, even in self-defence. Let's hope I'm not put to the test. I remember the rabbit I shot when I was a kid. I buried it and fashioned a wooden cross on its grave, and I've mourned it ever since. It was a needless kill, and the memory of it is a form of punishment. Does that sound like someone who could fire both barrels of a 12-bore at a human? Even so, the gun, fully loaded, is kept close by at all times. Who knows, least of all me, just what I may be capable of? I can't speak for myself today, let alone tomorrow. Just goes to show what possibilities are opened up, not all of them welcome or salutary, when all the chips are down – even saints can't trust themselves, so how can I? Augustine keeps coming back, like a mantra that refuses to be belied – 'There may be some light in men, but let them walk fast, walk fast lest the shadows come!'

Entry 38

About three nights since my last scribble. Each one as restless as the last. Not too surprising since I doze off during the day. I sit for a while, then get up and look out the windows – all round the house, like an unbreakable routine; I look through the living room window, then the kitchen window, then I climb the stairs and look out the bedroom windows, even though they present the same scene I looked at a few moments before. I take the gun with me as though I'm under siege and might be attacked at any moment. The windows are shut tight and the two doors, front and back, are bolted. I start at a noise that might be that of an intruder, forgetting that I myself am an intruder. The daylight hours seem more threatening than the dark. Reasonable, I suppose. As a child I was frightened of the dark, but in these times I have more to worry about in the light of day. Yet there's only so much walking around the place I can take. I sit, and then I doze off and wake with a start. Dozing and waking all day long. Dog at least has the sense to roam round outside, and where he gets to beats me. But he comes back. Always he comes back, my mute companion who listens to everything, says nothing and offers no opposition. He's just as restless as I am.

I've looked at the books scattered here and there on shelves and tables. Mostly cheap thrillers with the same template and only a change of names and places. Science fiction, too. What Wells depicts in *War of the Worlds* seems somehow understated when compared with the real thing – at least the invaders could be seen, and bacteria to which humans are immune were their downfall. Human civilisation and the planet we know are saved by friendly bacteria. The Virus is quite another matter – invisible and undefeatable, it almost makes Wells's narrative an attractive alternative. I smiled when I flicked through the pages inside their dusty, grimy cover, as though the story were a harmless fairytale, which of course, by comparison, it is. When horror is a reality, horror fiction has its legs cut from under it; it is defused and degraded, if not morally repugnant, like a species of cheap and uncomprehending voyeurism. Anyhow, I couldn't possibly red Wells now, let alone find some form of entertainment in thrillers. Such books have lost their ability to entertain and engross. The Virus speaks instead.

Restless nights and days. Yes, this house is not what it seemed at first. The safety it provides is more apparent than real. I have no wish to walk through cold days and sleep through bitter nights – but really we can't stay here. Safety is an illusion. How many illusions make up an average lifetime? We can't escape them, and no doubt we'd hardly survive without some of them. Where would we be without the illusion that we can live forever, or that a friend is a friend forever, or that love must last forever? Life would be different without illusions, and not necessarily better, by which I mean easier or more bearable. The illusion that the grass must be greener on the other side of the hill may be a useful incentive towards something truly better, but it might also be a highway to hell. Either way, we can't stay here.

The thought struck me that we might use this house as a kind of safe haven, as a place of safe return, or as a kind of staging post. Yes, maybe. Then the suggestion came to me again in a dream, not a nightmare this time. I dreamed I saw a man – elderly, tall and large of frame, with a kindly, bearded face – yes, this time I thought I glimpsed his face in a shadowy kind of way, the way of dreams. I suppose he looked a bit like the actor Findley Currie who used to appear in the old black and white movies of long ago when technology was in its relatively harmless infancy. He stood, filling the door frame at the front of the house, and he reproved me for pointing the gun at his chest. Then he said that the house was a safe house and that I was welcome to use it as such. Then there was nothing. Just another silly dream. I no longer trust dreams, though long ago I was advised by my grandmother that the *opposite* of a nightmare was true; no doubt she told me this to put me at ease; but if she was right, what are we to say of *pleasant* dreams?

The dream about the old man in the doorway was not as fevered as my dreams usually are. Should I trust it and use this house as a safe house, venturing a little here and there and returning? Or should we trust to fate and go further north or wherever our fancy takes us?

Entry 39

Running like a mad thing, crashing against obstacles hardly seen in the shadows, getting hurt, stumbling, falling, getting up and dashing forward again covered in cuts and bruises. The faster I ran the harder I fell and the more the obstacles multiplied. What kind of dream is this?! Some dreams feed upon cerebral archives, but this one is all about the present and my lingering doubts as to whether to move on or stay put. Even Dog seems to be tortured by the same uncertainties, now growling now whimpering in his sleep. Late last night I seemed to hear a deep booming in the distance, as if a large drum were heralding an invasion of monsters intent upon all manner of evils – but now I wonder whether that was the precursor of my nightmare or simply part of it. Nothing is certain. Nothing is absolute. I used to despise those who were certain of things that should be doubted. Now a little certainty would be reassuring.

Among the dusty array of books I glanced a history of ancient Greece. *Soma sema*, I remember, was the idea that the body is the prison house of the soul, from which the soul is released at death, though in life it is imprisoned by the body and all the attachments it forms. So death was thought of by some as a kind of release of something far purer, more real, than the body, something eternal and immutable, unlike the body which must suffer and perish. 'Learning how to die' meant releasing yourself from the attachments of the body, and, to the extent that you were successful in doing so, death would be easier and less to be feared.

Drivel? No doubt. But the close attachments the body forms would at least help to explain why we are so reluctant to welcome death. The more attachments we form and the closer we bind ourselves to them, the harder it is to meet the bear in the mouth; yet, he can't be avoided.

Yet, death must come, despite the body and its attachments. If living forever is an illusion, the reality of death must be faced. Such matters force themselves upon me because I must ask why I am so eager to move, to run, to get away. That dream – does it not mean that the harder you try to get away from things which are painful or unwelcome, the closer you seem to approach them, the faster they come to you. You rack your wits to escape from the tiger only to fall into the jaws of the crocodile. Your efforts to escape are not only futile but seem to bring closer the very thing you fear most.

Death must come. Avoidance and delay are what the instinct for survival is all about. Yes, of course! But we can run too hard. More hurry, less speed. The faster we run the more our pursuer gains upon us.

And so, I question the wisdom of hurry and dash. Danger and death, like the Virus itself, is everywhere now – behind, in front and on both sides, north, south, east and west. Hurry? But hurry *where*? And *why*?

Am I trying to escape from the evils that man is capable of committing, as though I might yet find a haven they cannot reach? There were evils in abundance before the Virus – man's inhumanity to man at all times and in all places is well documented. And much more besides about his dark side is still unknown, so well has he covered his tracks.

As for attachments, there are much fewer of these now than there used to be before the Virus; attachments now are starkly animal; the spiritual and the cerebral have evaporated, making way for the brute instinct for survival, which may seem reasonable enough if all you are is a brute, if all you want to be is a creature in a primordial soup of grasping, grabbing and killing. Who would have thought that the Virus would put an end to marital relationships, at least those that fed on a main diet of sex, and to every kind of relationship that hinged upon the exchange of sexual favours or on the physical as an expression of the spiritual. No relationship could even reach first base for fear of transmitting the killer bug to the very object of your deepest affections or of contracting it from the same source. And casual sex became increasingly causal, until it ceased altogether. All sex ended until the Raiders redefined it as unbridled lust in the form of violent rape and unbridled violence – all in a devil-may-care context in which all hope was lost, and with all hope, all love and all feelings which had the remotest pretension of being described as such. No wonder attachments between people were severely downgraded and of so little value – the hard, uncompromising cynicism of the trenches of 1914–'18 replaced the dreamlike hopes of the romantics, and the life of another became just one more bubble on the surface of a foamy sea of souls, easily pricked and just as easily forgotten.

Should we stay in this white-washed house until the worst arrives or should we move on in the vain hope of finding an untouchable paradise over the far hills to the north? How much does it matter *whatever* we decide? I glance at Dog, my mute friend, and there is no answer. Dog's life is as short and as uncomprehending as that of a Raider. But he stays by me and moves when I move and is still when I am unmoving. His thoughts are simple and clear, not troubled; his is a dog's life, after all – not so different from what life has become for all of us that remain. I have half a mind to reverse the situation and follow *him*! It would be just as well. But no, he will not move until I do.

There is no incentive for struggling on when hope has been abandoned, the hope that things may return to at least a modicum of normality, so that some of those things may be restored that give life a point to most of us – if only the hope of some civilised intercourse with beings of the same species. Otherwise there is only the instinctive drive for survival – and there is a limit to which the intelligent human mind can suffer the vacuum that instinct alone and by itself entails. True, the mountain men of the North American Rockies and the Sierra Nevada, the Cascade range and the Great plains tolerated great deprivations compared with their more 'civilised' contemporaries, and the hardships and isolation they endured were not for weaker mortals. But theirs was a life of their own choosing; and, in any case, they traded with both Native Americans and whites during the summer months and, at other times, were never so far from villages and townships that made a return to them impossible if they so desired.

But the Virus has deprived us all of choice. The door to your room may be locked, but, if you are ignorant of this, you can happily remain there; but from the moment you know of your imprisonment, that the door is locked, your room will in that very instant take on the character of a prison and you will panic to be released from it. That is the panic the Virus has engendered. People beat upon the iron doors of their cells until they fall back exhausted and despairing of any release from their isolation. They have been given a life sentence without recourse to appeal.

Entry 40

Woke up with fingers and toes next to freezing. Managed to forage more wood for the wood stove. Well, that's it! The weather has decided for us. We stay put! Just too cold to travel. We'll take our chances here. I am no mountain man. Dog would far better than I. But he's better at taking advice than giving it. He stays, too.

Napoleon's retreat from Moscow and the siege of Stalingrad come easily to mind. To manage the cold at the best of times is challenging; but in war! What gives dictators the right to …? Well, what a silly question! They have no right except the right explicitly or tacitly given them by those who will suffer most in consequence. It is one of the moral absurdities of so-called civilised man.

The Virus is a supreme dictator. It dictates not only that we should die but that we should die alone – no loving hand to hold in ours, no benign smile, no warmth of any kind, our existence bereft of all those simple expressions of sympathy and solicitude. We cannot even die fighting like Napoleon's men at Waterloo, or those in Stalingrad who were forbidden to surrender despite General Paulus's pleas to the Fuehrer. We cannot even stand on the scaffold or stand tied to a stake surrounded by fellow beings some of whom might even show or at least feel a little pity. Even a mountain man close to death might have been lucky enough to taste the hospitality of a tribe like the Crow or the Sioux, who were not slow to tend to the needs of those who had entered their villages in peace.

Yes, a stranger's hand while you lay breathing your last in a hospital bed was a welcome sign of apparently irrepressible humanity – but when the hospitals and all its auxiliary services folded, nothing was left. Perhaps it might strike us as faintly ironic, or in some important sense suggestive, that when we are born we necessarily share the event, but when we die we may well die alone. Such is the cruelty not of man, or not of man alone, but of the Virus that plagued us and plagues us still – that unseen barbarian whose wicked excesses are limitless and infinitely consequential. The capacity for expressions of humanity was one of its most important victims – when all there was to lose was finally and irretrievably lost and the god of love and pity fell silent in the hearts of all those who had once known him.

Entry 41

As for humanity, the lines of Gevorg Emin came to mind last night as I was falling asleep.

Not everyone's a man.
Like the jeweller's trade,
humanity is learned.
A man is not born. He's made.

What is learned is taught through word or shown by example. So, what can be expected if there is no one to teach us? The Virus has deprived us of education by depriving us of educators through word and example. How easy it was to unravel the complications of so-called modern and civilised life and eradicate the capacity to love.

Dog ran off in the early hours and didn't reappear again until later this morning a little worse for wear. He seems agitated. Halfway through the night I heard that booming sound again, which I thought was just a dream – it woke me up with a start and I couldn't get back to sleep, which is just as well what with the dreams I'm getting. Maybe the noise spooked him and he went off to reconnoitre. He keeps lying down and getting up again, as though he's expecting a door to burst open or a window to splinter. He's making me nervous and more alert than ever.

I've lit the fire – needs must, though if there's something out there, the smoke might attract the wrong kind of attention. But out where?! As far as I can make out there's nothing for miles around. I've had to burn wet wood together with the rest of the dry bits I've managed to dig out of the floorboards – it's either that or freeze to death. But nothing pleases Dog. I think tonight I'd better take a wider look round, locking Dog in the house before I go – he might run riot, and just one bark would give us away. I'll take the gun and just pray I don't have to use it or have it used against me!

Entry 42

Last night I tossed and turned as usual, losing the warmth I had built up by lying in one position. But then, I don't know how or why, I imagined voices singing gently. I think the voices of children. And the song they sang was 'O Come all ye faithful, joyful and triumphant'. And I swear I was comforted and fell asleep, as though the singing was a balm against which no discomfort could prevail. It came from those cerebral archives, from the days of innocence when, as a child, I expected nothing but wonder and delight in the days to come, for as yet I was taught to expect nothing less. Who can possibly be joyful and triumphant now?

Then I awoke with a start and remembered, painfully, that I had resolved to venture out and about while it was still dark, leaving Dog safely locked inside.

Soon enough I found myself outside the comforting walls of the white-washed house, and I first thought of heading a little further north in the assumed direction of the booms I'd heard before. I walked cautiously in a northerly direction. The booms started again, but it was coming from behind me – from the south! I backtracked and walked in the direction of the unearthly noise until I saw a faint yellow-orange glow in the sky. I walked further on. I was careful not to lose track of the way back to the white-washed house, noting the landmarks of shadowy hills and the occasional clumps of trees and undergrowth. It was dark enough to obscure my progress in the shadows, but the light of the moon enabled me to move forward. Another hundred yards or so and I'd stop and return.

The booms became louder. I stopped. I fell forward to the ground so as not to be seen and peered over a small grassy mound into a large hollow down below. I saw things I saw or half saw down south, the same unsettling things, but even worse this time. Strange painted creatures were dancing round a large bonfire, their half-naked bodies chanting and writhing in the glow and their shapes changing as the flames shot skyward. Someone, somewhere, was pounding on a very large drum. The whole scene reminded me of a picture I'd once seen called *Scalp Dance of the Sioux* by George Catlin. Catlin had obviously been at pains to depict the event as though it were a scene from Dante's *Inferno* – grotesque figures with satanic or contorted faces gyrating round a large bonfire which gave out a deep red glow against the dark night. Yes, this is how the scene struck me. I had suddenly been transported back in time to some primitive event only a few hundred yards from the whitewashed house. The contrast was alarmingly surreal. I didn't stay; I was not keen to take a closer look. I carefully backtracked until I was far enough away to stand upright and run. I ran fast until I reached the outskirts of the abandoned house; I was comforted by the sight of the familiar, a token of a civilisation, however battered and unkempt, light years away from what I had just witnessed.

Now I have to fight the temptation to take Dog and run as far northward as I can. No, I have to stop and take stock and try to make some sense of it all, if I can. And then run! Yes, there's no doubt that I should run. If only we could stay here undetected. Every instinct tells me that these creatures are moving slowly north and that they're bound to see the house and inhabit it or destroy it. If they find us here, we're done for. We must get out today!

I've called them 'creatures'. But they are human beings, *aren't* they? Is it that human beings can be defective, like an object? Can it be that they contain within them a defect that can be triggered by a change in circumstances – maybe even the merest change? Would it not be possible to speak to them without fear? Would they destroy us, Dog and me? Would they destroy the house with whitewashed walls? Have we not a common language still? Is there no hope at all? Is conflict, ruin, torture and death inevitable? Is there no bridge to cross? I think I know the answer to these questions, and that unnerves me. As for defects, they may be more or less dangerous, more or less complex, and they may often be revealed in a lack of skills: there are those who cannot draw for love or money, try as they might; those that cannot learn a foreign language despite the hours they may put in; those who cannot read music despite their fervent desire to do so; somehow their brains are wired differently, though they themselves through frustration and despair may prefer to calls themselves defective; some things are given to some and not to others; ad so there are things of which we may complain, but cannot put right.

But the inability to draw, to learn a foreign language or to read music are not at all the same as moral and aesthetic blindness, for these are a far more dangerous species of defectiveness, one for which there is no complaint from those deficient, since they are quite unaware of any deficiency or insufficiency and are consequently bereft of all desire to 'put things right'. The future or fate of the whole planet may therefore rest upon the shoulders of ignorance and consequent indifference, upon the existence of moral blindness and an inability to comprehend the kind of beauty of which Dostoyevsky speaks when he affirms that the world will be saved by beauty.

Entry 43

The booms were louder last night. So, we'll move out in a couple of hours, in full daylight, taking with us whatever we can find here. I don't know what's ahead but I fear most what comes behind. First, we'll go further north – I guess east or west will get us to the coast quicker, if that's where we want to be, and I'm not at all sure about that. Wherever we go we'll be moving more slowly than ever. Six decades and a half have slowed me down. Come to think of it, I don't know exactly how old I am. I feel older by the day; they used to say, 'You're as old as you feel' in which case I'm long dead, buried and forgotten – that's a bad joke, in fact, not a joke at all. But does it mean I still have a sense of humour?

Anyhow, does it matter if I'm slower than I was? I guess it does, if I'm right about what's coming up behind. Raiders have no respect for life, even less for lives they regard as spent anyhow. It all started when hospitals were stressed to breaking point and decisions about who should get what became an unchallenged routine. At first, the whole idea of choosing between patients was ruled out of court; then a case started to be made for it – pure pragmatics; and then no one talked about it anymore – it just happened, as a change in the weather just happens. And then? Well, then there was nothing.

Dog is frisky. He knows we must go. I've made up a kind of sleigh and harnessed him to it. The ground is flat and slippery, a kind of greasy grass, especially so until midday on account of the frost. I've packed some blankets, taken what's left of the tins and filled some bottles with water, hoping that the latter is still drinkable – to become ill now would be the end of it.

Entry 44

We're holed up in a small hollow, no more than a shallow dip in the ground, after a day's slow, painful march, stopping frequently to catch my breath. We left the white-washed house behind us. I looked back last night during the drumming noise. I thought I could see a faint red glow in the distance, bigger than that of an average bonfire. Had they decided to torch the white-washed house without a second thought – completely disregarding the possibility it offered for shelter for others, which is no surprise, but also for themselves?

We were right to get out of there when we did; a few more hours and … But I couldn't resist the temptation to creep back and see for myself. I tied Dog to a small bush and headed back, not all the way, just far enough to get a closer look. Sure enough the whole house was ablaze. The drumming noise seemed to be coming right out of the air all around, as though from some undefined place, over or under the very earth itself, pounding away from above and below remorselessly while the flames pricked the heavens like red-pointed spears.

And there they were again, those crazy, dehumanised figures, like painted demons of the night, ecstatic in their destruction of just about everything they could lay their hands on – even the dry-stone wall at the front of the house had been knocked down. I'd seen it before, but I rubbed my eyes like an automaton, a reflex of disbelief – but that was mixed with anger, too; our refuge was destroyed and for no reason comprehensible to civilised man – once again forcing me out of my reclusion, making me a man on the run. I retraced my steps back to Dog, as though I was going home after a bitter disappointment, home to a warm place and a few words of real comfort – though the dip in the ground was anything but warm and Dog can't speak.

Entry 45

Since they destroyed the house, it's fair to assume the Raiders will keep on northward like a plague of locusts – though of course I don't know this. Anyhow, I've decided on a change of direction – west. Maybe I can outflank them, unless of course … Well, nothing is certain. But the air's colder the further north we go, so maybe it's time for a change of direction. It's hard to make decisions. Sometimes I feel like throwing everything up in the air and going back south even if it means falling right in to the hand of the Raiders – I suppose that's a refusal to play the game of survival, throwing in the towel. Well, I suppose, no, I *know* she wouldn't like that. She's want me to go on, in the hope of, well I don't know what! But she wouldn't want me to give up, not yet, no, not yet.

She was always *positive* – that word's like an old shapeless hat, worn by too many heads. Always looking on the bright side. Always accusing me of cynicism and negativity. But the Virus took her early, at least early enough for optimism to make some sense. Had she lived longer, or if she could only see how things have turned out. Anyhow, she's deep in the garden way down south – she can know nothing, now or ever, though the dead can often speak louder than the living. Things have changed so much … I feel I am at the end of the world – I suppose she might say it's the beginning of the world, maybe a new world, and beginnings are thought to be more hopeful. She was never afraid to prune old plants, trees and bushes down to generate new and better life, while I was always reluctant to cut so much as a twig off an ageing tree. She said I had to be a more adventurous gardener and less afraid to cut away the old to encourage new growth. But she can't see what I see; she can't see what has become of things. How is it possible to hope when everything around you tells you that hope is groundless? I find it hard to feel any degree of optimism. But still, she's in my head telling me to go on. And the thing about an old shapeless hat is that it's too comfortable to discard.

We'll go west at first light and hole up somewhere by dusk. I swear I can sense the acrid odour of burned wood. Bad smells, like bad news, travels fast and far. That whitewashed house was far from perfect, but infinitely better than nothing at all – the story of civilisation; what the Raiders have done to the house is what the Virus and human bestiality has done to the civilised world, a world that was so often uncivilised but at least subject to civilised criticism by the brave and the righteous. Who is there to offer criticism now, and who is there to listen. There are no eyes to see, no ears to hear, except the ravenous and uncomprehending eyes and ears of the demons of the night.

Entry 46

Travelled west today. We're holed up in a wooded patch of ground below hills. Managed to make a makeshift shelter with some branches and two spare blankets. Must abandon the sleigh. It proved too much for Dog over ground that was full of bumps and tiny hollows. Have used some of the wood for a fire, and will carry the rest for next time.

Before descending to the wood, we needed to skirt round a large apparently oblong area, I reckon about 150x100 yards, fenced in by barbed wire. We saw several of these on the northward trek. They are mass graves for victims of the Virus. Once the Virus really got going, sufficient space and time for burials couldn't be found, and crematoria were the next to fold, not having the capacity and energy supply to keep going. Bodies had to be removed out of the villages, towns and cities into large rural spaces. Thousands were buried at a time, without ceremony, without even so much as a name tag, in graves dug out of solitary places as far as possible from surviving clusters of the population. With the general chaos and diminishing lack of manpower and organisation, these mass graves were finally abandoned and people were simply left where they died, chiefly in their own homes; houses became tombs and the source of further bacterial and viral infection.

From the top of the hill I could make out one or two more of these sites. I can only wonder what distant future generations of humans, if there are any, will make of them. Will they stare at them in sad wonder or take them for granted? Dog and I must give them a wide berth. I find the very thought of them distressing, let alone the sight.

Entry 47

We left the mass burial sites behind us a couple of days ago – thankfully! So distressing to think how many dead worlds they contain. I say 'worlds'. Each of us is fated to live in our own world – this is the head, the box, in which we feel and surmise and delight and grieve and hope and despair, and our eyes are the portals upon the planet we see in terms of the world we inhabit. How can we possibly help it? Each of us is a world unto himself, locked in through no fault of his own – something he can do nothing at all about. We are all prisoners of our own being, but prisoners who desire no freedom, prisoners to whom freedom is anathema; and so we fear death, the extinction of our boxes and all that they contain, for all that they contain define us and make up who we are.

These different worlds can indeed link up, make contact; bridges can be built between them. It is a pretty thought that the appreciation of Dostoyevsky's concept of beauty may be such a bridge – that the perception of beauty can cement one world with another, and here there would be grounds for hope, hope that the planet may be saved and that harmony between worlds may be achieved. But beauty is not the only bridge, for bestiality may also bring worlds together, as when a mob is led on by each of its constituent parts, each part serving to strengthen and entice another until all parts melt into one fearful whole which surges forward like an avalanche of ignorance and consequent indifference, intent upon the harm it must necessarily inflict upon worlds innocent and sensitised by beauty and compassion.

Worlds, good and bad, compete for hegemony, now one now the other achieving it, but seldom for long, and never for eternity.

The worlds Dog and I passed are buried and forgotten now, neither good nor bad capable of claiming victory. But the Raiders – yes, they are the living worlds of ignorance and indifference, and there is every indication that they bask in their victory. Yet what a sad and hollow victory it is – to survive and wield power on a planet that is uninhabited by beauty. What a soulless enterprise it is to rape and pillage and burn, eating and drinking like beasts.

O, this line of thought augers what I most fear – *insanity*! This way madness lies, as surely as it did for Lear. This is a storm, not a storm of nature but of man. True, it shows no sign of easing. Yet, still I cannot bring myself to believe that the very best that civilised man has accomplished – the unfathomable inspirations of great composers, the insights of prophets, the moral outcries of those motivated by their hatred of man's inhumanity to man, the writings of those of incomparable skill, all such things and much, much more – no, I refuse to believe that all this has been wiped from the slates of human endeavour, as though they had never happened at all or are of so little account. Before the Virus the battle was joined between worlds of beauty and worlds of ignorance – surely the battle is not lost!

I am looking for light in a darkened world, with the conviction that it does exist, if only I had the eyes to see.

Meanwhile, Dog and I move westward. We have used the last of the wood I've been hauling on my back. Winds are lighter. Warmer, I think. There are more wooded places to hide from nature and the remnants of man.

Entry 48

Still making steady tracks west, but more and more grudgingly –
asking the question, 'Why bother?' It's a survival trait, though perhaps
a pointless one. It's a reflex action inspired by fear, as when people
first started to move out of their homes to flee God knows where but
anywhere away from something they felt was pursuing them, as though
the virus was a foreign army on the march and heading straight for
them. The human brain seemed to make a tacit comparison and then
acted upon it. An army might attack in waves, sending first their inferior
foreign auxiliaries followed later, and if necessary, by the elite cohorts
and legions. The Virus seemed to act in a similar way by first testing
the strength of the opposition by goading it into attack and then, when
the confidence of the resistance was beginning to take hold, unleashing
legions that were unassailable by any of the available vaccines, rendering
all previous defences null and void. It seemed natural to consider the
Virus a deadly enemy that attacked in waves, seeking out the weak spots
in the defences, dealing partial blows, and then swooping in for the kill.
People wanted to be on the move, like children fidgeting in their seats,
but move where? This was an enemy that knew no boundaries, that
could cross seas and infect the very air we breathe.

So Dog and I plod on, though wondering all along why we should. The Raiders aren't a local phenomenon. Like the Virus which created them they are ubiquitous and may be as much in front of us and around us as they are behind. For all we know, those we left behind might have already caught up with us and left us in the rear, ready to surprise us at any moment, to stand in front of us and escort us to their hideous fires. I would make a stand with a handful of cartridges and a desperate aim – no, the very thought is ridiculous. My thinking is lop-sided and out of shape. I just can't think anymore. A man must stay strong for the sake of his family. Can I stay strong for Dog's sake?!

Everywhere is so cold, grey and desolate, yet no more cold, grey and desolate than what we have left behind. My brain stands still, but my feet move on. What on earth does that say? It's as though the very act of being on the move is an expression of persistent hope – an unwavering mood of expectation of better things to come, just round the corner maybe. Or is it just habit?

Entry 49

A day's plodding after all that wavering and doubt, we came across a small cluster of grey-stone buildings – a small hamlet, with a minuscule general store and a few very small houses; everywhere abandoned, I thought, until Dog started barking at what turned out to be a pig in a stone-walled pen. And then a voice called out from behind a small window in one of the houses. 'Don't touch 'im!' The voice belonged to Joseph, a man in his late 70s, I'd say, who rested a shotgun on the window sill and aimed it at my head.

Having satisfied himself that neither I nor Dog intended harming the pig, we took advantage of the hospitality on hand – if an absence of objection and rejection can be called hospitality. He lived with his wife, Louise, who was senile and bed-ridden. It was somehow refreshing to know that the Virus was not the only disease still prevalent. Joseph tended to his wife's needs as best he could; she was capable of no more than a blank stare and a naive kind of smile. He cared for her without respite, and for food he depended on what he could find growing or shoot, to supplement what he could still get from the remains of the food stocks in the general store. 'They all left,' he said. 'We couldn't.' I filled a bag with some provisions from the store, at his own suggestion.

He wasn't in the least bit inquisitive and showed no curiosity. 'It's just me, Louise and Old William,' he remarked when I asked about others. 'We get on all right. I consult Old William on most things,' he said, nodding towards the pig affectionately. From which I deduced that Old William, clearly a valued member of the threesome, was unlikely to become a culinary delicacy, nor yet a culinary necessity.

His remark, which long before the Virus would have been no more than a run-of-the-mill joke, seemed almost natural in the circumstances and failed to produce so much as a smile from either of us. Humour had breathed its last somewhere far down the line. I really do believe that Joseph and Old William get on well together, rarely disagreeing with one another on anything that mattered. 'I call him Old William,' he muttered as if to himself as we sat by the dying embers of the fire in the grate. 'He's far more deserving of a real name than most humans I ever come across' – a remark which I let pass and only ruminated on later; cynicism, a rejection of the human race and the humanity it once boasted? It was the kind of remark that could keep you guessing for the rest of your life.

There was no lack of humanity in the picture Joseph created of a loving, caring soul who relentlessly tended to a person who had become a shell of a woman and was not long for this world, Virus or no Virus, Raiders or no Raiders. Or by refusing to call the pig Snout or Trotters or some such, did he simply mean that pigs are profoundly undervalued creatures, regularly maligned by human beings who are far more deserving of such appellations than the poor creatures themselves?

Did I say a *shell* of a woman? Yes, but he loved her still, perhaps more than ever before. Even the vestiges of her were objects of worship. Men and women first seek the primeval pleasures of sex and the satisfaction of their desires for family and security. This truth has a wide application and seems too obvious to state. What then does it exclude? Love? Perhaps the best we can say is that love, as distinct from the passion of being *in* love, may be expected to grow from these primitive beginnings. But it hardly needs to be said that the expectation is all too often bereft of its realisation.

There are those who come to ignore the needs of their spouses despite the poetry of their vows and even in illness leave them to themselves, to nature, and to their God. Yes, but not Jacob. Despite this shell of a woman and the fact that soon enough he would be deprived even of this remnant, and also for all his trials, tribulations and loneliness and the greater loneliness that now loomed ahead, he still counted himself fortunate, not to say blessed, in having known her both at her best and at her worst. He loved her. And the love of another is rather like the appreciation of a book, which depends on the quality of the book and not a little on that of the reader. She had brought out the best in him, and this is no mean gift to bestow on another, a reciprocity of virtue. And so this struck me as a fitting epitaph for him when his own time should come, 'Here lies an unlucky man whose ill-luck might have been immeasurably worse.' And then it came to me that this very same epitaph might justly apply also to the great bulk of humanity.

That was not a place to linger. I felt our being there was an intrusion. In pre-Virus times, there was little to commend the little stone house in which the threesome lived, perched as it was on a steep incline, with three steep flights of stone steps to the rear which led down to a small, unkempt postage stamp of a garden which was itself encompassed by dark, grey-stone walls, a patch of untended earth and grass hardly lighter, cleaner or tidier than the minute interior of the house itself.

Both house and garden, the latter hardly deserving of the name, were oppressively dull and dim – yet, what was any of that now to the threesome?

We were on our way at first light the following morning. I'm grateful to Joseph for sharing with us the warmth of a fire in an old fireplace; for giving me a glimmer of humanity in a dehumanised world. Neither of us mentioned the Raiders. If he doesn't know about them, his ignorance is perhaps a blessing, and I want to keep it that way. He knows all he needs to know about the Virus, a scourge to which his wife is of course totally oblivious.

I think it interesting to note that in one of those fireside sittings with Joseph during which 'conversation' consisted characteristically of occasional verbal ejaculations redolent of Quaker 'meetings', I was about to say something which I knew to be quite false but checked myself just in time. I was about to say that I did not know who and what had made me who and what I am. But I know perfectly well who and what, the people and the events, have made me what I am. To relate the events would exhaust my already waning energies and is best left aside. As for the people, there is hardly one amongst them I would unhesitatingly call a friend. Friends are not those who hog conversation, cluttering their endless renderings with well-worn and for the most part idle clichés; association with such people, who after all form the bulk of humankind, may be tolerated out of courtesy, but never enjoyed.

Two principles seem to have been painfully hewn out of the amorphous rock of my dealings with fellow men, becoming mantras as distinct from clichés: first, that it is necessary to be 'as wise as the serpent and as gentle as the dove'; the second, immortalised in an ancient Buddhist scroll, is that I should 'fare lonely as the rhinoceros' since friends who seek nothing are as rare as hen's teeth. However, if we choose to live like the rhinoceros we shall be friendless indeed, since the world is vastly overpopulated with sycophants, scroungers, fair weather friends and those who seek association as a form of self-advertisement or self-therapy. Such 'mantras' are hard to swallow and harder still to keep down, which is no doubt why the wise constantly suffer from indigestion.

I do not know whether Joseph is a friend, only that he is not false. That much seems oddly to be suggested by the fact that he spoke neither too much nor too little. But it must be remembered that my reasoning is not to be trusted and that therefore my judgement in all things but the recognition of day and night must be suspect. I fast approach the conclusion, if I have not already done so, that I know absolutely nothing, nothing at all. As time passes I understand less, and I become more dismissive of the pronouncements of the wise – so hollow have they turned out to be. Even so, perhaps the best we can ever do is to look upon others with a little charity, upon the world in a spirit of generosity, and pray that we are right to do so.

Be that as it may, Dog and I plod on, leaving Joseph, Louise and Old William behind. There is nothing we can do for them, and our remaining would only serve to exhaust their supplies. The Virus has spared them, but the Raiders would not. We move on, but the doubts return. What is the point of all this? We could have stayed and taken over one of the abandoned houses. But, then, what would we be waiting for? Forever moving, forever restless, hoping to find who knows what, hoping to arrive who knows where.

From time immemorial, mankind has been broadly and vaguely divided into the oppressed and the oppressors; yet maybe the distinction so broadly and vaguely made out is false. It seems that everyone is oppressed by something or someone, and of all those things and people that oppress us, it may often be difficult to say who or what oppresses us most; and when we appear to be free of oppressors, we tend to oppress ourselves. And when we don't oppress ourselves, we oppress each other – a kind of parlour game gone wrong. A life without oppression seems unimaginable – this thought struck me as we left Joseph and his wife, Old William being the only creature who neither oppresses nor is oppressed. Yet this does nothing to invalidate Mill's insight that it is better to be a Socrates dissatisfied than a pig satisfied.

But this might be said, that if the Virus is an oppressor it has a long way to go to match man's own inhumanity to man. My travels on this globe have been limited, but I don't feel I've missed out. There are places where the evils man commits are doubtless worse than I have seen, and I have no wish to add to their dimensions by broadening my field of vision, though doubtless I have also missed what is good in man, though virtue cannot compensate. Before the collapse of the Media, the evil man does became a source of entertainment, outdoing the gladiatorial ring which was said to fulfil a social function. But we assume that the destruction brought about by the Virus is on account of what the Virus is and carries with it no reason, rhyme or purpose.

Entry 50

A full day of plodding against biting winds and sleet has made me think again. I was mad to move on. I should have stayed with Joseph, taking over one of the houses – anything, anything at all to avoid this cheerless, meaningless slog on a road to who knows where. Dog is suffering its effects, too. Tomorrow we'll head back. In any case, Joseph and I had better have a good talk about the Raiders. It's only a matter of time before they reach him. Both of us together might put up a fight. I've decided that my dogged determination to be forever on the move in the dead of winter is a kind of surrender, a resignation, an abandonment – it's not an expression of hope at all, but of weakness, a refusal to resist.

If we're not attacked, Dog and I will stay until early spring and move on then when the prospect of finding something better should make more sense. Moving on will never be an option for Joseph for as long as he has Louise to care for. Such devotion may never be found elsewhere, however far I travel; it needs to be supported and treasured. I understand exactly how he feels. Didn't I feel that way myself down in the basement and every time I looked out of the window of the living room on to the garden where she lies? But she is no more – except in my haunted brain, a perpetual image of some of the good things in the life that was, a reminder of the time I was happy and didn't know just how happy I was. Louise still breathes, and no doubt Joseph would say that the merest fraction of her is better than no Louise at all.

Yes, memories of happiness have not been erased despite everything. How true it must have been for most people, that we were so hung up on the mere routine of living with its preoccupations, its stress and strains, that we were quite ignorant of the happiness we held in our hands and were in danger of letting it slip through our fingers or even of mistaking it for something quite different, something quite inferior.

Joseph, Louise and Old William are a salutary reminder of what once was – and what once was is worthy of praise and worthy of defending. It must not be let slip without a fight, without resistance. To let it go without raising a finger would be like helping the barbarians to make a bonfire of the great literature of the ages, the words of great men and, through them, the overtures of a loving god.

When Custer made his Last Stand the best that could be said of him when all the worst had been set in stone was that he was courageous, and courage is a virtue, if not the chief of virtues. Better a courageous man who is wrong than a coward who is right. No, Dog and I will return. I'll explain everything to Joseph.

Entry 51

I am a recluse again – which is not at all a bad thing, for, though reluctant to admit it even to myself, I have known, long before the Virus became bent on the extermination of the human race, that the more dealings you have with this world and its inhabitants the more illusions you entertain, the more delusions you suffer, the more disappointments, the more busted dreams and broken promises you heap upon yourself, until, bruised, battered and torn, you begin a cynical descent into the dark wells of permanent depression before the jaws of eternity bid you enter, a fitting end to a life of false hopes and thankless strivings. Renunciation of the world and its inhabitants therefore has long seemed an antidote to that effete God of Expectation, the former at least curbing, if not extinguishing, the latter. Monasteries and nunneries must have been full of happy people; if not happy, then perhaps content; if not content, at least shielded. But now the Virus leaves no hiding place and spares none.

But I am not quite a recluse. I've taken a house about 200 metres down from Joseph, but on the same slope, which extends right through this small complex of stone houses. These grey-stoned houses are all the same – small, dull, dim, dingy, depressing and dark. Even so, they are palatial compared with the makeshift hovels that Dog and I have had to fashion. The main thing is protection from the cold winds and the rain and sleet – it hasn't snowed on the hills for some time now, and the patches that remain are beginning to melt away. Whoever lived here left in a hurry – there's a wood store for the fire, some tinned stuff in cupboards, some blankets, and of course a bed with a mattress which is like heaven despite the dust that covers it and the reek of dampness that seems to permeate it right through – impossible to dry.

The garden, such as it is, and like Joseph's, is at the bottom of several flights of stone steps from the door at the rear of the house; it's like living high up in the keep of a small medieval castle with a view to the sad, neglected, grounds below, though the main entrance at the front of the house is at ground level with the door opening on to the street. The thick stone walls offer the best possible protection against the weather, and once the fire is up and going, the whole house benefits, and the heat is kept in the walls long enough to sleep – and sleep more comfortably than I had begun to believe was ever going to be possible again. As for dreams, they still come, and, as usual, they are as bleak, confusing and as full of foreboding as ever. I sometimes wake up in sweats, cold sweats accentuated by the dampness in the mattress. Even so, we are safe from the elements.

Here we stay, at least until the weather improves and we feel stronger. Dog seems to agree having made his reconnaissance in just about every place accessible to a creature of his size and disposition. We eat together and sleep together and walk together. I still regret his inability to talk, but I look forward to some time spent with Joseph, who could do with some help. If the Raiders turn up, we'll face them together. I just hope, no doubt in vain, they don't turn up.

It strikes me that the word 'hope' sticks burr-like to everyone at all times, good or bad, since its use is universal and never-ending. In one of those rare, more loquacious moments Joseph related the story of a man who expected so little from life that he was beside himself with joy whenever anything at all, even the smallest thing, went right. More than this, that man would not allow hope to settle and grow; he imagined, said Joseph, that hope was a small white flower, and now and again he would stamp and twist his foot on the ground as though he were destroying that imaginary flower, because he knew that if allowed to grow it would become a monstrous weed which would threaten to strangle him to death, because a hope may be described as a weak form of expectation, and profound expectations, when unfulfilled, are capable of delivering mortal blows to the spirit. Joseph said it was possible to live with no hope whatsoever, so that even the word 'hope' was expunged from your vocabulary. As a variation on the same theme, it has been said that it is possible to love unconditionally, without the slightest desire, let alone the expectation, of being loved in return – for there is a kind of love that is not an 'investment'!

Yet, I wondered how that kind of life can come about and, more importantly, how it can possibly be sustained. Is the weakness in the story, or is it in my understanding? But Joseph said the man was a living example of how it was possible to live without any hope at all. He said that in this respect he lived more like Old William than your average human being; incapable of thought, and therefore of conceptions of hope, let alone their verbal expression, the pig would deal with problems as they came along, with or without success, but certainly without the encumbrance of reflection and the speculative complications which emanate from it; if in this respect the man had more in common with Old William, the fact might appear to throw some unhappy doubt on Mill's dictum that it's better to be a Socrates dissatisfied than a pig satisfied; unhappy, because it misses Mill's point entirely, namely that the human intellect is worth the high price it must often exact.

But, well, I guess you can be disappointed so many times that the word 'hope' slips out of your lexis or becomes a meaningless sound, rather as an exclamation mark becomes devoid of any significance if placed at the end of every sentence you read. At best, an expression of hope might become little more than a reflex action, or like a habit of long-standing that you just can't shake off, try as you might. This might happen to those who have always felt that though they are *in* the world, they are not *of* the world; people who give up expecting reciprocity of sympathy, let alone recognition, from a world whose values they cannot comprehend. For them, to continue to expect is merely a self-infliction of pain, a form of masochism that wears down the spirit and removes all joy of life. Far better, then, when hope, the predecessor of expectation, begins to grow from seeds thoughtlessly sown, to nip it in the bud and trample it under foot.

So much for hope. But what is to be said of expecting the worst? People do not hope for the worst. But neither should they incessantly expect it, for then life becomes a monstrous open prison. Old William expects nothing, neither good nor bad. Yet, the life of a pig is not to be coveted.

And so, the end of all this rambling is a plea: May God, a loving God, help us all.

I read this. I read this plea in Joseph's face as he related his story of the man who lived without hope and expectation. It was getting late and shadows played about his face; moving, flickering shadows, as the remaining light from the dying embers in the grate now and then relit as the wind gently spiralled down the chimney, as though Aeolus objected to the darkness of our thoughts and bid us reconsider – yes, as though the god himself despaired at dispirited mankind.

Entry 52

Been here a couple of weeks, I think. Weather seems to be getting milder and the days are drawing out a bit.

I can't really claim to be a total recluse. I spend some evenings with Joseph, who, after he's settled Louise down for the night, sits every evening directly in front of a blazing fire. Dog and I sit with him sometimes, listening to the wind outside, which seems to make wild music and the fire roar. The wood burns too fast, making it necessary to go outside frequently to the wood shed for more; we share the task, and Dog barks every time we open the door to the howling wind – as though he's beckoned to a place he'd rather not go by creatures he'd rather not meet. The jaws of a black hole.

We've talked about the Raiders. Joseph had of course heard of them but resolved to sit things out, hoping, as I hope now, that they'd either fade out of existence altogether, either because the Virus finally catches up with them or because they kill each other off in their wild rampages, like thieves who come to mortal blows over their spoils. He is prepared, needs must, to take a stand; and he of course he agrees that we should stand together.

Joseph has about him a curiously calm resolve – the kind of man who doesn't complain but simply gets on with things, although there seems little point in getting on with things at all in such a world as this has become. But what else is there to do? Sometimes I find him reading a Bible with the aid of a magnifying glass, and sometimes, though we've been sitting in silence together, he mumbles the words to himself; I look towards him half expecting him to address me, but he never does, unless I address him first. He mumbles a little, and then continues reading silently. It has become clear that he doesn't really want to talk about what he reads. But he did ask me once whether I'd read the Bible, and I replied that I hadn't, which would have been the standard reply these days should anyone have been asked the same question, which they very rarely would. He just looked at me over the top of his glasses, his eyes in a kind of squint, and asked if I'd ever heard of 'the peace that passeth all understanding'. I said I hadn't. 'You might read Paul's letters,' he said, and then fell silent, closing the Bible and stoking the fire. 'Paul's letters?' I asked. 'Yes.' He didn't explain and he never referred to it again, except to say, 'Well, it's the greatest possible gift. Like a shirt of chain mail; the arrows sent against you bounce off you like straws in the wind.' I suppose I passed the whole thing off as a piece of eccentricity. Anyhow, the wood needed to be replenished, and I got up; the door had to be opened and the howling wind reluctantly admitted. With the fire roaring again, I took my leave. And that was that.

As for peace, I've heard 'Seek and he shall find'. But I've been seeking all my life and found very little of it. Maybe I've been looking in the wrong place, or even been mistaken about what it is that I'm supposed to be seeking. Either way I've failed to find it – perhaps some of us are doomed to fail however hard we try. The jury is perpetually out on this one.

Well, there are people who believe that that kind of peace exists and that it's attainable, like those who believe in a God, whether of love or of retribution. I guess Joseph believes in a God of love. That's because he's a good man. I would never dispute such matters with him.

When it comes to goodness, to be in the bad books of a bad man is no bad thing. Joseph is a good man, so it seems to follow that being in his bad books is something to avoid if at all possible. I prefer to remain silent over my misgivings concerning religious belief. In any case, the proposition that God exists and is a God of love may bristle with difficulties, but what's the alternative? If, instead, you believe in man, that is equally, if not much more, problematic and disheartening. Joseph is a simple man and there is a beauty in his simplicity as there is in his silent readings of scripture and his mumblings to himself. Lamb's admonition to Coleridge comes to mind, 'Cultivate simplicity Coleridge; there are no hotbeds in the gardens of Parnassus.' I like Joseph as he is – a silent, gentle doer of good things and a thinker of selfless thoughts.

Entry 53

Tonight Joseph began to open up. He seems to trust me far more now. Anyhow, I told him how I admired his devotion to Louise and asked how long he'd been married. Forty-five years. I said nothing about ... well ... I said nothing about myself ... about how hard it was to leave my place in the basement – I can't bring myself to speak about it – it takes time – I still think of her, every day, and every day memories strike like sharp barbs. No, I said nothing about myself.

Joseph opened up, and I let him. He said Louise had left him, not once but twice, for another man! But both times he took her back, without hesitation and without question. I wanted to ask him how he could possibly have done that, not only once, but twice. I didn't ask. I just nodded as though it were only a casual piece of autobiography. But I ask myself how he could have done it. He said he was thinking of her wellbeing, that whatever was right for her would be right for him, that whatever she wanted he would want for her too – if she were happy, he would be happy, too, with the corollary that if he thought that a certain course of action was detrimental to her well-being he would oppose; but if there were no evidence of detriment, it was fine with him – whatever she wanted was absolutely fine with him. These weren't his exact words, but I think it's what he meant.

But I'm left wondering how to understand this. How could he possibly do it? – take her back just like that, with no remonstrance, no conditions, no resentment, nothing? Was it strength, or weakness? Was it love, or indifference? It's the kind of thing that could keep me awake all night – if I let it. His devotion knows no end, no limit – right to the last!

Straws in the wind, perhaps.

Entry 54

It's been another week, or thereabouts. I feel better, stronger, for the company I sometimes keep with Joseph. Mental and physical health must be maintained as far as possible. I must be ready for when the storm subsides, the wind falls, the rain stops and temperatures rise – I mean, for better times. You see, I've surprised myself. I've begun to think of better times when a short time ago I had given up on them completely. It helps that there's been no sign of the Raiders, no drum beats at night, no fires, none of that acrid odour of burning that lingers in your hair and nostrils well after the event.

The question must be what I think I should expect to see when all this is over? Since leaving the basement I've seen no sign of human life, no sure sign, maybe only the phantoms of my imagination – those darting, shadowy figures, human or otherwise, that have sometimes flashed by me, causing me to start and strain to see in the semi darkness, in the twilight hours – are they merely extensions of my dreams?

I said when all this is over. I'm not sure is this expresses anything, whether it has any meaning now. Will there ever be a time when the Virus is a thing of the past, half forgotten? The human population has been severely decimated and civilisation as we knew has … Oh, what's the earthly use of … . It's just a question of getting on with things, of surviving, of seeing things through, and then … well, then we'll see what we will see. That's all. If the Raiders find us they'll answer all our questions for us, and that'll be that. It's funny, but I don't want to talk about my fears with Joseph – it's better, safer somehow, to sit in each other's silences, and let come what may.

Entry 55

I dreamed I was in a celestial court defending the human race for its follies, weaknesses and sins. I believe I said life was hard and that every pleasure, though legitimate, carried a price tag; that nothing was without consequence; that small pleasures were hard won and even then uncertain and fleeting; that every pleasure was matched by unjustifiable pain, if only the pain of self-guilt; that W.H. Davies was right to describe man as a poor, frightened thing. I was an advocate against the charge that if Jesus was a fisher of men, the catch was not worth the effort, that he was fishing in barren waters. Mankind was not to blame for its follies for he is a victim of his own fears, fears exacerbated by the conception of a vengeful God.

I suppose it was all about the pity of things. People live in hardship and illusion, and when they shake off the mortal coil there is nothing left, no footprint in the sand on which they trod, sand washed blank by succeeding generations. The pity of it all. The pity of death and of lives not truly lived.

Once you begin to ask questions about the human condition, *really* ask them and not simply toy with them as though they were a transient novelty, you can never be the same again. Life and all that is in it takes on a different and troublesome aspect. Such perceptions of life are themselves painful, and yet the pain caused you is such that you could not exchange it for any pleasure. You're stuck with something without which you would be happier, but the happiness you lack would have subsisted in a kind of ignorance, a dazed happiness in which you would no longer have been yourself. Philosophical questions about the rightness of things is a mortgage you can never pay off.

I trust I have made myself thoroughly obscure – which is why I am tempted to tell Joseph about all this but will resist the temptation tooth and claw. His kind of simplicity must be preserved; insanity lies in reflections on imponderables. Which is undoubtedly why my brain is defective and can never be free from its defects. As I said, it's better by far for at least one of us to remain sane in our silences. In any case, it's a wise man who knows which questions to ask, and who knows the difference between a genuine question and a remonstrance, an expression of anguish or a cry for help. If you can't tell the difference, how can you know whether your answers are reliable? The logic of questions and answers is not so simple and is it itself subject to questioning and spurious resolution.

The bottom line, if there is a bottom line, is that if you should feel alien to the world in which you find yourself, as though you are on the outside looking in, as though you were observing the antics of fish in a fish bowl, are you becoming insane, are you already so, and what is to be done? Some have pointed out that in life there is no replay button to push, that the clock cannot be reset or put back; the same may be said of some cerebral paths, that once ventured upon there is not returning.

It's a heavy burden for those of an uncommonly sensitive nature – the mere reflection that man finds entertainment in his own capacity to destroy his own kind. How mean, morbid and wilful is the obsession with crime novels; yet they are amongst the world's top best-sellers. It shows how restless is the tiger inside its cage as it stalks imaginary pray and how merciless once freed to do its worst.

Now of course everything is stripped down to its bare essentials. Fire, rape and pillage scar the landscape of what was once more aptly described as a green and pleasant land. But no scars here, not here with Joseph, Louise and Old William. Little wonder that Joseph holds his pig in high esteem. For the damning ills of this world, pigs are entirely without blame, and considering the contempt in which, principally by some of certain religious persuasions, they are held, it must be unreservedly said that they are more sinned against than sinning. If things had been different, the anti pig lobby might have been tried *en bloc* in an international court of pigs, been found guilty of anti piggery and given a life sentence on a vegan diet. Do I detect a spark of humour here? Surely not. Vestiges of old times. Won't last. More cynical than humorous. And cynicism is here to stay.

I am resolved not even to attempt to speak to Joseph about my dreams and reflections, not even if he should ask. It's important to keep such madness to myself – as I have always managed to do. Last night, as I sat with him before his roaring fire, which gave a red taint to the entire room, I kept my thoughts at bay, simply by watching the flames consume the logs, contorting them into a hundred shapes before they became shapeless and disintegrated before my very eyes as if by magic, and as if they had never existed at all but had been figments of my own diseased imagination. Are not human lives the same, and is there a merciless God that watches from on high as we squirm and are extinguished as though we had never been? Such a question I would never dare put to Joseph; it would be an unjustifiable, not to say sinful, act. Instead we watched the embers in the grate when the candle he'd been reading by had snuffed itself out.

It was nevertheless an uneasy silence, for we know that it might easily be broken together with everything we have left. When Dog is uneasily alert, or when he barks, we stir and strain to see through the windows into the darkness, like the hunted in the forest when twigs snap somewhere in the shadows.

Entry 56

Sitting with Joseph earlier this evening, the thought occurred to me that it might be better after all if philosophical questions were left alone, like sleeping dogs. A philosopher once complained that such questions were asked far too rarely; perhaps his complaint was confused and misplaced, or perhaps we should say that academic questions should be confined to the coteries within which they are formulated; questions of right and wrong are different, far too rarely asked, and should be pursued with conviction.

The Raiders don't ask questions of right and wrong, they don't quibble over what should or should not be done in the interests of humanity; because for them the concept of *humanity* has lost all moral content, and the word simply signifies 'all living things that can be termed *homo sapiens*'. As for those who easily degenerated into raiders, I daresay the term was always bereft of moral connotation.

There's still no sign of the Raiders, though I continue to sleep uneasy, and my constant getting up and lying down disturbs Dog as well. He grunts every time I move. It used to be said that there's no sleep for the wicked. The contrary is of course true. The wicked are amongst the very few who get a good night's rest. The good have troubled nights, as do dogs and those who fear the snapping of twigs in the dark.

I lay awake at night and wonder at what point on the continuum a man becomes a Raider, how far a man must be pushed before the defences of civilisation come down and all vestiges of humanity are lost. These idle speculations help while away the sleepless hours but are otherwise less than helpful. We are stuck with what we have; we are where we are, and the nightmare is real.

Yet, speculation is inevitable. The Virus took first the most physically vulnerable, and then those who thought themselves above the authority which advised caution and imposed restrictions, and those ethnic minorities who considered vaccination either a satanic plot to get rid of them or else a lack of confidence in their God to deliver them. But the Raiders? Who amongst the survivors became Raiders? Not only the simple-minded or the rebellious, but those also who had led comfortable lives and commanded the respect of those they considered lesser mortals. Must they not have been bankers, lawyers, teachers, politicians, company directors and all manner of high flyers with all the privileges and rank that their positions implied?

Lower, middle and higher classes of society were somehow rolled into one, all becoming painted figures dancing round bonfires in the shadows of midnight, indistinguishable from one another, like unworldly demons on heat or as though subjected to an irrational and incomprehensible ecstasy of spirit. Were such creatures to be discovered who had never experienced anything better, it might be more understandable; but to have fallen from a higher estate to this – that is the question that will not be settled so easily and that plagues me without resolution night after night. To think that they once spent their money on expensive holidays and absurd meals in top restaurants, that they courted the favours of those above and were contemptuous of those below, that they believed themselves to have achieved the unachievable, that they had reached a level of celebrity undreamed of even by themselves – to think all this and to see them now! Is this what fear and despair does? Is this the inferno that comes of hopelessness? Or, was there an essential ingredient that was missing already, long before the Virus exacted its horrific toll?

And so I ask again, at which point on the continuum which has sanity at one end and insanity at the other does the demonisation of civilisation begin to make itself felt? Were human beings so constructed that their own demise was easy to bring about once the self-destruct mechanism was set in motion. Or, again I say, was there an essential element deficient long before the mechanism could be activated? Nor should we forget the adage that the road to hell is paved with good intentions. William Clarke Quantrill may have begun with the notion that he was helping to right the imbalance between the affluent north and the impoverished south, but his Raiders soon became the scourge of the nation and their raping, pillaging, butchering sprees became one of the blackest pages in the annals of the American Civil War. How and why should a reasonable point on the continuum descend into the unpardonable?

Despite the severity and apparent universality of our decline, is there no possibility of reversal? If the decline is reversible, how is it to be reversed? Is there a key that can reverse the apparently irreversible? I would put none of this to Joseph, whose guesses and speculations would in any case be at least as good as mine. Despite the turmoil in my own defective brain, indeed because of it, Joseph must be left in peace. I must act the simple-minded, as though the only thing of importance is to survive the present moment. I guess if we could live in the present moment, never minding what is past or what may come, we should be less than human and much more of the animal. Obsession with the past at the expense of the present may be unwise, but to ignore the past is unforgivable folly, and to care nothing for what the morrow may bring seems sheer arrogance. Someone once said that the past is frozen, the present is fluid and the future borders on eternity; but much can be learned from the frozen wastes of the past and the unwillingness to learn makes it pretty certain that the mistakes of the past will be repeated; as for eternity, that's an idea most of us would rather not entertain, even if we knew what it meant.

Entry 57

Everything that's happened has caused a sense of timelessness everywhere, maybe like weightlessness in space where what we call gravity fails to work. There's no point of reference, nothing to hold on to. All points of the compass merge into one – north, south, east and west dissolve into nothingness. Even the pioneers in their wagon trains moving west over the vast and empty plains had an occasional point of reference – a rock, a hill, a carcass, and places where the land noticeably rose or dipped or curved. But sitting here in what I've come to call 'my place' gives me no anchor, nothing to set my compass by, and sitting in silence with Joseph in his place seems no different. There's just a great mass of sameness. Where has everything gone? Or is it just a step further along a path of encroaching insanity?

Louise is deteriorating rapidly now and seems to have fallen into a sleepy stupor, only occasionally opening her eyes – so Joseph tells me. She used to be capable of getting up from her bed, then she was unable to stand at all, and now it's hard to watch her reject the thin broth he tries to feed her. Joseph tells me these things in his half-mumbling fashion, as though addressing no other but himself. With her in this state she's trying company, but without her he'll be devastated. Someone once remarked that a man was not born to live alone, that there's something unnatural about a stone that's forever rolling. I know it's right, and I know the pain of sudden loss and how that can never be fixed.

Everything has its price, and love carries the highest price tag of all. To go on living without the love of one's life is hard; that is the price for having loved. True, the comfortable, long-term attachments of the connubial nest may inhibit the achievement of independent flight; but only the cynic would quote Rousseau ('The slave in his bondage loses everything, even the desire to be free') to justify a life lived alone or in utter detachment from the affections of love; on balance, such affections win the day, but the loss of a partner in death gives a new, solemn and sobering slant to the adage that it is better to have loved and lost than never to have loved at all; an adage that may naturally be doubted, hopefully only temporarily, in the profound grief that attends loss.

I think it won't be long now before Joseph will need to 'consult' Old William on how to go on without Louise. When the time comes, I hope I can be of some use, that I'm still sane enough offer some comforting words.

The bitterly cold north-easterlies have given way to warmer air from the Atlantic which, in turn, has brought us strong winds and heavy rain; but at least the air is balmy, in contrast to the cutting, biting, piercing winds that have howled about these houses for what seems an age. At last the hard winter seems to be relenting. It's strange to mention the Atlantic, as though it's a real thing and still exists. In these lonely circumstances you learn to forget things you can't see or feel, as though everything has ceased to be, and only you are left in your immediate surroundings, until something comes along and bites you in tender places – like the Raiders, who are real enough and never too far from your thoughts.

Entry 58

I would have hoped that merely thinking about a thing doesn't help to bring it about. But the inevitable must happen. It seems as if the bitter north-easterlies have carried poor Louise away with them.

There was a loud knock on the door this morning. Poor Joseph was standing in the doorway looking utterly lost and dejected, and all he could bring himself to mumble weakly was, 'She's gone.' I've never seen such a look of despair, in eyes that might have belonged to the merest ghost of a creature half starved and at the very end of his own existence. 'She's gone,' he repeated, as though he couldn't believe his own words or hardly knew what they signified. I helped him inside and sat him down by my own fireside for a change.

You can't say anything at such a time, so I didn't try. We just sat there in silence in the early morning watching the flames in the fire. He held a mug of tea which went cold and unsipped. I might have told him about … Yes, but I didn't. She crowded my mind, that wonderful being who lies so still in the garden not far from the basement. But I said nothing. I couldn't bring myself to relive in speech what I had pushed back and deep down in my mind, a memory more deeply buried than my beautiful … No, I said nothing about any of that. In any case, there seemed to be a kind of superior wisdom in silence, silence of a certain kind. I don't know how long we sat there; the fire had to be built up a couple of times I think. Then he said he had things to do. I made to offer help, but he just raised his hand to stop me and left without a word. I wanted to follow him, to force my help upon him, though what form that help might have taken I had no idea. I knew that any gesture from me would, at least at that time, be an unwelcome intrusion. But I was long in thought about how Joseph would fare and how I might help him; how we might help each other. I knew he felt less than half a man, and I knew how that felt. But right now he needed to be alone.

Entry 59

Having left him alone all day, I visited Joseph late last night. I let myself in and found him sitting in front of a fireless grate. He clutched his Bible as usual, but it was unopened. After a while he said, 'I know what to do – where to put her – there's a nice spot up there – between two trees – she'll be looking down on me from there – and in the summer I'll sit with her.' I said I would help. He nodded slowly.

Entry 60

This morning the deed was done. The ground was hard but we managed it. Louise was buried with the simplicity with which she and Joseph had lived, and the tree on either side stood like sentinels. The place was, as Joseph had said, a kind of hillock and overlooked the tops of the houses below; from there you could see for miles around. Joseph had fashioned a crude cross which he hammered into the ground; then he stood there, cap crumpled in his hands though a sharp chill was in the air, as though he were a recalcitrant pupil waiting to be reproached. 'Lord Bless you,' he said, eyes fixed on the cross, and there I left him standing.

I returned to his house, lit the fire and waited for him. At length he sat before the fire, again clutching his unopened Bible. 'I knew it would happen,' he said, 'but …' The sentence was never finished. He fell asleep, which is how I left him. Sleep is said to be one of the best of medicines, which I'm sure it is, if it is not bedevilled by nightmares and restlessness. Perhaps Joseph's simplicity will help him sleep the sleep of the innocent and the good, if such a thing exists. Ah! – if only you could wake feeling as well as you've ever felt, like those mornings in childhood; what you would give for just one morning such as this! But waking happy is a forgotten memory. Is it still possible for Joseph?

I shall check up on him this evening.

Entry 61

It's been about a week since Louise passed. Joseph isn't eating – seems to be just wasting away. Philosophers have done their best to offer some consoling reflections on the nature of death. Montaigne assures us that death is less than nothing and that the time after our death is no more ours than the time before our birth. Socrates, if Plato is to be believed, at least considered the possibility that death might be an alternative form of existence.

Religions promise a life after death in a place called Heaven or Paradise where we shall once again meet up with all those we have loved in life. It's to be noted, even so, that those who talk much about Heaven seem to be in no hurry at all to get there. And then it's said, with more general and secular significance, that time is a great healer – it may be so, but when a loved one passes, the adage seems to lack application and buckles under the counter adage that absence makes the heart grow fonder; grief can actually grow with time, as memories of past associations become clearer, sharpening the sense of loss. If death is, as some say, a part of life, then life is not all it's cracked up to be, and if there is a Creator he or she or it has a great deal to answer for. Those who bring children into this world are asking much more of them than they care to acknowledge; the burdens their offspring will carry are enormous.

Joseph manages as best he can, like a sick man in bed who tries to alleviate his pain merely by shifting his position, rolling with difficulty from side to side in the vain hope that this might offer some mitigation. I notice he leaves his Bible on the small table beside the fireplace. He seems to tolerate my company rather than indulge it. He was always a man of few words, but now he rarely says anything beyond the strictly necessary. Perhaps he'll learn to speak again – I don't know. Dog and I call in on him every day and will continue to do so. I had it in mind to propose our moving in with him – but it's doubtful whether he'd want that; he's a man enveloped in his own company, immersed in thoughts of his own now that Louise has passed. Even Old William has taken on a sullen air, and grunts more sparingly.

With the first signs of spring, Dog and I might move on – though again the questions are where? and why?

Entry 62

My dream last night is worthy of record, being quite unlike the stressful amalgam of confused ideas I usually get. Indeed, by comparison, it was quite coherent, and also suggestive.

In my dream I found myself walking through a town I must have known, past shops which were familiar. I guess it was a warm day for I carried my jacket over my shoulder, while on the other shoulder hung a small canvas travel bag. I had just been speaking to a familiar face, someone I might have been somehow offended by who seemed most anxious to appease me and renew our familiarity; his attempt was not altogether successful, and I walked on. I walked into a shop I knew so well to be a tobacconist specialising in good quality pipes and tobacco, only to find to my horror that the stock had been entirely replaced by cheap chocolate and coloured balls of sugar under glass counters. The tobacconist had also had a section of old and rare books; but that too was no more; my horror intensified.

I thought I might soften the blow with a whiskey or two in a nearby bar, but then I found that my jacket had slipped from my shoulder somewhere along the sidewalk. I quickly retraced my steps and spotted my jacket lying on the ground. But when I picked it up and dusted it off I found that my wallet was no longer in the inside pocket! Someone had, it must have been in a flash, seen the jacket, rifled the pockets and stolen the wallet. Cash, credit cards, etc. had all gone, no doubt irretrievably, and my first thought was to phone the bank, report the theft and stop the card. But then I remembered my shoulder bag and checked the inside compartment; there was the wallet, safe and sound after all. My relief was indescribable.

Not only was this dream clear and coherent relative to all others I am plagued with, not only did it have a happy ending, but it was also highly suggestive of times past, of times I had known, of faces, places, things familiar and comforting – despite the awful transformation of the shop and the shock of apparently losing both jacket and wallet. It was a dream of old times, before the Virus came and destroyed and disfigured everything we knew, finally turning everything into a savage hotchpotch of survival do-or-die. And so it was a friendly dream which brought a little balm into this harsh reality. Will I have such a dream again? And will the things depicted in the dream ever return; even a store selling inferior candy would be better than no store at all, no candy at all. If the dream could have been recorded, I do believe I would willingly play it back, especially at my lowest points. But I consider it to be a one-off.

No, things can never be the same again. Dark shadows have come over the whole of what we fondly considered to be civilised life, like the shadows formed by the black clouds that glide over the Great Plains heralding storms and flash floods, except that the shadows that darken our civilisation are not simply passing through. Speaking of shadows reminds me of my boyhood addiction to Tolkien, who makes Haldir the elf speculate on the future of Middle-earth:

'Some there are among us who sing that the Shadow will draw back, and peace shall come again. Yet I do not believe that the world about us will ever again be as it was of old, or the light of the Sun as it was aforetime. … Alas for Lothlorian that I love! It would be a poor life in a land where no mallorn grew. But if there are mallorn trees beyond the Great Sea, none have reported it.'

I marvel that I can remember these lines yet have difficulty recalling what I did yesterday. Yet the memory of books that are deserving of the name is as precious to me as any other. Who is there now capable of writing books of note? – or of even so much as speaking the language with respect for words? There is no one to write words of beauty, or any words at all for that matter – and as for poetry, well, that belonged to a bygone age, far, far away through the mists of time when the thought of beauty and the beauty of thought still had some relevance. Alas, alack! My hand trembles as I write – with rage? with fear? with despair? with lamentation? All of this and more.

Entry 63

Since the last entry, I guess about a month ago, there's been nothing but a cramped routine. There's been very little change in Joseph; he seems to have begun to make a few simple meals for himself, but hardly sufficient I should say. He visits Louise's grave every day, without fail and at exactly the same time. I've seen him up there even in the rain, sometimes sitting on the hill like a dazed or enchanted shaman, sometimes even standing, stock still like an armless scarecrow; he makes sure the cross is firmly fixed before returning to his dark little house; but his is anything but a stultifying routine; on the contrary, it seems to keep him going; it's almost as though Louise didn't pass at all but simply decided to move out of the house and up the hill and between the trees. Even the word 'pass', a mere euphemism, suggests that death doesn't really happen, that those who have died have just opted for an alternative venue through boredom or exhaustion with the last. Such is the inconceivability of death, of what death is; well, let's face it, as if we could imagine *nothingness*, our own in particular!

When the time seems to be right, though these days one time seems as right or as wrong as another, I've decided to talk to Joseph about our leaving together; I mean, if he can possibly bring himself to leave

Louise where she is, as I left … Well, anyway, I'll put it to him – gently and slowly and as rationally as I can. After all, there may be a place where real human beings can still be found, untouched by the consequential barbs of the Virus, people, *real* people I mean. Maybe people who read Bibles, are fond of books, who can remember some of those things that made us what we were as distinct from all those vices that make us what we are now, people who are still capable of living in peace and harmony with one another far from the Raiders and their fires and gyrating, twisting, painted bodies and unquenchable thirst for blood and their lust for a satanic form of compensation for a degenerate life of boredom and hollowness. Yes, maybe there are still some vestiges of the civilisation we once knew, our own Middle-earth. Dog, Old William, Joseph and myself – yes, we'll make an odd assortment of travelling companions. But the alternative is to stay here and waste away. Surely, there must be more than that!

Yes, I'll speak to Joseph, maybe tomorrow. I'll break the idea to him bit by bit.

Entry 64

It's been at least a week since the last entry. I've been watching Joseph carefully, observing his daily visits to Louise, everything as before, not a day missed. He does seem to be getting weaker by the day, in spirit as well as in body. Even so, I took the plunge and began to talk to him yesterday evening. I mean, about the planned exit in the hope of finding something better than this, about out leaving together.

Well, he just sat in silence listening to everything I put to him. I was careful to put things step by step. I made the best case I could, even though, as I listened to myself, I thought my brief anything but watertight. He listened to everything and finally said, 'Well, there's Louise, isn't there?' Then he fell silent again and stared into the fire in the grate. I had no answer to that question which, anyhow, wasn't a question at all. After another long silence, I just repeated myself, softly and gently. Then at length he muttered, 'Well, takes something thinking about, doesn't it?' I just nodded and didn't approach the subject again. Throughout all this there was no trace of interest on Joseph's face let alone a smile of agreement on his lips; he just sat in his armchair expressionless, as though we were back in time and he was half listening to a talk on the radio on a subject in which he could have had no possible interest, as people used to do when they switched on their radios and televisions simply as a source of background noise as a poor antidote to feelings of isolation and loneliness.

I left him supposedly pondering over the idea. Time would tell whether he'd come round to it. But I felt we didn't have all the time in the world. Somehow I sensed something menacing on the horizon, like one of those dark clouds approaching over the Great Plains. There was no hard evidence that anything was about to happen; I had no obvious reason to suspect anything sinister. But such feelings have become commonplace to me now and are similar to those I get almost every night when waking from a troubled sleep; feelings of intense anxiety as though the wolf is at the door and nothing in heaven or earth can prevent the door crashing down, so that all will be lost, all that there is, though all that there is may be ever so little.

Why did I feel that we didn't have all the time in the world when that is precisely what we had? Nothing makes sense, or that sense things have is getting too hard to decipher – no doubt another symptom of an increasingly defective brain. I have heard of a philosopher who, it is said, feared two things above all else: first, false friends, and second, becoming insane. I used to share the first fear; now I share the second as well. There is no doubt that things are deteriorating. I have glimpses of creatures, animal-like, human-like, and things neither animal nor human, all taking shadowy form and fleeting into and past my field of vision; hallucinations I can well do without; sometimes I turn quickly and find nothing, nothing at all. Yesterday I turned on my heels quickly and Dog, thinking I was responding to something real, turned round with me; there was nothing, of course, but Dog looked at me as though he had trusted me and now found his trust groundless.

Entry 65

Perhaps I have it. Second sight. If so, I don't want it. *Menacing* did I say somewhere?

Early yesterday morning I watched Joseph climb the hill as usual. I saw him sit at the bole of the tree to the right of Louise. There was nothing unusual about that. No, but then, when I looked through the window it must've been a few hours later, he was still there, sitting against the bole of the tree, his head inclined back on the trunk as though in peaceful sleep. Nothing much unusual about that either; but then it started to rain, and the rain then fell more heavily; yet there was no movement from Joseph at all. I decided to go up there, shake him awake and bring him back lest he caught his death of cold. But Joseph was already past caring about the rain or anything else. Poor Joseph. He was already cold and a little stiff. My first thought was to carry or drag him down; but then, I realised he'd want to be next to Louise, and then I'd need to carry or drag him back up. I lay my coat over him, and left him – not for long, but I needed to come to myself before attending to him.

I managed to do what was necessary this morning. There was no rain, but yesterday's downpour made the ground softer and I dug a grave as deep as I was able, covered Joseph as best I could and somehow got him down into his resting place. It took a few hours before I could regain composure enough to fill the grave in. Tomorrow I'll make some kind of cross and do for him what he did for Louise.

Well, there they lie, together. Everything I'd said to him was of course irrelevant. I understand that now. He could not have left Louise. She kept him going, so when she was gone, well there was nothing left. Hopes of leaving and finding something infinitely better must have rung as hollow to Joseph as the American dream must have once sounded to the very wise and the very old.

It's funny – I was waiting for Joseph's reply to my grand and hopeful idea. Well, he's given an extremely definitive answer. I was hoping, as much for him as for myself, that we might find something together that could salvage a few blessings from this great, unholy mess of our lives. But may God, if there is a God, rest his pure, simple and beautiful soul. I miss him deeply and bitterly already. Who would have thought that I would have found such a depth of companionship in a friend of very few words, a friend whose total silence is now eternally assured.

And the question is, what to do now?!

Entry 66

I'm still here, in my sepulchre of grey stone.

I miss him, though it's only been a few weeks – Joseph! Funny thing is, already I can't remember his face. Not clearly anyway. The harder I try the more elusive the image gets. Is it important to remember? Does it matter? No, but only because at the end of the proverbial day so very little really matters. Things matter to those to whom things matter, it has to be said.

But I distinctly remember something he said and something he used to do. After sitting with him some evenings he would get up and see me to the door, and as he made to close the door behind me I heard him mutter, 'Thank the Lord for all things.' I used to wonder what 'all things' meant and whether it really excluded anything, whether it was just a phrase that couldn't possibly be literally true, rather like 'She's been *everywhere*' or 'He knows *everything*'. I guess he meant all things for which the Lord should be thanked – and that too, of course, begs an obvious question. It's a question I didn't dare ask him; some dogs are best left in somnolent postures. He was just voicing his simplicity, his contentment – though how he could possibly be content with his lot I can't say. How comforting it would be to say, 'I do, say and think as the Lord directs' – a kind of mantra, but, there again, one that begs an obvious question if you're the questioning kind; and I don't think he was the questioning kind. When Joseph thanked the Lord for everything he was of course counting his blessings, and it is no doubt testimony to his simplicity of soul and his propensity for contentment that he believed he still had blessings to count.

Yet after Louise's demise, I didn't hear him say, 'Thank the Lord for all things' – but neither did he get up to see me out. No, but he was directed, perhaps not by the Lord, but certainly by Louise. Even when she was still breathing but in a bed-ridden and vegetative state, incapable of coherent speech, Joseph said she directed him, guided him, by her voice which was in his head, telling him, advising him, what to do and how to do it – not in any dictatorial manner but, on the contrary, in the gentlest of tones. Joseph said so, and as if to underline the point, he would tap his right temple with his index finger. 'She's in here! – speaks to me!' Thereafter, he would tap his temple and I'd know what he meant. Even that evening, after trying to persuade him that we should leave together to find something better, he tapped his temple, slowly, as if to say, 'It depends on what *she* says.' Maybe Louise herself was directed by the Lord, in which case Joseph was on safe ground. Now he lies under it; and both are directed by the Lord.

Simplicity. Contentment. Yes, but I have a defective brain and lack both. Too restless. So is Dog. As for Old William, he still sulks about in his makeshift pen, and I don't know how to feed him; nor do I want him to feed me. If Dog and I are leaving, maybe the best thing to do will be to open the gate of his pen and invite him to wander where he will and fend for himself. A pig, I think I must have heard it from somewhere, likes to be his own boss; I can't see him snorting along with me and

Dog; he'd lack all discipline and order and be off somewhere on his own as soon as my back's turned. No, I think the kindest thing would be to scrounge up whatever edibles I can find, leave them in the pen with the gate open, and make off with Dog.

Entry 67

Dog and I are getting ready to leave. The time has come at last.

Old William is no longer a problem. I left the gate open. He was still in his pen the morning after. But now he's gone. I wish him *bon voyage*. He'll need all the luck in the world if he happens to come up against the Raiders. They won't welcome him as one of their own, though perhaps they should. No, they'll call him Porker, hang him upside down, bleed him out and roast him for dinner. Poor Old William! Let's hope Joseph isn't looking down from above on such a spectacle as that. That would be something for which devilry, not the Lord, should be thanked – unless of course you happen to be prejudicial against pigs because you are vegetarian, or because you believe your God commands that you should despise them and should wish them only on your worst enemies – on second thoughts that, too, would be a form of devilry. The best way to treat Old William, like any other pig, would be to look after him kindly while he lives and, if you must consume him, to do so with respect and gratitude – but this of course is asking too much, now more than ever. All such talk is now quite irrelevant, as are most things that belong to an increasingly receding past.

With Old William out of the way, Dog and I are facing the open road, or, rather, the open country – well, depending on which direction we take. North? South? East? West? We'll toss a coin.

We'll take with us whatever seems most needful, from our house and from Joseph's – I'm sure he wouldn't mind. I feel uncomfortable entering his place now – everywhere empty, and even Old William's pen is now a vacant lot. People may feel a kind of reverence when they enter a church – either that or scorn or indifference, but usually a kind of reverence. Lincoln said that blood consecrated the ground at Gettysburg. Well, it's not just blood that makes a place holy. Anywhere where people have loved and laughed and suffered and struggled together against the relentless barbs of misfortune, living together through love and self-sacrifice, is a holy place. A house that was once a happy family home is therefore also consecrated. I feel a kind of reverence when I enter Joseph's grey-stoned house – as though the ghosts of those who loved and suffered there sanctify it. An empty house that was fit to be called a home is like an empty church – it demands respect and quietude! I suppose we now invite the corollary that a house that was not a happy home is a hell – so be it.

They had no children, he told me. Well, at least he and Louise were spared the very real possibility of experiencing the death of their children had any existed in these darkest of times. No parent should see the loss of his child – bad enough that children should see that of their parents.

I shall take with us Joseph's Bible . I think he would want me to. I took it earlier today. I found it open and some lines of Psalm 82 are underscored:

'Defend the poor and fatherless; do justice to the afflicted and needy. Deliver the poor and needy; rid them out of the hand of the wicked. They know not, neither will they understand; they walk on in darkness: all the foundations of the earth are out of course.'

I guess 'they' are the wicked. But are the 'poor' those who are poor 'in spirit' or those who are poor in pocket? Perhaps both. But then, the poor are said to be always with us; and again I must ask, *which* poor? … No, I must stop asking questions – Joseph wouldn't like it. My defective brain is unlikely to come up with decent answers. There is something handwritten, in the best copperplate, on the flyleaf of his Bible – whether by Joseph himself or some other I wouldn't know:

'Within this sacred volume lies
The mystery of mysteries.
Happiest they of human race
To whom their God has given grace
To read, to fear, to hope, to pray,
To lift the latch, to force the way.
And better had they ne'er been born
Than read to doubt or read to scorn.'

Faith is in. Questions are out. At least, so some must have thought in the year 1851, the date this version was published. Such certainty is a great comfort to many, to others alarming. Now, opinions either way are as irrelevant as rational discourse.

Whether you've a religious turn of mind or not, if we take the Ten Commandments as our measure, the evils man has committed, is committing, and will doubtless forever commit, are incalculable and unspeakable. The little good that man does serves simply to keep our heads above eternal, black water. At least, this might have been the judgement before the Virus – before all hell was let loose, before ravenous tigers were set free.

Entry 68

My fingers have taken to trembling again, but with good cause! Yes, good cause. It can't be right. I know my brain is defective – but it can't be as bad as this. Surely the time is not yet. Not yet! There were different phases in different parts of my life. I used to think I was mixed-up and that the world wasn't. Then, I changed my mind and decided that the world was mixed up and I wasn't. I couldn't reach any kind of finality: was I sane in an insane world, or was I insane in a sane world? Now maybe it's been decided for me.

I went to pay my final respects to Joseph and Louise. I thought I'd stand by their graves for a few moments before Dog and I leave. But their graves weren't there! My first thought was that I'd come to the wrong spot. But no, everything was as it should be, the trees, the view down to the house, everything as I expected it to be – everything was as I had expected it to be, how could I possibly have imagined it would be otherwise? Except, the graves! The graves and their makeshift wooden crosses weren't there, and there was no sign of them. It's not as though the graves had been desecrated. They just weren't there at all, and there was no sign of their having been there, for the ground was completely undisturbed. I even retraced my steps back to the house and from there made once again for the hill and the spot between the two trees. My bearings were obvious. It was impossible to be mistaken. But where, then were the graves?

Am I, then, insane in a sane world? Or could it still be that I am sane in an insane world? Maybe a world in which conspiracies abound, conspiracies so bizarre that even the conspirators are subject to them?

Uncertainties such as these are intolerable, enough to make murderers of saints and untameable monsters of murderers. It's all part of the general mix in the wake of the Virus. The Virus has shown beyond doubt the limits of human endurance. It has shaken the confidence of man at its very roots. But still I must return to the simple fact that the graves of Joseph and Louise have disappeared into thin air in a world where things do not disappear into thin air. I must live with that absurd fact. Maybe it's easier than you might think – after all, there is so much to have to learn to live with.

Yes, so much to have to learn to live with. No wonder man has sought solace by wallowing in mediocrity, all the better to shield him in the more sober of his waking hours from the harsh realities of the human condition. Mediocrity and familiarity are natural bedfellows; they complement each other. Was it not like this before the Virus? – that a child frightened of the dark, of forces he could understand and with which he was unfamiliar, would grasp his teddy bear tight and was relieved when the light was switched on and he was presented with the soothing sights around him, of familiar, easy, unthreatening things, and the touch and comforting words of mother or father, of all the things he knew and had come to trust; things that were safe, reassuring and full of light. Yes, it was just so.

As with the child, so too with the man. The jump from mediocrity to genius is a leap too far, and what we cannot understand we attribute to the mysteries, and then have recourse to the familiar and the safe. We see in the glass too darkly and are unwilling to press the issue.

The ambitions of men seemed driven by vanity. Vanity! That ally of mediocrity. Mediocrity – that spring of cheap, false fame, a fame that stands not on a foundation of rock, but, like the house of proverb, on shifting sands. Is such fame amongst men something to be coveted? In such a world, anonymity is much prized by all those who have a just claim to wisdom (and by wisdom I do not mean pragmatism). Oh, teach me to treasure anonymity and be free!

I truly believe that from the first breath I took I was blessed with complete and irretrievable anonymity. Yes, it was a great blessing; but for much of my life I mistook it for a curse. But in a jungle inhabited by ravenous beasts, who in his right mind would want to make himself known? Would not wisdom dictate stealth and the utmost caution? Are not the beasts themselves endowed with camouflage to hide themselves from fellow predators? No, far better to move unseen, unknown and therefore unmauled, free of pretension, free of conceit, free of desire to be anything other than a breathing, sentient being – until the end comes, as come it must for all humans and all beasts. But if this breathing, sentient being is also capable of *thought* – well, anonymity is not enough to guarantee peace; his thinking is likely to stalk and ravage him; his existence is likely to become tortuous, unsettled and excruciatingly painful. The human brain imposes a heavy responsibility; it is delicate and most troublesome in the wrong head.

What nonsense!

All this is idle, like cogs in a machine, which turn without touching. What do I do *now*? That's the question. Am I an insane creature in a sane world, or a sane creature in an insane world? Does it really matter which is which? Maybe not. I'm still alive, I *think*. Is there not an advantage in still being alive? – having a brain that still functions, even if only after a fashion?

Where is Joseph, and Louise? Such a question is like, 'Am I mad or sane?' Just how does one begin to answer such a question, if indeed it is a question and not a cry for help? If it is a cry for help, who now is possibly in a position to offer help or explanation or any comfort at all?

The very wind that blows, the temperature that falls, the rain that beats – all or any of these things is an angry foe who beats against your door – a flimsy door, I must add; a door that rattles in its frame and promises to collapse with a little further intimidation. Oh Lord! Those who faced lions in the gladiatorial ring might have found momentary comfort in their faith and in a promise of eternal life. But God help those who have no such faith, no such promise; who in the name of some all-loving god will help *them*? And if there is no such god, why is it that good men have written, poets have penned, philosophers have speculated, while the world itself has taken an inexorable course towards pain and destruction? Oh, the pain and the pity of the human condition!

But then, of course, I am defective. I am a brain that never lost its moorings, if only because no moorings were ever vouchsafed it. The small boy who, seated upon a hill of coal, seemed to be chosen by some, perhaps malignant, god to be witness to the failings of mankind, was doomed by his own prophecy to be a silent and ineffectual prophet of doom.

Do I remember that small boy? Oh, yes. Very well, despite the passing of many years. As small boy he would wander from his home, and one day he found himself seated upon a small hill, which turned out to be a heap of small coal, somewhere deep on the Welsh valleys. He sat there and he wondered, wondered about the world which he had not yet seen. He thought he might make a difference to that world, but he did not know how corrupt and how impermeable that world was; how it excluded generations previous that were far superior in wisdom and goodness than he was himself.

Being just a boy, what could he possibly have known about the depths of moral wisdom? How could he possibly have known that men far superior to himself had tried and failed to make of the world a far better place than he had himself found it? He was wet behind the ears, fully green in his comprehension. Yet, he felt and thought and later acted as though he were himself the precursor of the salvation of the world of men. Ah! Is it any wonder at all that his life should become one single and repetitive reminder of the limitations of good over evil? – that he should fail in his endeavours, as surely as the horse that misunderstands the starting pistol and shrinks back into the ranks, as surely as the regiment that misunderstands the order to advance as an order to retreat?

I don't know why I continue in this vein – it's just a waste of time and of ink and paper.

Dog and I must move on. It's just that why we should do so is still not clear to me. Moving is not the same as improving. I am reminded again of that man, sick in bed and wishing to move on to the other side, thinking that by so doing his pain will be mitigated.

But where are Joseph and Louise? The question begged to be answered. I shall try tomorrow to find them. I shall do what I did before. If I do not find them … But I hope to high heaven to find them. Whether I find them or not, dog and I will move on. South! Yes, south again! Where else?! I don't know what I shall find there. But I must return, return to the beginning – to the basement and, above all, to what is in the garden, buried deep – because she was the rationale of my very existence. How could I have left her? I don't know. I am ready to go south again, come what may. As I said before, all points of the compass have equal value. Equal value! Now, who, in his right mind, would have thought of saying such a thing? Yet, it is so. Past, present future; north, south, east, west – nothing seems to matter in these beyond-darkness times.

I am so glad that these silly notes of mine will never ever see the light of day. No one at all would ever understand them. No one could possibly benefit from them. Nothing matters. My fear of being read by someone else is as irrational as could be. Even Martians, assumed to be of superior intelligence, would consign them to the wastepaper basket of human scribbling. They are not worthy of investigation, of time, of energy. May the Lord, be he a Lord of Love, be praised, for the smallest of mercies.

Dog and I must leave this place. As soon and as smoothly as possible. Tomorrow – no doubt! Yes, and we must be up at the crack of dawn, ready to meet whatever we may need to confront. Back southwards. May God speed, if there be a God worthy of worship. You know, it used to be for me, as it is for you, that the way forward is relatively straightforward, with only certain bumps along the road ahead. But what does it mean, this 'straightforward road ahead'?

You see, this is the problem of insanity, and of not knowing whether you are sane or insane.

Joseph, Louise! Where are you? Were you anywhere at all? Were you a figment of my imagination, and is my imagination to be trusted? Surely you existed! Did you not? Oh, let there be a sign that you existed. If you did not exist, then why did you appear to me as though you did?

I do not trust my memory, my imagination! I trust nothing. Not even myself! Now, isn't that a tragedy? Think! When you do not even trust your own imagination!

Yes, I am mad. Deranged. I am no longer capable of judging events correctly, if ever I was. I am all at sea – losing faith, not with the crew, but with myself. My ship is barely at anchor in seas of misfortune. May God, if ever there was a God of love, bring this vessel to safe harbour.

Entry 69

Gun, Dog and Bible. We'll travel as light as possible, the better to travel fast – down south, where I belong and have always belonged. Back to my roots, back to the basement where all is quiet, modest and bereft of all vanities. And back to *her*! I should never have left, never dared to venture into the badlands of the north. True, I sought to escape from the southlands, but no point of the compass has anything better to offer. Besides, as I stood just now between the two trees up there on the hill, where I know despite appearances Joseph and Louise are interred, I saw smoke in the distance and heard the beat of the drum – it must be the Raiders; they have come to the northlands, like a shadow creeping inexorably over the landscapes, plundering everything in their path.

I think it's safe to travel by day, first light tomorrow – but no later. The weather has improved and the days are getting longer. Each day we should make good ground. Finding shelter of wood or stone is not so important now; we are taking enough covering for the night. Dog is ready. Tonight I shall sleep the sleep of the wise – knowing now where my roots lie, knowing where I started and where I should end, all vanities dissolved into the ether, all pretensions cast aside; it's a good feeling – I mean, feeling there's nothing to say and nothing to do except survive a little longer; though of course there is no reason other than natural instinct to stay alive; but the longer we survive, the longer the Raiders must wait for our blood and bones. Food is the problem, but we shall take what we can and find the rest en route. Back in the basement there's enough to keep us both going – ah, the simple comforts of the basement!

After all, the basement is freedom – freedom from vanities, yes; but that means freedom from the obsession with having to *say* something, or *do* something, as though the ills of the world may be dispelled or even entirely removed by your own efforts, and this must surely be the greatest vanity of all! I have considered all points of the compass; I've gone north; with east and west, never the twain shall meet. Now I return south. Surely I have been like a machine that does not know when to stop; you switch it off, but in the next instant it seems to switch itself back on. Or like the teacher who retired after 40 years' work still believing that he could change young minds for the better if they could only disregard his white beard and his walking stick and focus instead on what he had to tell them. Vanity! Or like the writer who thought he could change the world for the better with his pen but without a comprehending readership. Or the priest, who persisted in sermonising to somnolent congregations; congregations which would, some wise man once said, have snored through the Sermon on the Mount. Ah! To be free of such vanities – there in the basement where all is tranquil, quiet and safe. We make haste to the basement!

And yet! And yet, what then of Socrates and the pig? When Mill said that it is better to be a Socrates dissatisfied than a pig satisfied, he was not advocating a life in the basement. No, that's true. But perhaps the life of a pig has something to be said for it – at least it is free of painfully unfulfilled vanities masquerading as selfless ambitions that cannot possibly be realised, free of all the clutter, all the debris of the mind. The Raiders cannot be swayed by virtuous word or deed – and there the matter stands, without debate, argument or resolution.

My defective brain has no hope of sorting such things out. Dog and I must continue southward; we must get to the basement before ... ah, now that's an unpleasant thought! We must hope that the Raiders have not destroyed the house and the basement with it. Maybe the smoke and drum we heard further north means that the Raiders are continuing north, that they've finished their unspeakable deeds in the south. Yes, but there is more than one group of Raiders – there are many – their numbers are legion. But maybe we'll be spared, somehow. And surely, they haven't found her resting place – that's the key thing.

If Dog and I can safely make it to the basement and can safely remain there, all will be well. Of course, it means a daily routine of bare survival, and nothing more. No challenges other than this; nothing to think about; nothing to stress over; no complications; all will be ironed out as smoothly as pebbles; life will be ... well, it will be the life of a pig, or as nearly as a human being can get to it.

In fact, such a life would resemble the life of a Raider, would it not? I would become a Raider albeit in isolation from all other Raiders. Raiders might still get up to all their vile deeds, but I would not be one of them. No, not one of them, but not through moral choice or superiority; because, having the brain and habits of a pig, whatever Raiders might do would be of no possible interest to me; being a pig my brain would, as it were, be a morally blank sheet, a *tabula rasa*; pigs are incapable of moral judgement and are therefore free from the necessity to praise or condemn. Is that *freedom*? Is a pig free? We make his chains? And we? We make chains for ourselves and for one another.

Such thoughts confuse me – and that's because Dog and I have yet to reach the basement; when we do, all will be well. I wonder how Old William is doing and what he's up to. Old William doesn't make decisions. Decisions are made for him – so I can't ask, 'Where did Old William decide to go?'

Entry 70

Started out this morning and made good progress over safe ground – southward. I stopped every few hundred metres and looked back, like a wanted man looking over his shoulder. But it pays to be careful. Every step forward is a step nearer the basement and safety. But there are no shortcuts, which is just as well since shortcuts tend to be bad news.

I think, if the going stays good, we'll be at the house in two marches. The sun was warm today and the green folds of the hills would have made a fitting subject for a landscape – back in the days when people actually put paint on canvas to capture such scenes; that fact that they did so seems so strange now, when all that is relevant is the life of a pig. Such a life leaves little room for anything other than eating and sleeping.

Onward!

Entry 71

It's taken three days to get here. The house is just the same, well, apart from all the windows – there's not one left intact now. But the basement is all-important, and that's just how I left it. Dog seems to feel at home. But he does have the tendency to run up the stairs and out of the house in one of his restless moods. I must teach him to be cautious and to come with me rather than give in to one of his flights of fancy. If he is seen he might either be killed or traced back here.

I have paid my respects to her, several times now. All is well. I'm sure she's as pleased as punch to see me back, and no doubt she understands how my flight north was in vain; if only she could rise from her bed of earth and speak!

Dog and I have been making good use of the foodstuffs that I had left behind here in the basement – all of it good. Now of course we have good shelter from the elements, come what might. We shall not move from here. Here we shall stay, forever. Yes, come what might – and who knows what might come?

Entry 72

One week of peace and tranquillity – this must be what I called the freedom that the life of a pig gives you. Well, decisions are in danger of being made for us, it seems. Last night there was a great deal of activity, and not far from the house. Dog started to bark, and it was quite an effort to calm him down; thankfully, he wasn't heard, or at least nothing came of it.

The screams were the worst, but whether screams of pain or of total madness I can't say. The effect was terrifying – it went on until the small hours, and then this morning, once again, the air was full of the acrid odour of burnt out shells of houses or of wood. I assume it's the work of Raiders. If I'm right, all my hopes of escape or of safety in isolation down here in the basement are thrown into question.

Now, if I'm a pig, I'd retreat into a corner and wait – if there's nowhere else to run. If I'm not a pig, it seems I have some decisions to make since I may well be forced into a position of having to make them.

I must decide which I want to be, which I need to be, which I *have* to be – pig, or man?

Entry 73

I've barricaded the door that leads to the first floor and the small window that looks out from the basement on to the garden, and we have enough provisions to last us for a while. But we can't wait here indefinitely. They'll force the door and then they can burn us out. I guess it's the same pattern they've followed all along. It just so happens that we're next. Looks as if we've returned just in time for our own demise. Perfect timing! When irony knocks the door it knocks it off its hinges.

Well, if we can't wait here until they reach us, we'll have to go out to them. Looks as though I've decided to abandon my anonymity with a vengeance. But first we'll wait. Who knows, either they don't know we're here after all, or they know we're here but have their sights on something bigger and grander! It pays to wait. It also pays to be honest, and if I'm honest I must acknowledge that I am full of wishful thinking. Wishful thinking is invariably a form of denial; I must be aware of that.

It's just as well I brought the shotgun and cartridges, though I cursed the thing en route. We'll go out with a bang if we have to, and, if I put wishful thinking aside, it increasingly looks as though we'll have to.

Entry 74

It's night. We're waiting for them to come. Waiting. How much of a lifetime is spent waiting? Many waited for the Second Coming, which never came. Many for godot. Many for things to change for the better. Many for a change in the direction of the wind, or of the tides. Many for the merest signs of affection. Many for love. Many for the hangman's noose.

Dog and I – well, we're waiting for the Raiders, waiting for the end. But meanwhile there are thoughts to comfort and to calm the mind. Memories – embellished of course, as they invariably are, if not twisted and contorted; for memory is an unreliable beast and is not averse to a little torture, which it inflicts on the unwary and the despairing and the hopeful all alike. I have found it impossible to tame the beast. But at least I can rest content in the knowledge or belief that what I remember is not wholly false – and by the fact that there are things to remember at all, however vague and disjointed the images have become; and by the fact that I need to remember them. However fragmented, some memories seem to act like a balm to the soul.

As a boy I visited my aunt on occasions and found, on frosty mornings, Old Mister Cobbley sitting in her living room, close to the fire which glowed red with coals. Deep in an armchair he sat, smoking his pipe with occasional grunts of satisfaction interspersed with a smoker's cough. He spoke with a soft growl. 'If you ever buy a new pipe,' I remember him saying on one occasion, 'remember to stick a red hot coal in the bowl – it scorches the bowl and helps to prepare the way for your first smoke.' I was a mere teenager and thoughts of smoking a pipe were as far removed from my psyche as sharing a bed with a mermaid. 'Don't let it burn the bowl too much,' he was quick to add. 'Course, don't smoke the coal!' he ended, with a rough chuckle which made him cough. Rightly or wrongly , this advice was never heeded.

Old Mister Cobbley was fond of giving out pieces of advice on such frosty mornings. My aunt would give him a cup of tea; though he refused biscuits, no doubt because they didn't sit very well with his pipe. Lord knows what he smoked in it, but it smelt of old socks and the smoke filled the room. Those were days when smoking, even indoors, was not only allowed but almost expected. Not that my aunt smoked; she disliked smoking, but it would have been an act of thoughtless cruelty to deprive Old Mister Cobbley of his sweet sojourn by the fireplace, especially when he was so overflowing with well intended, though irrelevant, pieces of advice. The good fellow was old and had no doubt seen too much with too little reward. He hadn't long to go. He might at least be granted old socks, as those on death row are given the freedom to choose their last meal. This was not the only occasion when I was the beneficiary of his advice about how to treat a new pipe – he repeated it on different visits to my aunt, perhaps because he thought the matter of the utmost importance to a young man's future development, or, much more likely, because he was, like all old men, losing his grip on events, sinking slowly but unstoppably into dotage and senility.

But what interests me most is that I should have such a memory at all, and have it so long, and as clearly as any memory can be held, albeit it frayed at the edges.

It's the same about the man who was always referred to as The Pole, who lived just a few doors from my grandmother. This giant of a man, somewhere in his late 50s, would walk heavily along the street and up the hill to where the allotments were sited, where he kept a few chickens in a coop. He would collect what eggs there were and walk back again. The man seemed to be wordless, never replying to salutations other than with a nod. He was a man with a mission, which was to collect the eggs, and that's that. His mind seemed impenetrable, his clothes modest, his gait slow and ponderous. 'He's harmless, though,' I seem to remember my grandmother saying. He had a wife and, I believe, two daughters. His daughters were very seldom seen abroad; his wife, never.

The Pole was enveloped in an air of mystery. Is that why I remember him, even though I was in my early teens and my head should have been, and probably was, full of quite different, possibly grander, things?

I do not and can never know – only speculate. But this is true, that the memories of Old Mister Cobbley and The Pole have stuck with me all this time and are indelible items in my cerebral library of images.

I think of them now as we wait. But I can't hold on to them for long. They come at will, they come when called. But there is much to rock this doubtful boat. Dog is restless and makes his way to the door of the basement and back again, forever pacing like expectant fathers of old. No, it's not the call of nature he answers, but a very different call – that of fear and expectation. He knows that nothing lasts, that all things must come to an end, even this intolerable form of existence. Yet he must wait, as I must wait, as we must all wait – not for salvation but for the end. The end is no salvation, simply the end. Just as death is the end of the game of life and not an event within it.

A game may continue even if there is an incident during play; but when the game finally ends, it cannot continue, unless, of course, you imagine that another game starts – but then you're into afterlife and all that stuff, a real nest of confusion if ever there was one. Confusion upon confusion, which is why some people resort to philosophy to untie all the knots. Unfortunately, after the demise of philosophy with the rise of technology, those who are confused are irrevocably so. People were confused even when philosophy was alive and well; now, with philosophy unceremoniously laid to rest, their confusions have been transmuted into mediocrity and they cling to the worthless for comfort, to the trinkets of life, as if they could ever possibly replace a more meaningful existence. Dispense with philosophy and you dispense with confusions, but when you dispense with confusions you are left with mediocrity – not with Socrates, but the pig. This is the merest hint as to the prevalence of the hidden ironies of life – those that can only been guessed at but never confirmed, for confirmation requires thought, and thought is philosophy.

I hear noises outside. Is the door secure? Dog and I depend on its being so.

Entry 75

No one's burst in yet. Dog and I continue to wait. It's like waiting on unfinished business, in a world that's full of unfinished business. Some unfinished business shouldn't have been started in the first place, and some begs to be completed.

There were shouts last night, but muffled and rather distant, as though in other rooms in another house or another basement. I don't think that can be; no other place in the neighbourhood is occupied – as far as I know. But then, things might have changed a lot since we came back from the northlands.

Changes. So many changes. Changes can elevate, they can enhance, they can denigrate, they can demoralise, they can destroy. There have been changes for the better amongst so many that were for the worse. Progress has always been piecemeal, fragmentary and sometimes in reverse order so that what looks like progress is in fact retrogression. I write of what was. Now there is only static decline, a stagnant pool of the worst of mankind, if mankind still exists. We might as well have been invaded by an alien and hostile species which has repopulated the whole world – as though a crazy gardener were to dig up and dispose of all the flowers and plant weeds in their stead.

Dog and I can't possibly be waiting for any changes for the better – of course death has been called a release. But a man released from prison has the outside to look forward to or to dread. But the release that death gives is nothingness, not even a blank canvas – just an infinity of nothing, no pain, no pleasure either.

This morning I checked our defences again. I still have the shotgun and the cartridges. I sat on the floor and counted the cartridges. One, two, three, four, five, six, seven, eight, nine, ten. Maybe that's enough. But enough for what? Dog has his teeth and his frustration; his bite is far worse than his bark. We shall stand or fall together.

After counting the cartridges, I looked through the small basement window on to the garden, standing on a chair to do so. The sun was shining on the unkempt, overgrown, weedy and entangled grass – picture of what everything has become.

But if I were to venture out there and tidy up the place, cut the grass and trim the hedges – well, that would be a very normal thing to do, and it would give every appearance to a visitor that nothing at all had changed, that everything was as it should be, and that small scene might even be enough to give them the impression that mankind had not degenerated at all, and that what they could see here was the same everywhere. And if that visitor was told that it's not at all the same everywhere and that everywhere else is a complete mess, this postage stamp of a garden, being tidy and well kept, would give him a spark of hope, wouldn't it? Yes, I think it would – it just might. I'm beginning to get the crazy idea that I should tear down our defences and walk right through the door, up the stairs and out into the garden and potter about there and set things straight – as a kind of beacon of hope.

Entry 76

I slept on it, in a sleep as uneasy as usual. I decided against civilising the garden. Not worth the grave risks involved. I had thought that doing up the garden might remind any Raiders who came across it of better times, as though it might bring back a civilised system of values that has sunk beneath the debris of the Virus, but I forgot that any such system has sunk irretrievably. Do the Raiders deserve any quarter? And hope would be quarter. Do they deserve hope? Do they know what it is that they should hope for? Did they value what once was? Are they to be given no responsibility at all for the loss of what once was?

Isolation is dangerous, but not simply because it deprives you of companionship and society. After a lifetime of daily and routine close encounters with people of all sorts, after a life crowded with people, isolation is like looking at them all afresh, as though through the wrong end of a telescope, and you might believe you get a more accurate perception of the whole picture. If one life is lost, this has consequences for other people, maybe more dire consequences than we are capable of imagining; but if the whole of so-called human civilisation is lost, what difference would that make to the universe?

The danger of prolonged and complete isolation is that it might result in the most jaundiced view of human kind – or at least of the greater bulk of human kind; you might want to say that he or she, these or them, are worth saving, but the rest aren't; but when you get to making distinctions and differences, you are in deep, murky and dangerous waters. In the attempt to keep your head above the maelstrom you resort to generalisations of the most fearful kind – and if there is any wisdom and goodness left after such reflections, you will abandon your generalisations with contempt.

Whether the human race is good or bad, or partly this or partly that, we are stuck with what it is. The universe however is indifferent. Indifferent to the human race. Indifferent to its composition, its moral complexion, and to its fate. But isolation may well deprive us of our faith in so-called human nature, and there are many who would trust their dogs and cats more than anything that walks on two legs.

I trust Dog. That's because he doesn't know how to lie, how to deceive, how to cheat, how to be cruel. And if that makes him unfitted to be a member of the human race, I can only say that he has a lot going for him. As to what he thinks of the human race, I can't say – except that on that subject his mind must be a perfect blank; for if not, he wouldn't want to hang around for longer than it takes to form a judgement.

No, given what things have become, I am not encouraged to put the garden right. It would simply be a signal to the Raiders that this place is occupied, and they would act accordingly, almost as though they would want to punish those who seek to restore order, albeit the order of a small garden.

The very idea that I should want to improve the garden in these circumstances is further proof positive that my brain is entirely defective. I must try to take such thoughts with a pinch of salt and just let them pass like sand through my fingers. Yes, sand through my fingers. Like the sands of time that are running out.

Entry 77

More muffled shouts last night, outside but close to the basement, almost as though people occupied the house above us, or as though people were fighting their way up and down corridors. Such a fevered imagination. But I shall make no move to verify or to clarify. Security remains the order of the day. What I find astonishing is that no Raider has cottoned on to the fact that there's a basement here and that we're inside it. Uncanny! But as long as we're safe, what does it matter?

I dreamed of the seaside last night in some fevered kind of way, maybe because I was thinking of sand. Sand and foam, sandy beaches, and the sands of time. That any dream about the sea should be fevered is quite appropriate. I have always had a love-hate relationship with the sea – no, not hate. Much more like fear. Fear and dread. Perhaps I never loved it at all, but only what usually went with it – the sound of seagulls, the fresh, salty air, that strange feeling of newness and freedom that goes with a walk along the beach, even a pebbly beach that hurts your feet, the discovery of shells and the realisation that there is beneath the waves a life that you can hardly imagine and never ever understand, just like Dog can never understand the lives that human used to lead. How could a dog understand the hopes and fears, the pleasures and pains of human life?

At first, in my dream, I enjoyed all the things that a walk along the beach might entail. Then before me the sand fell into a bottomless pit and I was swallowed up with it and washed into the deep, black, cold sea – as though the sea was jealous of the attention given to everything but itself. The sea, like fire, may be a good friend and a bad master; but it also demands respect, and it prefers you to fear it than ignore it.

When I awoke I wondered what the seaside is like now – now that the Virus has reduced every fond memory to ashes. No more walks along the beach. Deserted beaches. Deserted cafes and joyrides. And after thinking such thoughts, I counted my cartridges again. One two, three, four, five, six, seven, eight, nine, ten.

Entry 78

Noises again last night. We kept very quiet, Dog close by me. Still safe.

I thought of expectations. If they are unreasonably high, is this evidence of a defective brain, a machine that's gone wrong somewhere down the line? Seems to me, it's like the difference between a real musician and a mere dabbler. A real musician insists that his instrument is in tune before he'll agree to play it – after all, a stringed instrument that's out of tune is an affront to the music to be played and to the instrument itself, not to mention an assault on the self-esteem of the musician; no, it has to be right. A real musician about to play his violin to a packed audience may understandably refuse to get started if his instrument isn't up to scratch. Nothing less than perfection will do for his instrument, for that is a precondition of everything that is expected to follow, and 'everything' includes the performance of the musician himself. But a dabbler will make do in front of his friends if the violin doesn't sound quite right – perhaps even if one of the strings is missing.

The difference between a violin and the human machine is that imperfection is built in to the latter, and to such an extent that it would take insight, depth of feeling and supreme effort to correct the imperfections which are integral to the machine and substitute for them a level of performance which are foreign to it. The best that seems to be attainable are states somewhere between the poles of perfection and imperfection, somewhere invariably closer to the latter than the former; and even then it is hard to maintain, let alone improve upon, those states that have been attained.

But these reflections are themselves suspect and evidence of a defective machine. After all, there is hardly universal agreement on what constitutes perfection! In any case, it seems we must learn to be content with a violin that plays imperfectly, and sometimes very badly, if we are not to discard it entirely. Of course, you may discard it, but then you are an outsider; you must be prepared to live a life in isolation; as for friends, your high standards will render you friendless; discard the violin and you discard the music of which it is, however imperfectly, capable. Perfection is incapable of living with itself; it requires the imperfection of its surroundings to comprehend its own status. And what use is perfection in isolation from everything else? Besides, those who may consider themselves far above the common run are invariably blind to their own faults. Human beings have had to learn with so many imperfections both in themselves and in others and in the world that surrounds them – a world which they make and which partly makes them.

The Raiders are like musical instruments in states of advanced disrepair and quite incapable of correcting themselves. Once again history has shown that the step from reasonable imperfection to unreasonable brutishness is very short indeed. Why did I expect anything else? More than this, I am ashamed to say, the Raiders hold up a mirror to my own imperfections. 'Be not a stranger to thine own self' – yes, but the trouble with this delicious piece of advice is that you might get to know too much and that what you know will be indigestible.

Where is my courage to resist? How comes it that fear rules the roost even in a world which is dead and beyond resuscitation? Even when the only reason for survival is an animal response to discomfort and pain? Dog and I are cowering in a basement, because, I believe, the world is no longer inhabitable by civilised man.

Yes, but it was once inhabitable, was it not? Does not the world deserve to be preserved if only for old time's sake. What it once was – is not this worth fighting for? I should like to say, 'and for what it might become again' – but I lack reasoned conviction, reasoned optimism. But sometimes it pays to be irrational, to hope against all hope, when your back's against the wall and there's nowhere else to turn and nothing else to do or say.

I must somewhere acquire the courage to be irrational. Where can I find it? If the Raiders were rational they would help to restore a rational world. But their reasoning is limited to that of the brute. What must happen when rationality is up against irrationality, when rationality has no hope at all of getting through, no hope of removing the barriers in its way? Perhaps the rational must don the garb of the irrational, just as force must counter force when reasoned argument has failed, provided of course that reasoned argument is in favour of the good and against evil. And here we must assume that what is good and what is evil is beyond question in the hearts and minds of the rational and that the hearts and minds of the rational are true. The force of argument must of reluctant necessity sometimes translate into the argument of force, which, we must admit, is a dark indictment of the human machine.

Dog and I must prepare for battle – like men on the battlefields of old fixing their armour and sharpening their swords and lances while praying all the while that the battle will not ensue or that, if it does, they will be spared by their God, or by sheer luck, or by a simple twist of fate. Courage must on many occasions be led on to the stage like a reluctant pig by its ears. Our pig must be pushed from behind with many a groan, huff and puff. Old William would not have been partial to the prospect of a fight – perhaps he sensed that one was coming and made haste to avoid it.

Where is Old William now? In a safe and happy place, it must be hoped. But there is not now nor ever was a safe and happy place for pigs. Not in this world.

Entry 79

I recall it very clearly – last night's dream, and the oddest I've had so far.

I dreamed the Raiders knocked politely on the door. No, they didn't burst in at all. There were three or four of them and they were all dressed in white robes, yes robes I think they were. And they were smiling – benignly! No weapons, no screaming or shouting. It seemed they knew all about the basement all along and were just choosing the right time to come and see us. They were so polite that Dog didn't even growl let alone bark. Then they produced a piece of paper. They said it was a kind of petition signed by them all, apologising for having tortured and terrorised people, having burned property, having denigrated civilisation and put in its place a hell on earth. They asked me to be witness to their petition and promised a future better and brighter than anyone had even known, and they regretted that they had all helped to elevate mediocrity to such an extent that it had become impossible to make out the good for the bad. Having signed it, they left without further ado. I felt ashamed for holding the shotgun, which I lowered and tried to hide in a corner of the basement. They didn't seem to mind. No, they just left, smiling all the while, as though they were emissaries from heaven and understood everything.

I remember feeling relieved. There was hope after all. The Raiders were not as impervious to reason and goodness as I had been supposing all along. And there was no need to fight. Dog and I were spared the trials and tribulations of martial conflict. Now all was peace and understanding, and civilisation was capable of being restored, simply because I was not the only one who believed in it; not the only one who believed that it was well worth restoring and looking after.

Yes, but it was only a dream. What does it mean? Such dreams as these are destabilising and are grounds for false hope, and a hope that is false is worse than no hope at all. Destabilising! – as though the circumstances for real weren't destabilising enough! Once again, my brain is playing tricks with me, like a machine that won't start and then appears to start only to stop again. If only the dream were a precursor of what will be. To be comforted as a child when nightmares disturbed my sleep, I was told that the opposite of dreams is true. This was not a nightmare, and I am convinced that the opposite of what I dreamed is true – just a confirmation therefore of my waking nightmares. Yes, my brain is letting me down.

At the same time, I feel constrained to hope against all hope.

Entry 80

They appeared again last night – those men in white. This time they presented no petition, and they said nothing – nothing to me. They seemed to be in conference with one another in a corner of the basement. Then they left and I awoke.

These dreams of Raiders dressed in white must be false if they seem to offer hope of some enormous change of character. I imagine three mirrors arranged in a triangle and in them are reflected beauty, truth and love. They reflect each other mutually, as though they are three sides of the same thing, which indeed they are and must be. True beauty is not the attractiveness of surfaces and appearances, however welcome, enhancing and even engrossing these may be, but a beauty of soul. True love is not the desire for sex, however pleasing and inevitable this may be, but the love of goodness for its own sake. Truth is not the indisputability of routine fact, but the mother of all truths, namely that love and beauty must be the cornerstones of a civilisation that is going places in contrast to civilisations that are static and ambling along and in which man's inhumanity to man goes unredressed and undiminished. But if Raiders should stand inside this triangle of mirrors, their images would be unreflected, their forms less than shadows, for theirs is a form of existence which allows man's inhumanity to man to become the norm, masquerading as the necessity for survival. They have lost their bearings and the compass that might have restored them.

No, I cannot allow myself to have faith in dreams such as these. It would be like bathing in a sea of false hope. But why did the white Raiders not speak to me in my dream this time? Were they afraid that I might reject their petition as false? Are they plotting something? Were they deciding my fate? Such questions are absurd to ask of a dream, as are any answers equally. I think I would feel much better if I were to stop taking my dreams less seriously.

But the reality is hardly less palatable. Dog and I are still waiting, waiting for something to happen we know not what exactly. We can only surmise. One thing I shall not do. I shall not step outside the confines of the basement. The basement is our only hope, and it was so from the very beginning. How foolish we were to venture out northwards, trusting the compass to find our way to something better, as though we were following a false marsh-light. True, Joseph was a friend, at least of sorts, a kind of remnant of the things that defined the civilisation that has been lost – but only a remnant, and a fragile one at that.

Many like Joseph put their faith in holy books, little realising that holy books need to be reviewed critically and constantly, that they are no more than guides to betterment and not in themselves the alpha and the omega of an improved civilisation, a civilisation that wants to go places. Such faith in any written word would be like trusting the walking stick to do all the walking, the lighthouse to do all the manoeuvring in stormy waters, the marsh light to magic you to your destination safely on dry land. Nevertheless, Joseph's heart was in the right place, and a civilisation that strives to go places is in dire need of people whose hearts are in the right places. Hearts and heads, righteous passion and brain, must work in harmony if the world is not to become a lop-sided phenomenon – either a superfluity of mere cleverness, or one of pure sentiment. Pure sentiment is like wanting to save a drowning man but lacking the wit to raise the poor fellow's head above the water. In a world that purported to love God there is now no greater hell.

For all that, Dog and I went northwards, and that yielded little or nothing. Will the time come when we should try east, or maybe west? I shall ask Dog and see if he wags his tail or hides his head between his legs.

Entry 81

Yet there is hardly need to move. Our every need is met here, just here in the basement. It's as though food and drink miraculously appears before us when needed most; like clockwork, you might say. I must have opened tins and prepared things, but I can't for the life of my remember doing so. Yes, of course, yet another indication of a defective brain, of a brain that is deteriorating inexorably. There's no other explanation.

Somehow we are sustained in a world that is bereft of selflessness. I recall the tale of the man who professed to worship Satan and was reviled for saying so. Yet his life was altogether saintly; but his words were given greater weight than his deeds and he was burned at the stake. His profession to worship the Dark Lord was merely his way of rejecting the hypocrisy of those who *said* they worshipped God. He might have been acquainted with the reflections of Mencius, 'When I was young I listened to what men say; now I listen to what they say and I watch what they do'. Words and deeds; which should we take to heart when they fail to match? Whom do we believe, the speech or the maker?

Meanwhile, Dog and I continue to be sustained. Here in the basement

Entry 82

Sustained by food and drink, Dog and I. But not by hope. Hope melted away long ago. Hope, like love, truth, justice, was a word much used but little understood – like a hat worn by so many heads and is now shapeless yet no one wishes to discard. People were like lost children, peeking round every corner perchance to spot the familiar and the reassuring – until the persistence and the unrelenting brutality of the Virus crushed hope underfoot like a cockroach, allowing what once were human beings to divest themselves of their humanity, retaining only their outward shape and losing that which separated them from lesser forms of life, indeed becoming less than the lesser forms of life, becoming the lowest of the low, since animals cannot be blamed for their brutality having no better starting point from which they might fall. Animals cannot fall from a state of grace; they cannot lose what was never vouchsafed them – a more than rudimentary language, making possible the foundations of intellect, with its multifarious possibilities for the creation and expression of love and compassion and the spoken sophistication of feelings. The sophistication of language is the sophistication of feeling, the creation of language the creation of feeling, for it is not as though all feeling came first and its expression second.

The twin drives of mankind towards true love and mutual destruction were well known by the ancients. Plato knew as much about so-called human nature as successive generations, perhaps more. He dared to say that the object of education was to help us to love beauty. What? Plato out of context? Yet still we may use his words to ask: how far has education succeeded? Yet, without it, the demise of civilised life would have come quicker than it has. But he also said that only the dead have seen the end of war. He knew well the complexities and frailties of man. He knew how human nature holds within itself its own salvation and its own destruction – he could not have known which would get the better hand. The Virus has decided the issue – irrevocably it seems; which is why hope is as hollow as a rotted oak.

I fear losing Dog. He looks around dolefully, as though he knows some kind of end is near, though of course he knows no such thing. It's almost as though he needs more than food and drink to sustain him, to keep him going. But can a dog know hope, even if there were grounds for it? Of course not, not by my reasoning; but perhaps my reasoning is simply a piece of unreasoning. This is what happens when all hope is lost, when hope loses all sense and meaning. When you lose hope, when you abandon it as a meaningless chimera, you begin to question everything else, everything on which hope depends. It's like taking the corner stones from an edifice; the whole structure begins to crumble and fall. A table requiring four legs may stand on three, hardly on two and never on one. The abandonment of hope is the dismantling of all that is worthwhile in your system of values. It is a bleak and abject surrender. Wars, even the most just of them, cannot be won where all hope has been abandoned.

Is this what I have done? Have I surrendered everything by abandoning all hope, by calling it hollow and meaningless? Dog has not left me yet. As long as he stays I believe I can trust fate a little longer, a little further. I believe I can raise myself up from this bed of despair and challenge any Raider that dares to threaten our space.

Yes, that's right. And now I remember that this is just what she would have wanted, she who lies close by, out there, deep and warm. I might have hesitated while she lived for fear that the Raiders would discover her and torture her or worse. But of course she is beyond hurt and has been so ever since she was interred. Her spirit lives on, very much so. She would want me to resist – for the sake of what was and, just maybe, for the sake of what might be again, somehow, sometime.

Hope is such a precious thing, even when groundless, even when irrational, it is like a warm light in a cold room – yes, even when hollow. It must be held on to, at all costs. I'm sure she would say this. She would say this even if things are so bad that the words seem senseless, as though she were trying to articulate a piece of nonsense. What is irrational must be fought with the irrational. Yes, have I not said it already? The best weapon to use against irrational bestiality is an irrational hope for its defeat. Hope, even when irrational, is the best weapon in our armoury. What else, short of victory, can raise us up? And we cannot fight the good fight unless we raise ourselves up from this bed of despondency.

I must tell Dog not to be so despondent. We shall face the Raiders together, come what might.

Entry 83

Yes, I am encouraged by the thought that Dog and I will stand together until the end in the name of what has been lost and what may yet be again.

All this time I suppose I have been depressed. But what is depression? Is not depression rooted in egoism? In ambitions thwarted, dreams unfulfilled, hopes lost? Is there a form of depression that owes little or nothing to egoism? Depression is selfish; it feeds upon itself and it shuts out the suffering of others. But what is the *object* of depression? Surely that is a question that begs to be asked. For if the object of depression is the loss of all that constitutes a civilised form of life, surely that cannot be mere egoism!

There are forms of depression that shut everyone else out, and there are forms of depression which invite everyone else in. The former are at best unfortunate; the latter are at worst the remnants of a civilised intellect.

I believe I am no longer depressed, because Dog and I will stand together. And if we fall it will be because we rose up!

I thought I heard footsteps above. But the basement is still secure. I wonder, if Dog and I still stand a chance, whether we should make a beeline for the outside and bend eastwards or westwards, out and way. No, we must stay and make our stand.

I think I have forgotten how to pray, and that makes me feel thin, weak and vulnerable. Besides, I have never been able to take Plato's strictures to heart and give them a practical application: pray for the right desires before you pray that they be fulfilled. I have never been sure what the right desires are; and therefore I have always been hesitant in my prayers, and more than doubtful about their fulfilment.

Entry 84

Why do I fear Dog's departure, his refusal to stand? Is fear of loneliness a weakness? Why do we fear it? Is it because there is strength in numbers and therefore less chance of defeat, hurt and destruction? The natural tendency is to bunch together when under attack, even though this invariably turns out to be counter-productive. I need Dog to stand with me, but this is no guarantee of victory. What chance could we possibly have against the Raiders who will stop at nothing to subdue and eradicate for sheer amusement? What end do the Raiders have in view? Is it subjection and destruction for their own sake? Or do they imagine an end further to that?

But there can never be an end that could possibly justify the sacrifice of human lives. 'The end justifies the means' is a sentiment shoved into the mouth of Machiavelli – not that he would have contested it. 'Exitus acta probat' was a Roman precept long before that. But the means is as thoroughly subject to moral judgement as the end to which it purports to be directed. Moral judgement can and should rule out the means, however laudable the end is thought to be when those means threaten the uniqueness, and that is to say, the sanctity, of human life.

I ramble. My brain runs before me like a dog unleashed. It hurts my head.

Many feared loneliness because it was a harbinger of insanity. Television, radio, domestic pets – all played a role in keeping the worst forms of loneliness at bay. We cannot it seems live entirely alone. Even the death of a pet was like the loss of a limb; the loss of a loved one left people paralysed with grief. But in so many cases force and length of habit was mistaken for love – and if it was a kind of love, it was not unconditional.

That ancient Buddhist precept, 'Friends are few and far between; fare lonely as rhinoceros,' is hard to adopt and harder still to sustain. How much harder life would have been if it had been a universal watchword. But are we to say, better a false friend than no friend at all? A large number of marriages would appear to have proved the point.

She however was a true friend, she who lies deep and warm. To prove it the flowers still grow over where she lies, some standing tall like sentinels, the flowers she loved and lovingly cared for, all reluctant to share her grave lest she be forgotten beyond recall. The rhinoceros is a fine beast, but it is better to have loved and *won* than never to have loved at all. Win or lose, death exacts the punishing penalty of loneliness and grief; a pain above and beyond all others and such that makes it easier to condone the independence of the rhinoceros over the never-ending, all-consuming desire for partnership; yet for the vast majority of human beings it is always the latter that takes first preference.

Once again I am reminded of the indescribable pain of solitude that delivered irreparable broadsides with every lockdown in the attempt to quash the Virus. People felt the searing pain of loss even before the

Grim Reaper had his fill. People died twice – first in spirit, then in body, as though death in spirit were a dark angel intended to torment those destined to die in flesh, like a hard-hearted jailer on death row taunting those about to face the chair, the gas chamber or the *cruelly* humane 'lethal injection'.

Isolation interminable was responsible for death in spirit, after which death in body seemed an almost welcome release. The world is now but has always been a frightening place, despite the beauty spots, despite the hopes and ambitions of the young and not so young. It is something that has had to be endured; and this is made possible by sharing fear, by living together, by a common language. When communication ceases, when companionship is outlawed and impossible, this fearful place becomes unendurable. It may be endured a little longer by those with inner resources, by the ignorant, and by the thinkers who might entertain the idea that time will pass and with it the horrors of the present, beckoning a new dawn and greener pastures; but to all a sense of hopelessness will eventually come. Man was just not meant to live alone. Better the companionship of a beast, a creature of the forest, than isolation and lonely death. The Virus ensured a relentless and, then, a permanent isolation. People passed their waking hours in lonely anxiety, they slept an anxious sleep, exacerbated by intolerable dreams, and they woke once more to the fretful hours of daylight.

Let it be set in stone, that the human condition is best served by people standing together in mutual concern, kindness, understanding, compassion, tenderness and – in a word – love. Oh, what an ill-used word! Only then can it be meaningfully said that death shall have no dominion. Without it, Hobbes's description of life in the 'state of nature', being nasty, brutish and short, too readily finds application in man's much vaunted 'civilised' existence. It is not simply the possibility of war, however brutish war most certainly is, nor yet disease, inhumanity, cruelty, poverty and famine that should move people together in ever greater harmony. It is the reality of death, not simply death by any of these means, but death *per se*, that should bind people together in an unbreakable and harmonious bond of friendship, sympathy and helpfulness. And what of happiness? Well, to be worthy of its high repute, happiness should be evangelical and reciprocal. Happiness in a social vacuum is vacuous and chimerical. If it is thought to be an elusive fish, it is almost invariably because it is sought in barren waters. Happiness should be shared with others since others are in so many instances its very source and object. What value should we place on one who is described as 'selfishly happy'? Is he not diminished?

Ah, what did I say about expectations? Can any expectation be more excessive than this, that such a bond of friendship, sympathy and helpfulness should exist or even be at all possible? Whence did it come, this expectation? What nonsense am I trotting out in these scribbles? Has my life in the basement robbed me of all my faculties? Yes, too long in the basement. Have I, despite everything, managed to forget the Raiders, even momentarily? How can a brain become so defective? Have I not seen and heard some of the worst that man can do and is doing right now, outside the basement?

O, incorrigible brain! Smaller versions of the Virus infect brains, like those that entangle computers and render them less than useless. To entertain expectations that exceed possibilities is a drain on your resources. It saps you of confidence and of energy. It weakens you and makes you doubt the validity of even the most otherwise elementary and unassailable patterns of thought. You are left a pale shadow of yourself, thin, emaciated, with eyes that long for refuge from the sights and sounds that were once routine, once ordinary, and now made extraordinary by your inability to believe the horrors of what you see and hear. Damn these expectations! Damn the impossible!

I have a sudden and overwhelming desire to sleep, to sleep deeply as never before. Dog knows it and sidles up close. We may share our dreams, who can tell? He is most fortunate that he has never, and never will, share my absurd expectations. Sleep, perchance to escape them!

Entry 85

Horror of horrors! Dog's gone! I woke to find him gone! He can't be far away. Perhaps he sneaked out and is on his way back right now. Any moment now I might hear him squeezing his way through the door. Or has he been caught? If he's been caught I know they'll torture him and kill him. They can't do that – but they will! Time and again I told him to be careful and not to leave unless I'm awake.

I'll wait. There's nothing left but waiting, anyway. And if, no *when*, he comes back, I'll tell him not to be so rash in future. I'll remind him that we must stand together and, if need be, fall together. That's all that's left – a small degree of resistance which will change nothing. But it's better than nothing. It would be the last bleak, meek, weak clarion call of a civilisation that's gone forever. Yes, I know it's gone forever. The Raiders have made sure of that. The Raiders, created and inspired by the Virus – the Virus, that monstrous beast that still runs riot and ravages what's left of this once human population. Not long to go though, hey Virus? You've almost done a complete and permanent job. Only the Raiders left – that last, poor, almost unrecognisable vestige of human life on the face of this fragile planet. Well done, Virus! – I guess you must be proud of yourself. And when you've finished here, you might be lucky to find some other civilisation somewhere else in this universe which you can work your evils upon, and on and on you go until all decency is gone.

Poor Dog. He's been with me for so long, I can't remember a time when I was without him. I don't know how I managed before he came along – badly, very badly, no doubt. He was, no *is*, my rock. Yes, even if he doesn't return, of course I know he *will*, he will still be my rod and my staff. He's indelibly written deep down inside me, somewhere in heart and head, head and heart. Though always silent he was by my side, never leaving it. Maybe if I speak his name he'll come back. But I shall not shout his name lest it attract the attention of the Raiders. There is still a little time left. I must not leave the basement before my life is complete. It is not complete until I have said all I can say, done all I can do, and been all I can be. I shall resist, and then perhaps my life will be complete. Of course, it is the intention of the Raiders to render every life incomplete – their own existence, though itself temporary, depends on it, feeds on it, thrives on it.

Now I hear noises again. Something, perhaps Dog, is coming. Oh, let it be Dog, so that we can stand together – together, if need be even 'til death. Did Camus say it is better to die on your feet than to live on your knees? Yes, but Dog and I think it best to live on our feet. Here he comes, I think!

Well, it's not Dog. I just have to get used to the idea that he won't be coming back. I remember that eight-year old kid during a day trip to the seaside. He stood on an 'I Speak Your Weight' machine and inserted his penny. It told him his weight. But it also produced a slip of paper on which was written, 'You will always have the courage of your convictions.' He hardly understood what the words meant, but he never forgot them. When he came to understand them, he was still not old enough to know what those convictions should be. But the years passed and he came to know; and that was essential – just as Plato so sagely says, 'You must have the right desires before you pray that they are granted.' Yes, he came to know something about the philosophers of old. But at the age of eight he knew nothing at all – so it's a wonder that at such a tender age the words 'You will always have the courage of your convictions' had been printed so indelibly, so unforgettably, on the *tabula rasa* of that young mind. But some things are objects of wonder simply because we insist on making them so, other because we have no other reasonable choice.

I guess life is something we are stuck with, and we must make the best of it – with or without Dog. Now I hear the familiar noises in rooms, more like corridors, footfalls and the shuffling of feet. Perhaps now it's my turn. And perhaps then I shall be free. I remember that line of Huxley's, 'It is better for a man to go wrong in freedom than to go right in chains.' But best of all is to go right in freedom. And, if you can hold on to what matters most, you can be both free and right, even in chains, for there is a kind of freedom that is immune to bondage.

People have dreamed of freedom, of being free; but I have been free in dreams, even in the most fearful of nightmares. I should like to dream now, if, and this is my only condition, my dream is as unreal, as surreal, as any dream can possibly be, as surreal as Adolf Hitler singing in gentle, humble, and unmistakably reverential tones, 'All Things Bright and Beautiful, All Creatures Great and Small'.

Do I dream *now*?

Do I hear the splintering of wood, the cracking of rocks, the rippling tinkle of broken glass? Does the wind howl and the rain make rivulets on the window of the basement? But is it still the basement? The whole place has become a vast, shadowy, cold, comfortless, grey-stone room, like the deepest, darkest bowels of an ancient ruin of a castle, long abandoned, a place made immeasurably less inviting by the large holes at the base of its thick, crumbling, outer walls through which sea-water pours relentlessly into the dark holes through the flooring, flowing fast and furious to places unseen and unknown. The noise of continuously gushing water is excruciatingly painful.

God, what sort of place have I been sent to? Where is this terrible place? It might be the Chateau d'If, the fortress of San Nicola, or Castel dell'ovo, – but in their final death throes, having strived for so long to stand against the ravages of time and sea. But, no, it is a place generated by a brain conditioned by its plight and circumscribed by a plain basement; it is the product of a diseased imagination striving to rise above its confinement in this dark, ungodly place. Yes, this ungodly place, wherever it may be.

Do I wake or sleep? Pray God I sleep and dream a nightmare!

Entry 86

I suppose I must have survived the castle. God what a gloomy, soulless, heartless place! At least now I can I breathe, and the grey stone walls have melted away, and here again is the familiar basement. Some men dream of pleasant things, perhaps of romance or lustful sex. They may even covet such dreams. I have become a sexless amoeba, unattracted to the opposite sex and infinitely less to my own. Therefore, the pleasure of sexual attraction no longer exists for me and cannot be a salve here in the basement. I am, as it were, a tabula rasa on which no gender can be written or impressed. And so, it seems, I am capable of viewing the world in black and white, as though the intricacies and nuances of what separates one man, one woman, from another is of no account. All the complications of human relationships have been reduced to a simple denominator: the desire to live in peace, all differences swept aside as though they were of no significance – as though we are all, at bottom, amoebas, so that even all pretences to war become quite meaningless hindrances to peace and tranquillity.

The realisation that you are an amoeba is sudden, though the process towards becoming one has been long in existence – just as you can suddenly find yourself at a destination though the road has been long. A vessel slowly empties, and suddenly you realise that it's empty; there's not a drop left. Much time passes, and suddenly you realise you are not the person you once were. The transition seems shocking and unaccountable – but we forget that every condition is the consequence of things unnoticed and therefore unaccounted for. The tea is ready because it has been brewed.

Becoming an amoeba is like having seen something in a certain way all your life and now seeing it quite differently, if you see it at all. And then the whole world seems an entirely different place; human relations are separated off from you, as though you are viewing them as curiosities to which you find it difficult or even impossible to relate – things which you previously took very much for granted. You are given a cold view of the planet and its inhabitants; the planet itself takes on a strange, even alien, aspect. If you were a fish, you would be questioning your element, puzzled by its texture and by everything, animate and inanimate, that inhabits it. But when you become an amoeba, you wonder how it can possibly be that one human being can be physically attracted to another, whether male to female, male to male, or female to female. The whole panoply of attraction suddenly becomes quite incomprehensible – suddenly and irreversibly. Yes, that's right, irreversibly! Do you not see, then, how different the world has become! How different and how incomprehensible! How different and, probably, how intimidating! How threatening! Which is another way of saying, how alien!

But my brain, you understand, is beyond all help now. My thinking is distorted beyond all recognition and beyond all salvation. You must not think like me; to do so would mean the end of everything you know and feel comfortable with. And that would never do, because it would mean the end of everything you consider to be life and living. Don't you see? Even if I am right and you are wrong, life must proceed along all the old lines if it is to be worth living. If like me you become an amoeba, well the end of the world is as good as the beginning, and nothing in between is worth the toil that centuries of human life have invested. But the old lines are not possible for me. The Virus has seen to that. It has destroyed all the old ways of thinking and feeling and being. What human life remains finds itself in a desert initiated by the virus and worsened by its own shortcomings. We are all at sea, a sea of sand – dry, infertile, and quite beyond the fringe of salvation.

Isolation! Yes, that's the rub! The creeping weapon of the Virus. You feel you are living in isolation from all that you know, because all that you know has changed and been replaced by alien forms. It's as though the Virus had a mental capacity and, with it, the ability to devise a deadly strategy of 'divide and rule'. The success of such a strategy is measured by the mistrust and hostility it engenders amongst those to whom it is subject, and those to whom it is subject are not simply individuals within a nation but nations amongst themselves. A nation, fearful for its own security, is apt to forget that no nation is safe unless all nations are safe. And so, the virus divides nations are easily as it inspires hostility and mistrust between individuals within a nation. When despair, total and ubiquitous, is thrown into the mix, it becomes everyone for himself; and this ensures the success of the strategy of 'divide and rule', one that mutates to 'divide, rule, and destroy', and this on a global scale.

I am glad I am here in this basement, even without Dog, rather than in that cold, dark, heartless, grey, stone cavern of my nightmare. Perhaps here I can live out my days in peace – without all those silly, divisive trappings of so-called civilised life. If I have become a genderless amoeba, this is nothing short of divine release. The shackles of desire have melted away, finally and irrevocably. Sophocles might well have applauded it.

But what happens if we see men as mere catalysts and women as mere vehicles of human reproduction, when all feeling is reduced to animal passion and love is left out, so that love is bereft of all its multifarious modes of expression? Has this finally happened, as though man has been stripped of all skills, talents, intellect and all their accompanying vanities? Has much-vaunted 'civilisation' with all its accoutrements been reduced to animal passions, the twin instincts of survival and procreation? Has the capacity to see the best in people weakened as the Virus has strengthened? I fear it might be so. I know it is so. It is so much harder now to see the best in people, if only because the best in people has ceased to be expressed – because it has ceased to exist? But is it really possible for human beings to grow *down* and be less than half the size they were, with half the potential, half the capacity, half the humanity? Maybe for this reason the word 'hope' has slipped out of our vocabulary, like so many others. Language, like human relations, has lost its potential for beauty and has become merely a cold medium of exchange, like messages in Morse. It feels like the end of the world. Poets are redundant and Parnassus is thick with weeds.

Yet I am still here – in the basement. The castle has passed with the dream, until next time when it might return with a vengeance. But I am still here. It seems a long time since I ventured outside the basement, not even for those salutary daily walks. Instead, I hear voices as if in corridors; and the basement seems to have grown smaller, the walls closing in upon me; and the more I fear it is so, the more they close. But the basement is still a safe place, safer than anything outside. I write this word 'outside' – a word I clearly remember, but now I'm not so certain of its correct application.

There are places on this planet that inspire fear, dread and loathing – but not simply places that are the coldest, the darkest, the hottest, the most desolate. Not at all. Amongst them are places which someone might take for granted but which are loathsome to you, and yet you cannot give a rational account of why they are so, nor perhaps will you ever be able to give a reasonable explanation. A street of houses, ordinary and unremarkable to everyone else, may make you wince and shiver with fear and dread – a fear and a dread which rise like monsters from the darkest depths of your psyche, and all they require are the simple triggers of what to all others are the entirely commonplace – which means, of course, that they are not simple after all.

The virus has caused the commonplace to become despicable. What is commonplace about the advent of raiders and their loathsome activities? Yes, even they have become commonplace, as when the most tragic news is falsely mitigated by sheer repetition and becomes the norm. But some very few of us can still use the word 'falsely' and apply it correctly – a lingering vestige of hope.

In general, the distinction between true and false has become at best blurred, at worst undetectable. We spend so much of our lives lying both to ourselves and to others, and the lies we tell ourselves are the lies we pass on to others in the guise of truths. So accustomed are we to lying that telling the truth is difficult and so often painful, which at least in part explains the prevalence of false hope and the scarcity of good writers – false hope is a survival tool readily employed by homo sapiens, but denied all members of the animal kingdom. Lies are too easy to conjure and to spin; in politics and elsewhere, the ubiquitous success of propaganda trades upon ignorance and the craving for the wrong kind of simplicity, it feeds on the desire for security and on the lack of a critical faculty. Not hope, but *false* hope, is the last thing to die.

Truth is always unpopular, even when accessible. Dostoyevsky might have said of truth what he claimed of beauty, that it will save the world. But that could never happen, not while homo sapiens are in their infancy; and if they ever break out of their infancy they will no longer be homo sapiens. Meanwhile, the very concept of truth was conveniently replaced by another more palatable – for people began to speak of 'his truth' and 'her truth' and 'your truth' as though truth had no anchor in objectivity but was as varied as varieties of grass, and so 'truth' simply became an alternative word for 'opinion'. In this way, people saved themselves the trouble of critical thinking and self-criticism. Reflection was a useful tool only insofar as it enabled you to express what you felt; but the very idea of your endeavouring to establish whether what you felt was right or wrong, true or false, was a step not only too far but also quite unnecessary.

The Virus and its effects have finally put truth to rest; since the dawn of man it was progressively ailing, and few thought it worth the effort to revive it, and so it lay for a long time like a neglected patient in some dark corridor without so much as a passing gesture. Now it is buried deep in some forgotten corner of a dark wood.

It has been said that truth is the first casualty of war; if so, that is because it is first and foremost the immediate and very human progeny of that toxic mixture of politics and fear. In our own little lives fear has mastery over veracity, except in those rare moments when its back is turned and courage surfaces like an Excalibur to momentarily overwhelm it.

The walls have stopped closing. A reprieve.

I must sleep.

Entry 87

I think I slept. It's hard to say. The difference between sleep and wake is harder than ever to make out. The place is threatening – more than ever – and not the refuge I once thought.

Why didn't people rise above the Virus, their humanity intact? Why did they sink into an abyss of selfishness and hatred? What monster of the deep turned the tide? Can it be turned again? Turned back?

What can bring about a change in those who do unspeakably inhuman deeds – those who turn against what good parents have always endeavoured to teach? A painting? A poem? A gentle smile, perhaps? Something that reminds them of what they have lost and what they should recover. Something that turns on a light in the darkness. How can the blind regain their sight? Something that obliges the face of evil to see at last its own reflection and despise it. The capacity to see beauty is the groundswell of selfless hope; without it hope dies; selfless hope must be rooted in the perception of beauty, of something greater than itself, something that is worth striving for whatever the odds may be; something worth appealing to despite everything. Some who were about to burn at the stake, when all hope of reprieve was lost, may nevertheless have spoken their last words to a loving God – their appeal was to something greater than they, greater than the terrible moment. Their appeal may have fallen on deaf ears, on no ears at all; their God may have been chimerical. But their appeal was greater than hope of personal salvation, earthly or otherwise.

If God is left out, what is there to believe in that is the foundation of all selfless hope? The restoration of humanity, perhaps; the restoration of civilised man and the beauty of which he is capable, which is to say both the beauty he is himself capable of creating and that which is there to be perceived. The perception of beauty requires a man of beauty to behold it, just as an inspirational man is one who is himself inspired. If artist may paints a scene of unspeakable cruelty, he does so to record it and enable others to see it that it might not be forgotten, so that what is remembered may never be repeated. Why does he bother? Because he is unwilling to allow beauty to be tarnished, to allow life to be negated or human life to be de-sanctified. Such are the sketches of instances of abominable inhumanity in the genocides that blacken the pages of history. Only an artist who reveres the beauty of life can paint such scenes, every brushstroke, every imprint of pencil or pen, a stigmata redolent of the Crucifixion.

The pages of history? Why should we read them? Presumably to make sense of the present and surmise the future. Too glib? Well, as for past events as they unfold in that monumental, depressing and repetitive tome, we might learn better to forgive the forgivable and endure the unforgivable – yet there are things that cannot be endured. As for the future, we may look upon it with a dubious mixture of hope and dread, like a novel whose ending may be too easily guessed.

There was a man who said he was not keen to die but felt consoled by the fact that the beauty he was leaving behind would continue to exist. He was not of course comforted by thinking of the ugliness which he knew all too well would continue to exist; the comfort he found was in the beauty of nature and that of which man himself is sometimes capable according to his sensibilities. He would not have been a Raider. Raiders cannot say such things. They have thrown off the mantle of humanity and dressed themselves in the robes of the disaffected. Their number is now legion, and I fancy I have seen them dressed in white. But do I wake or sleep?

I find myself writing nonsense again. Words fall on to the page like glass marbles from a bag and from there they roll on to the floor and disappear down cracks and crevices in the walls until they are all gone and the page is left blank again, nothing said, nothing worth saying. Defective!

I think I dreamed of Dog. Yes, I know I did. He came up to me, looking lost and forlorn. I gently placed a collar around his neck and attached a lead. I walked with him to some place that seemed pleasant and safe. And then he turned to me and spoke and thanked me for my kindness. I held his head gently in my hands, looked into his eyes, and said goodbye.

Entry 88

But what is there to leave behind that I should find consoling? The world has changed since those pious consolations had any validity. As for the beauty of nature, the trees are burning and no birds sing. Nature has been ravaged in a long process of exploitation – yet on the geological scale it's been accomplished in a flash. The beauty of nature requires sensibility to be perceived. Sensibility was always in short supply, but now it is non-existent. Nature and human nature have suffered the same fate, deteriorating in unison; and never to return, unless one believes in the power of irrational hope to drag things into being again which really have no earthly chance of restoration.

No, all that's left now are crumbs from the table; the feast is well and truly over and no one's inclined to clean up the mess left behind. Crumbs from the table, inert ashes from the fire – so what is there left to console me in the last hours of my demise? Perhaps that's all there ever was! Just crumbs from the table and ashes from the fire – in which case my own expectations have a great deal to answer for.

I need to sleep to escape my own logic. The surreality of dreams is a kind release, even when it stings and shocks and makes the blood run cold.

I thought I heard Dog barking upstairs. It raised my hopes of his return. Then it stopped and I waited. But he did not return. Perhaps it wasn't Dog at all but just a remnant of a dream, as an afterimage is a remnant of what was once seen and is seen no more.

But there are more noises than usual. I think I shall gingerly move about, and maybe tomorrow morning, when all is quiet and still in shadow, I'll venture out to the park, my old haunt, for old time's sake – if, that is, the Raiders are nowhere about. It might be uplifting to say hello and goodbye to the few trees that remain – those last sentinels of a better world gone by, still standing, though bound for pastures of nothingness, as are we all.

Entry 89

Went to the park. Saw no one. No Raiders. But it was in the shadows before dawn. Some trees still standing, others burned out or chopped down. And now no birds at all. On my return, as the light came up and the shadows melted, a thought I saw some yellow flowers, daffodils I think – didn't stop to look closely. Yellow flowers!

But I was happy to return to the basement, unseen at that! Safe again, for a while – but it's strange not to be welcomed by Dog. Where is that poor beast? As I lie here now my brain runs backwards through time to places, times and faces that I once knew – a roller coaster of images. It's painful. I try to think of yellow flowers and that seems to alleviate the pain and induce a calm kind of sleep – no, not sleep, but something between sleep and wake, as though I have taken some opiate, some strange oriental balm that makes me sink down into the mattress and feel weightless. And when the yellow flowers slip through my cerebral fingers, the roller coaster returns and, with it, the feeling that I am being taken to a place I don't wish to go.

Yellow flowers. I must hold them tight, but not so tightly that they suffocate, wither and die. After all, they are my lifeline now that Dog has gone.

Entry 90

Mind and body. Poor mind that is now so defective, hanging by a thread of yellow flowers. But my body offers so little consolation – this poor structure that has served me for so long, so deserving of respect, so long in suffering; the flesh once firm now hangs as though ready to depart, exhausted by time and circumstance – this poor, bony, skin-clad frame, with what remains of a brain to navigate, this poor assembly which has seen so much and done so much and achieved nothing. But it is fitting that mind and body should shake off the mortal coil in unison; they have been together so long that it would be an act of cruelty to separate them now – what would the one do without the other but pine and fade away in cruel solitude?

The forced separation of one thing from another, of parents and grandparents from children, brothers and sisters from one another is an unspeakable cruelty – an abomination brought about by wickedness and a total lack of humanity, a heinous crime for which man can be blamed. It is what the Virus has done – but the Virus is neither wicked nor blameable; yet it has done the unspeakable, with countless and grievous harm.

Only some yellow flowers stand between me and total extinction. At least, I think they were flowers and that they were yellow. Sleeping and waking are like mind and body – two sides of the same coin. It's hard to know which side will show when next thrown. Too close to call.

Footsteps! I hear them, distinctly! Is this a sensation within a dream, or is it real? Is a dream the antithesis of reality or an aspect of it? Is it reality seen through a different lens? It is possible to mistake the one for the other? Can we dream by mistake? Can I dream your dream in error? Can I promise never to do it again without permission?

Still I hear them. The footsteps, down a corridor, and doors opening and closing, and then more footsteps down the hollows of a corridor. Is this a dream? Does it matter?

Entry 91

I heard it said, long ago, yes, long ago, in those far-off days when I lived and knowingly breathed the air of day and night and could tell the difference between sleep and wake; I heard it said that we should live in such a way that when the time comes to shake off this mortal coil we might truly say that we have done all we could do, that we have said all we could say and have been all that we could be, so that we can say that our lives have been *complete*. What a blessed life such a life would be, and so different from the common run in which our lives are ended incomplete, perhaps cut short through no fault of our own – not to mention all those who die without ever having lived at all though they are as old as Methuselah; most of us manage to live a little, but, for the most part, we remain unborn, or are born too early, or too late.

Yes, a blessed life indeed – to have said all that you can say; and, if it is really worth saying, then let it be said more than once, if necessary in the same words and in sentences of identical syntax, and let it be shouted from the rooftops. But, first, you need to know what to say, and, sometimes, what you feel you need to say most is so crushing that you are obliged to make an inarticulate grunt.

But words, their number and repetition, are not everything. Neither is longevity. Every day in the years of long ago, my father's enlarged and framed photograph hung on the wall on the landing of our house. I would greet and salute it every time I passed it, morning and evening. He died young and beloved of the gods, and, though he was a man of few words, and those soft and gentle, what I learned from him was more valuable than anything subsequently taught me in the whole system of education to which I was subjected. He was as noble as his portrait, a man of integrity, courage and humility, and of talents and wisdom unacknowledged. Maybe the effects on those who loved him during his few years on this bedevilled planet were such that his life was, though short, *complete*. He did not live long enough to know the man who is his son; yet his gift to me is priceless; not the gift of life, but the knowledge of how to live it; all the errors are my own.

A picture may hold within itself the qualities of sainthood. Such was his portrait, which was burned by Raiders, together with everything else. But it's indelibly printed on my memory, though everything else has faded. *Ho un timore reverentiale di mio padre* are words which don't even begin to cut it. The Raiders have ordained that our lives should be incomplete, just as they have ended the development of a civilisation that might after all have been going somewhere, given half a chance and with a fair wind. We are all in reverse gear, and even the few that are left, those so very few who began with good intentions, have succeeded only in paving the way to hell – it's hard now to distinguish between them and the Raiders they fear.

Entry 92

Stare at a portrait long enough and it seems to come to life – the eyes become less expressionless, and the mouth seems to move, to form words almost imperceptibly, but silently as though in the faintest of whispers. If he who is pictured could step out of the frame, say his piece and step in again, it would be a dream worth dreaming – oh, to be instructed by the dead who had much more to say than their time allowed, to be embraced by them who were given so little time for embracing! That is a fitting subject for dreams – conversations with phantoms, with the spirits of those who were not permitted to linger long; not long among the living where they were little counted and soon forgotten.

What did Joseph say, that little man of few words? Did he not say that the more good a man tries to do the more evil he will meet, that the more he endeavours to move forward the greater the resistance he will encounter? Well, such a world is not good enough for good men; yet, without them, the world is good for nothing at all.

Yet this is where we are! The all consuming fires of ignorance burn brighter and hotter day by day, and the supreme end cannot be far. I judge this by the turmoil in hollow corridors and by the darkness. I have half a mind to try my luck again and strike out north, south, east or west – who knows, this time I might find a haven, however small and fragile, to spend a little time among those who, though beloved by the gods, have not yet departed.

If I am safe here, I do not know it.

Entry 93

The man in the portrait was broken by war. How else could you explain his reading of the New Testament 34 times before the gods took pity on him? It was an attempt to find sense in the senseless, meaning in the meaningless, and I fear it did not work for him. He could neither understand nor forgive man's inhumanity to man – man's senseless striving over his fellow man. There was no escape, no salve in the New Testament.

Escape! Why do I vacillate? Do I fear the Raiders? But are they outside, or are they here on the inside? The basement is no longer a safe haven. Of course, it never was. Only in a dream, however terrifying, are you safe now, and then not for long, for when you wake you wake to a nightmare.

Entry 94

I remember that long ago I sat cross-legged looking up at my father's portrait. I believe I said, 'I've done my best. Yes, I think I can truly say that I've done my best, that I've done all I could. The rest depended on appropriate responses from others, which were not forthcoming – I can't be blamed for that. After all, my life was full of illusions; all the doors I bled my fists upon were false impressions in a wall of continuous and unyielding granite.'

But these words were an expression of compassion to which I felt entitled, and not an outpouring of craven self-pity. After all, the lives of so many of us are full of unrealities, of imagined, illusory events, thoughts, beliefs and dispositions – and of bitter regrets with which we flail our consciences mercilessly, yes, until the blood runs, and even then we are dissatisfied and un-consoled. Yes, the effects of things unreal are all too real enough.

Things done or left undone, said or unsaid – such are our regrets that make up the walls of the poor cerebral cells in which we incarcerate ourselves or are incarcerated by others. We seldom think that what we strived after and failed to achieve was not worth the effort in the first place, and that in the larger scheme of things their importance is at best wildly exaggerated and at worst non-existent. But, if such consoling thoughts are entertained, there are those who will cry 'sour grapes!' – those who are content with their own lot and are blind to the need for improvement, those who condemn the perceived failures of others, those who fail to grasp their own insignificance and resort to cynicism as a substitute for compassion.

I dream I lie prostrate, weak and unable to break out from these walls – imagination is my only release, but the ability to imagine requires cerebral energy, a resource that is now reaching its end. Do I dream, or do I only dream that I dream?

Entry 95

I must have dreamed the impossible. As I lay half in and out of sleep, I could have sworn I saw Joseph as the sleeve of his white coat brushed against me. And then he was gone. As in a dream, I wanted to speak, but could not. I wanted to shout, but no words came out, a soundless scream – more disquieting than a nightmare from which there is no escape.

The basement seems smaller, very small and getting smaller, as though the walls were closing in – just enough space for the bed on which I lie. I am afraid to sleep lest I wake in some small dark hole in a deep place where I can never free myself. I wish I could get up and make for the door, at least where the door used to be. I would make a break for it, even leaving her behind, because she would understand and let me go. I can touch the walls from where I lie, and all the strength I ever had seemed drained away. So I just lie here, in anticipation of I know not what. How can a life without great fault end like this?

The answer is that lives without great fault are in the hands of those that are devoid of sufficient virtue to resist corruption and inhumanity.

But all is well – for who would wish to live in a world without love, apart from those who are already incapable of it?

The Virus created pathways towards the abolition of love, so that only bestial relations remain. If, as was once said, beauty is in the eye of the beholder, the world now lacks beholders, and so beauty itself, lacking the ability to be perceived, has ceased to exist. No beholders! 'All the world's a stage' said the Bard; but now the stage is all but empty, almost all having made their various exits; only the villains of the piece are left, and their numbers are dwindling daily. What a miserable world it has become – a theatre devoid of lovers, heroes and admiring audiences.

But all is well – for who would wish to live in a world without beauty, apart from those who are incapable of perceiving it?

Too weak now to scribble. Fragile! The fragility of all those virtues good people have strived for and died for and stood for is depressingly, alarmingly fragile – the Virus has revealed and exploited our weaknesses.

But, fortunately, I am still able to say so! There is at least one who can still call a spade a spade; one who can still recognise the face of evil for what it is! And so, the Virus is not all there is. No, sir, it is not all there is! For only love can defeat logic, overriding what our heads persist in telling us, that all is lost. As long as we can hold on to love we stand a chance, however slim; all is not lost if the outcome depends on what we can still do with a will and a passion. Hope is not hope without the will and the passion to back it up, just as courage is of no use without the strength to exercise it, nor strength without the courage to utilise it. And love is the foundation of will and passion, as the centre of a volcano is the source of the hot lava it emits.

Too weak to scribble more nonsense, propped up in a bed which seems to want to move. The time for spouting nonsense is fast coming to an end, I know. Does the bed move? Down corridors, perhaps? To greener pastures? To the end of the world? I think …

Entry 96

Maybe one day it will be written that darkness came over all lands, though not for the first time, and remained until the next rising of the sun, which shed light where no light had been, giving new hope to an embittered species and fresh horizons to a different and better world – a world which I am not permitted to see.

I dreamed of a vast field of tulips in full bloom. As I approached them their blossoms turned into the smiling faces of people some of whom I recognised, some very few of whom I had loved; I wanted to speak to them, to hear their voices, but they turned back again into tulips, and I awoke smiling too. Is this my last dream?

Entry 97

But what now is to be said about she who is buried here and eternally sleeping? Ah, I remember only too well. When the light went out of her eyes, it went out of the world, too. The lie is persistent – when people say that a human corpse is peaceful. There is no peace in the eyes of the dead. There is nothing. The eyes of the dead are blank, hollow, empty; they are the eyes of a waxen doll. They should not be gazed upon, not by the young, not by the old. And so, she was best buried, deep and out of sight – best remembered as she used to be, with eyes vibrant, alive, watchful and wise. It is always best to remember the best. Buried but not forgotten. Best buried, for if those dead eyes could see, they would have shed tears of anguish and distress, like the rain that is said to issue from the eyes of a loving God.

It was good that her eyes could no longer see the end of all the beauty and all the pleasantries that she, like everyone else, took dangerously for granted. Well, she took too much for granted and was in good company in so doing, for the numbers are legion of those who take far too much for granted. Perhaps she at last understood that; perhaps at last her expectations were beaten down like plants vastly overgrown. Perhaps she understood, near the end. Hopelessly weak in mind and in body she would stand in her thin nightdress before the long mirror and speak in amicable tones and with gentle gestures as though in conversation with her own reflection, perhaps debating with her own image how all those good things she had known could possibly come to such a pass and how they could all come tumbling down. And then she would stand weakly shaking with amusement, as though she understood at last the comic tragedy of human life – the tragedy that all who are born are destined from that very moment to die, and the comedy that so much is done to hide this fact amongst the baubles and playthings that form the trappings of our sorry state, while love, the only reliable balm in the pharmacy of life, is so often the victim of war, resentment, hatred and self-deceit. The conversation would come to an end and, still staring into her long mirror, she would gently rock with laughter, no doubt at the absurdity of the human condition of which she herself was part. This was the ritual which the Virus, irreversibly compounding her existing frailties, would soon bring to an eternal end.

Yet, there is of course another who is buried here and all about – one that some have named Beauty, others have called Truth or Love. Is she in eternal sleep, or will she one day rise again? She will rise if there are voices loud enough to demand that she does, and voices louder still to herald her return. Her eyes are not closed, they pierce the earth that covers them; they see what has been done and they despise it. Spades and shovels will not disinter her; only wisdom can – that spark that ignites the souls of thinkers and, by inspiration, the soul of mankind. Wisdom! Yet another word that slips from the pen too easily; for it is hard to hit a target that moves in the dark. All devices must be put to work to find the right word. 'Wisdom' must do for the want of any other, and time is shorter now than ever it was. If wisdom is a plant, it is of the most delicate of varieties, every day facing annihilation for want of nourishment and tender care should men turn their backs on the garden of the world and grow fat on their neglect. This sleeping Beauty is truly in the eyes of the beholder, and mankind must once again learn how to behold it, and when it does, Beauty, Truth and Love will rise again and will remain like tender plants.

But perhaps it is too late for pious sentiments. If a garden is overgrown, who is there to tend it and restore it? Even as life slips away, we grasp at hope like straws clutched by a drowning man. Yet, even he who at the hands of beasts faces the firing squad and in an instant will be no more – even he looks to the heavens, as if to hope not for himself but for those who, like him, believe that life is worth living, worth the trouble, worth the pain and that it is, after all, better to have loved and lost than never to have loved at all.

But so what?! What if all things grow so dark we cannot see? Is there not an inner eye that still beholds Beauty and continues to love it? Even the mere memory of what was is worth grasping, worth holding on to when all else fades from view. Was there not a time long ago when opposing armies ceased the slaughter, when enemies came together to exchange smiles of friendship, Christmas greetings, photographs of loved ones – all this before their generals demanded that they return to their positions and strive to kill one another? In all that senseless, wicked maelstrom of slaughter, Beauty refused to sleep and rose however briefly, and in doing so, promised to rise again.

The walls of the basement are melting, slipping away … Walls that were closing upon me seem to open and vaporise … paper, pen … everything slipping away … melting – things I don't wish to see. The time has finally arrived. Thank God the eternally dead are unsighted and cannot rise again to see everything in such a state of destruction.

Destruction, or creation? Could it be *creation*?

For wait! If the end has come, it may be only one end among many. Perhaps the end of despair and the creation of new hope!

For of course Bunyan was, is and always will be right, 'Be ye watchful, and cast away fear; be sober, and hope to the end'; his words are well chosen, whether or not we share his hope that the Gates of Heaven will admit us. Whatever we say, write or do, or fail to do, we return full circle to his sentiment; for there is nothing else; there is no worthy alternative, whether the hope is for some divinely assured Life Eternal or whether it is a faith in the redeeming features of human nature and the more morally supportable capabilities of man.

So, what though the end has come! We must hope beyond it, and then some, all the way through infinity until no one remains to hope at all. And if no one remains, there are no problems to solve. In the meantime, we must hope beyond hope. We must not focus on the worst in man but on the best, not on what he is at his worst, least of all on the worst he has done, but rather on what he may yet become. Are these pious sentiments? Yet, pious sentiments are all we have, and they are all we need.

And in my most vivid dream I looked out upon a green and grassy space where crows were picking to shreds what once were raiment of black. Was this a dream of hope or of despair? Not of despair! Not crows, but ravens – envoys of hope bent upon the destruction of those shrouds of black despair that bind us and stick burr-like to the human psyche when that tender plant, overshadowed by the darkest clouds of duress and incomprehensible pain, has forgotten how to hope. We learn to hope again by remembering the best in man, even if the best has been achieved by the very few and the very best by even fewer; the ability to see the best in man, if only through a glass darkly, enables us to live a life that is worth living, enables us to live and not merely to breathe. Joseph was right; you cannot live your life forever regretting that man is no better than he is, for that creates a myopia that stifles hope.

Milton had even Satan say, 'What though the field be lost, all is not lost.' Cannot we, who are yet better than Satan, say the same? But I am tired and must now sleep; as the curtain falls I believe I see splinters of light in the dark canopy of heaven. Now pray your God I am not mistaken, that this vision is not another idle dream.

But you should not pity me; no, it is I who pity all those I have seen – the Raiders and all those who have cried to a non-existent God for help He cannot therefore give. No, do not pity me – for I have still the faculty of thought, and my thoughts save me; they separate me from the animals which must decay when they breathe their last. I have hope that my last thoughts may be amongst those that have thought the same, the thoughts of those far greater than I – yes, those who that have thought the same. This I might call the 'spirit' – and the idea that the spirit might endure despite all that is done to extinguish it – this is my greatest hope and therefore my salvation. Do not pity me. Pity instead those who are bereft of thought, and therefore of salvation.

The faculty of thought is the beginning, not the end, of civilisation.

But memory is the reservoir of hope; it is where hope is inspired and resourced. Memory is not always unreliable; they are not only of the worst in man. Many memories are of good things, of the very best of things, and they are true and crystal clear: memories of love, of friendship, of self-sacrifice, of devotion, dedication and selflessness, memories of the best that mankind can be. With such an armoury hope can endure the many onslaughts of despair; with such exemplars we can emulate the best in others and in so doing become the best we can be. Such memories are the nutrients of growth and re-growth; and from such fertile ground hope and inspiration can emerge and re-emerge like snowdrops from the icy depths of despair. Let our memories be preserved! After all, I know myself by my memories. My memories tell me who I am, and who I am not.

Entry 98

And this, the last entry, is I have no doubt, the most important of all, coming as it does in one of the few nights remaining. While there is ink for my pen and paper on which to write, this entry must stand as testimony to all that has gone before while the remnants of sanity are still extant.

Answers sometimes come in dreams if they come at all. Such as these must be awaited; they cannot be pushed, bullied or so much as pursued. They have their own volition and must be obeyed.

An answer has come at last to a question long and painfully asked: why should we continue when all seems irretrievably lost? Why bear a life in a world into which we were thrust without consultation or permission when that life seems altogether futile.

In my dream I was an infant and found myself in a room of sorts in which were seated all the loved ones I had known: my dear grandparents and parents, aunts and uncles, and infant friends. I passed from one to another, and, embracing each, told them I loved them. What is allowable in a dream would not be so otherwise. How fearful it would have been for a mere infant to offer protestations of love with such a pressing degree of conviction, with such solemnity, such authority, as though he were a miniature adult announcing the end of the world or the beginning of a new! Yet such was the dream. Then, now older, I made the same protestations to subsequent friends, and even to contemporaries I had known and disliked, and then to my teachers. Older still, I made known my love to people I had met along life's path, those I had liked and those I had not. In this way, the dream allowed me to make my amorous rounds to all and sundry.

I make this of my dream, that it is an answer to the question why we should live. For we should live for the sake of love. We should live for love's sake. There is no answer more compelling than that we should strive to live for the sake of love. There is no answer stronger than love.

For many, this answer is no more than Piety teetering on a very narrow ledge. People *should* live for love's sake, but they *do not.* They live simply because one breath must follow another; they live to obviate the pain of not taking the next breath. They live because the alternative is unthinkable – both inconceivable and unacceptable.

But I have no defence. No further argument. No further ground. No further premise on which to support the statement that we should live for love's sake. The statement is bedrock and stands or falls in its own right without recourse to what men fancy are the *tools of logic*. Its strength lies in its appeal, and its appeal lies in an intuitive grasp of its obvious merits, in a perception that has no need of further grounds.

Have I been unusually lucky to have known love while many have not? But I have not always known love. Those who have not known love should be shown it, that they might live for what *might* have been and for what *might* yet be, not simply for what *was* or for what *is*. This is not sufficient. For those who have known love must also *show* it to those who have not, so that merely to speak of it does not ring hollow. Those who have seen little of love must be allowed to live for the possibility of doing so, for herein lies hope, hope and the *sense* of life. Let all be shown love by the example of it – which is why we should strive to love even the unlovable.

It is not enough to die for love's sake. If love worthy of the name is as important as the wise have claimed, it must be lived for also, unconditionally and unreservedly. And if all this is wrong and demonstrably faulted, then let night follow night and the light of day be snuffed out until the end of time and the demise of man.

Yes, but could all this be simply the product of confused thinking? Yes, of course, for what can be expected of a brain made sterile with a cocktail of dubious vaccines, opiates and, above all, endless solitude and soul-destroying isolation?

Soul-destroying? Or should I say head-destroying? Is my problem a variation on the theme 'Head (Reason) and Heart (feeling)'? The head often tricks us into thinking that the heart is in the wrong place, and the heart often deceives us into believing that the head has no place at all. The heart and the head don't always act in unison.

My head has been battered by isolation and left for dead. Or is my problem that the heart must function without the head, or function with a head that is forever in a state of flux and imbalance? If so, I am like a musician who is all heart and who, ignorant of musical notation and of how it relates to his instrument, frequently fails to remember where on the keyboard the next note is to be found, let alone what it is called; he must play by ear, and he never plays the same piece in exactly the same way or with exactly the same notes throughout.

But the heart and the head are two sides of the same coin. They constitute a false dichotomy at least to this extent: though they may not always *act* in unison, they invariably *suffer* in unison.

Whether it emanates from all heart or from a confused mixture of heart and head, I feel compelled to reaffirm that we must live for love's sake. At least my confidence is unshaken by isolation and questionable cocktails – though it is true that one might be very confidently mistaken! But if a musician plays only by ear and never plays the same piece in exactly the same way, might not each version be equally palatable, equally memorable, equally delightful, equally deserving of the name 'music'?

In how many ways can the statement 'We must live for love's sake' be played? Do the variations matter if they are all on the same theme? I think not – or so my head, or my heart, tells me. Joseph might have settled the matter, perhaps by saying nothing at all. In his absence I can only repeat the statement in the manner of a mantra and be content to do so, my critics being an audience of zero.

It is comforting to know that a mantra such as this is impervious to the Virus and all its variations, as it is to those who would question it and those who would reject it. Logic cannot touch it. You accede to the mantra without hesitation, without question, or not at all. It is rather like the proposition that no child should suffer sexual abuse; there are those who would accept it immediately as though it were an elementary proposition of arithmetic, like $2 + 2 = 4$; suppose you came across someone who wished to discuss it first, let alone someone who refused to accede to it? Given that he understands the proposition and is not a philosopher, how would you, how *could* you, go about getting him to accept it? Could you even begin to understand his doubts, let alone his refusal? He would be hard to make out, like an amorphous lump seen through the wrong end of a telescope.

But if it is said that we should live for love's sake, there are those who would say that it all depends on what is meant by 'love', and they would not all be philosophers. Questioning the unquestionable is as part of the human condition as the refusal or the inability to contest the contestable.

Words have their limitations, yet all we have are words. We strike at the target, but the target is in shadows and is always on the move, from side to side and up and down, and sideways here and there. We aim in the dark but aim we must, and in this may the God of Love help us all.

We ask why we exist when all is in chaos, when all is imperfect, when all is violence and despair. Then let us say that we exist to be loved. Ah, but even tyrants are loved. But are they truly loved? Is the word love rightly applied here? Suppose we say, we exist to be loved and to be worthy of the love we are shown? Dictators and tyrants may be loved, but they are they really worthy of that love? Or is the love they are shown not worthy of the denomination of love? We exist to be loved and to be truly worthy of that love. There is no greater rationale of our existence than this.

There is no science, there is no wisdom that can omit love, rightly felt and rightly earned. I see now a passing of worlds, and it is hard, nay impossible, to say whether we are at the threshold of a new world or the passing of an old. It is a twilight world in which everything or nothing is possible; it is nightmare world, full of shadows of what once was and what may yet become. It is a fog of possibility from which one of opposites or contraries might emerge; the better, the worse, or nothing at all. Hope is a silly word, a childlike allusion, as though to a marsh-light that may or may not be found; hope must be grounded, not in fancy but in what once existed, so that what once existed might exist again, perhaps in better or refined form, just as a straw must be strong enough to support a drowning man.

These drugs have killed me, almost. I must try still to rise above them and name them for what they are before they themselves render me nameless.

And now I feel the shadows forming once again, with head and heart jostling for survival in what has become an alien world.

~ ~ ~ ~ ~

BV - #0056 - 270622 - C0 - 234/156/18 - PB - 9781780916293 - Gloss Lamination